Poem   79p

OUTPOSTS

— Taxus —

Other poetry books by the author include:

Forget The Country You Came From *(Singular Speech Press)*
Straw Bones *(Beginner's Mind Press)*
Wear This Country As A Stolen Coat *(Brushfire)*
Measuring Time *(Trout Creek Press)*
The Village Painters *(Adastra Press)*
Without Shoes *(American Studies Press)*
Corn Dance *(Europäischer Verlag, Vienna)*

OUTPOSTS

David Chorlton

OUTPOSTS

First edition 1994
© David Chorlton 1994
All rights reserved

ISBN 1 873012 64 0 *(paperback)*
ISBN 1 873012 65 9 *(hardback)*

Cover painting by the author
Cover design by Joe Pieczenko

ACKNOWLEDGEMENTS

Thanks to the editors of the following publications,
in which most of these poems first appeared individually:
*Abraxas, Bone and Flesh, Bristlecone, Chaminade Literary Review,
Coe Review, Contact II, The Current, Dog River Review, Fennel
Stalk, Free Lunch, Galley Sail Review, Green Fuse, Hawaii Pacific
Review, International Poetry Review, The MacGuffin, New Laurel
Review, Nexus, Old Red Kimono, Outerbridge, Oxford Magazine,
Panoply, Pembroke Magazine, Poet Lore, Poetry Motel, Santa Clara
Review, South Ash Press, Webster Review, Wire, Xenophilia, Zone.*
Also a broadside from *Lilliput Review,* and the anthology
Six Guns (Longhand Press).

Published by
TAXUS PRESS
at Stride
11 Sylvan Road
Exeter
Devon
EX4 6EW
England

Contents

BREATH

On unclaimed land, evolution is still
grinding stones.
Bears consider the changing
shapes of men, while fish
leave the valleys to fly.
Deer shed their feathers,
the shell falls away from an elephant's back
and skeletons move into the flesh,
beginning as fern, then turning
through phases of wood
and chalk. Copper
forms the backbone of an animal roaming
underground. When it shakes
ice from its fur,
the land buckles, making new crevices
where man sheds another skin
and longs to stand.
He breaks each of his bones in turn,
resetting them as he grows.
Ribs are a loom on which
he weaves his lungs.

THE STONES

Pushing through the surface of dry
country, stones reach the light,
black, veined, jagged or worn, to soak
in heat, unable to hold

the pressure driving them
out from under ground. Nobody sees
them arriving, but surely
they raise their colours from deep

beneath the desert. They are
the sharp layer covering
animals asleep in the earth, fragments
of a continent trying to return.

METEOR

Beneath a meteor
nocturnal animals rummage in the trash
while coyotes cry
as if from another star.

A moth
has come to rest on the open page
of a book whose reader
lies asleep. By the light

of his dreams he passes
through a world of dormant fires

and in the forest around him
silent wings are marrying
their speed with the darkness.

THE EARLY HOURS

A sleepless night. The electric moon
rolls between clouds. In the streets
a few cars trickle, humming
aimless tunes. Across the city

dreams are sparkling in the dark,
as brilliant as crickets
whose knees outsing the clocks

that are so old
as they step
back and forth in living rooms.
Sleepers wander

where they would not go in daylight,
like the Chinese traveller

who loaded his boat with books
and sailed across the moon's reflection,
never to return.

THE BRIGHT SPECIES

The brightness of insects on a balmy night
when they are drawn to the warm
lights about the house
survives as a code,
undeciphered, once written
with a luminous pen, then rolled
into miniscule, transparent bodies
and dispatched to the domestic
corners of a home. Too small
to make noise,
they settle on the porchbeams
and fly from the window
to the doorframe. Evolution
left them green, or striped, and continued
without them. Crawling,
they explore the woodgrain.
The monkish ones remain for hours, long
and still with wings
draped behind them, while
the brilliant shades surpass
all their surroundings. Once,
they could have been larger
than the tigers of their time, and having
chewed whole forests down
began to fade
until they reached this present size
with the scrolls inside them
so small their history
can never be confirmed.

OUT OF THE SUN

A bird might breathe through its wings
or lizards grow
to the size of buffalo

were the Earth more iron
and less ice. Planets

fly around us in clouds
of sulphur, with extinct
volcanoes and a core of liquid rock
under miles of sea. By the grace

of air
we exist. In a universe
pulsing radiation

we are made of stars.
Meteors
sizzle to our arms,

carbonaceous chondrite
snagging on the atmosphere,

landing in Mexico
near somebody cooking
over slow heat.

FULL MOON

With no clouds across the salty moon
we can see the silver troika
racing across its fields, the filament

at the centre burning, and our desert
reflected on the sunstruck
space. There is light for the owl,

a nail in the sky to navigate
a passage by, and a silence
so white a mantis

alighting on a crater would crunch
into its dust to make it crack.
Wind rummages in mesquite. Animals

created for the dark are moving through
what land remains them. They make
no noise but a whisper, like that
of skaters on the lunar ice.

WEDDING ABOVE THE TREELINE

The ashen shadows of drummers in bright turbans
slide across the shorn slopes
as the first crystals form
in an autumn bride's breath. Her husband
to be has pulled

the skin from a ram's head over his own.
Animals of burden loom in the smoke
behind them. On a pole

a red scarf soars
into the darkening atmosphere
while flames along the ground illuminate
the wooden masks that dancers wear.
Fire is the music

so high in the world
that the air fades to nothing as they breathe it.

THE GATES

A city locked for centuries
is open. Inside its walls
nothing has changed since the last

disillusioned monk threw his bibles in the snow
and set off on a life
of wandering. The gates
swung back behind him, and froze

together while the citizens
lived quietly, cradled

in a long winter
through which they perfected their crafts,
died in small houses
and raised their children to be strict.
The generations

blew like fallen leaves
through the streets, and left
the thick walls intact
for those who followed to be safe

from time.
Now the gates have cracked.
Animals are running free.

Into the forest they go, with the hair
on their backs raised high.

THE SKATERS

On frozen moats around their towns in the north,
skaters glide. Their slim grey faces

are set into the folds
of scarves, so bright
as to claim all the light around them.
At the speed of frost

they pass each other, steering
and balancing with hands
behind them as their black coattails

flare. A silent winter long,
from billowing fog they hurry
on hushed steel, coming close, then whispering

away. Nobody speaks
on their private journeys, believing
that the ice beneath them runs so deep
it will never erode, and their country

has a sun of its own, cold
and shimmering on a clear lake of sky.

TARASCON

A gardener in front of the battlements
is picking green flies from his irises
while the river drags silt

and wind hits the stone
but cannot budge it
from its stern foundations. He presses

the flies between his fingers
and smears them on the grass, stopping
briefly to marvel
at the immensity of the walls
leaning against

the sky with nothing left
inside them to protect, nobody
watching the horizon; only
a man with flowers at their base,

possessed by his duties,
intent on staying his course.

WINTER'S GUEST

Fog has swallowed the landscape. Bony trees
stand angled at every turn
in a road searching for its end.
Sounds fall short

of any listeners. Across the silver grass,
bootprints trace a disappearing path.
Between the brittle vines,

threads of ice
lead to invisible fields.
In a half sketched doorway, two women
wearing unmatched woollens
move their lips

and then return to blazing kitchens.
On such days, even fire
is a private world

and every journey leaves the traveller
to trust in the curves
along the road he has chosen.

WITH THE WINDOW OPEN

Water runs from a wooden spout
into a trough, outside
a house whose ceilings press
low against the cool bare space
where travellers sink

into linen, and listen.
They are surrounded
in their sleep by wolves
but do not know it. They snore

while bears rummage
in their bags, and vipers
curl into their shoes, then

wake up and splash
their faces in the well,
clearing the silver from their eyes,
still unaware

that nothing in their dreams
could have saved them.

THE CONVALESCENT

Directly from a long sleep,
the kind that accompanies an illness,
the patient steps
onto an unpaved road

and walks until he cannot remember
how he came to a landscape
of red soil, rock and songbirds

where the leaves lie
with their silver sides down.
He stops

to listen. A sudden wind
turns the foliage around
and the hills flash with reflections
that wash every image from his eyes
for an instant, until

colours return
and the birds who held
their breath in the squall

have voices again, a stream
running over stones in their throats.

BYZANTIUM

My friend in his old coat
is leaving for Venice again

to wear the mist
and become a stone in time.

He shares the fading centuries
with himself, and keeps

his money in an alpine bank
for the day he finally locks

his door, when his job
has made a foreigner

out of him, and having
stood once at the portals

of Byzantium, he steps
without companions

into its golden flames.

ARAHOVA

Grapes cling to the windowframe
of a woman's house, where she spins
at her wheel with hawks

circling down from Parnassos.
She never lifts an eye to them
or looks down
into the olive groves so far
away in their valleys that trees
grow as mist

and darken as soon
as the mountains rise over
the sun. This is the time

the woman takes a chair outside
to work until she has
no face
but a scarf

that was hers before her birth.
Black

is all the weight she has,
sitting between night
and day, breathing cool air in, warm
air out as darkness falls

and wool lies across her lap
like soft lightning.

EARLY MASS

Green shutters hang loosely in the silver
fog on a morning square
in Picardy, as the dull bell

swings in its tower
calling early risers
to their pews. In their cold

kitchens, the faithful
yawn above the flames
that warm the first coffee, as clouds

of sleep issue
from their mouths. These spinsters
for whom Sundays are a feast

of chaste marble,
wear their church clothes
daily. Waking

a few steps at a time, they pass
the unsure contours
of streets in muffled light,
with only their shoes to guide them.

A SLOWENIAN WEDDING

On the doorstep of an inn
whose yellow windows burn high
on a secluded hillside,

a bride inhales night air
then wanders through her village
unaccompanied, past long barns
where straw is steaming in the warm
darkness, as the celebration

goes its way without her.
The groom slips away
through the back door, and into the quiet
forest where he listens

to a train gathering speed in the distance,
letting go of its otherworldy cry
while the villagers all
sing in a single room
and he goes

to where he cannot hear them.
After the train, the only sounds
in his world are those
of his own black shoes
and the red fox in the undergrowth.
Meanwhile,

his bride sits in the open,
pulls her rustling skirts together
and looks up into the sky
at a field of poppies growing on the moon.

IN THE NEXT COUNTRY

A bed is floating on the fire blue
tiles in my house of chalk
and straw, where ancient
scents are heavy
when curtains part. In the courtyard

is a chair beneath the arch
set deep
in shadow and dark voices
when traders come to offer

jewelry and news
from other countries, and they talk
to their shoes as I send
them away. When the lemon
wind stirs, I wander

through yellow streets
to the striped door
of a house with cheap embroidery
and copper trays. From sweet

grainy coffee
I turn toward the secret water
lying far from any road
where egrets
drink among the golden reeds.

BETRAYAL

meet me on the other side of the rain

it is a curtain of strung beads
across the doorway to a coffee house
where the rugs are embroidered
with our language and a moustache
is your passport

i will open my coat
for you to steal relevant papers
taped recordings of our leaders
and a list of their vices

i will whisper in the dark
and kiss you on both cheeks
as i pass you the keys

enter the system tenderly
the streets are winding

when you claim the city
wear soft shoes
and do not wake us

we surrender every time

DOUBLE AGENT

inside my cuff are the plans
for taking the glacier

in the sole of my shoe
are those to win it back

when the moon fills to half
i will call from a roadside phone
to grant permission
for the invasion of ice

when the ibex have been driven beyond cold
i shall tell my other army
to release the land with fire

i slip between governments
liberating countries and sharing
intelligence with long grasses
shorebirds and leaping
animals that balance on the slimmest ledge

mine is the invisible voice
whose accent shifts
according to the secret it shares

at diplomatic parties
in the neutral shadows of back streets
behind the factories where missile parts are born
in a cleft between rocks
with a clear view of the test site
i make my connections

playing policy
against policy

swapping photographs of home
until nobody knows anymore
what it is they are defending

BETWEEN THE DUNES

in a soft country
of slopes and creases
the citizens wear liquid robes
and drift between oases

the compass always points to sand

the sand has banked
and tumbled through the years
washing over cities
and swallowing the paths
of people wandering to consult the palms

their history is buried
their future is water at a shadow's edge
their living moments

are cinnamon
olives and white linen
there is no government

for those ruled by grains in the wind

THE BORDER

The guard in his wooden
lookout tower has raised
glasses to his eyes
and scans the flatland
on his side of a border
that runs between two empires.
He turns the searchlight
through an arc that burns
the stubble. On the foreign side
the wheat
is brushed by a golden wind.

A refugee has crossed
so many borders, he becomes
invisible where countries change
their names. When he stops
in the shadows to catch
his breath, pieces
of a border lace his shoes.

Waiting to be processed, travellers
hold their passports open
as they stand in line
with the barrier down. Rain
falls onto the pages in a light
that takes the colour from their faces
as they perform
the ritual. First they give up
their names, then they forget
where they came from
and word for word their language
is washed away. They walk
through an open door
into a narrow room,
into a country in the dark.

Illegals feel their way
through moonlight
on a desert split
between cultures
that never meet. They crawl
toward a future
in a land without time.
They dig
themselves a passage
through the border's roots.
On the other side
the world is a single country.

WITNESS

for   Ignacio Ellacuria S.J.
        Amando Lopez S.J.
        Joaquin Lopez y Lopez S.J.
        Ignacio Martin-Baro S.J.
        Segundo Montes S.J.
        Juan Ramon Moreno S.J.
        Elba Julia Ramos
        Celina Ramos
            Murdered, 16th November, 1989
        Ita Ford
        Jean Donovan
        Maura Clarke
        Dorothy Kazel
            Murdered, 2nd December, 1980

Our word for eating
does not translate
into your language
when it is earth
that is eaten. I have seen
my people fill
their mouths with soil
and swallow it to bury
their appetites. Their stomachs
believe for a while
but nobody says grace
until they take their guns
into the hills. Clothes
hang from trees
beside the roads, where
I recognise my disappeared
brothers by their shirts. You,
whose God is dead,
expect us to pray
but where there is
no faith without justice,
not the church

but our people are dying
and vanishing as if
they were airbrushed
from the photographs we
would place on their graves.
I could not shield
my face from the glare
of four white handkerchiefs
lying on the road. I knelt
to pick them up
and found beneath each one
a name scratched
on the ground. Your government
sends money for so many
weapons in such a small
country, while those
who come to help us
pay their way with their lives.
When spectacles are all
that remain of a man
on the grass outside his house,
I believe as I collect
the broken lenses
that these are the eyes
through which you see us.

THE LISTENER

for Rena

The mockingbird has no secrets
when it sings in the dark
and its innocent voice
fills the trees. Your telephone

rings. Pick up the receiver.
A listener
is balanced on the line
like a tightropewalker.
Half your voice

is diverted to him.
He makes notes
with one ear for each
caller. He represents

national security
and wants to know the who
and when and why and what
of all you do. On summer nights

the songs change melody
as they slip between the leaves.
When you know

someone uninvited waits
for your every word, speak
in a lover's tone; make
your tongue trace circles
in his ear.

THE COUP

Our senators deliver speeches of fine rain.
The newspaper
has the same date every day

and blames insurgents abroad
for the drought at home.
Our meals are censored.
By the time a rumour circulates

it bears the state's approval.
Waiting for the underground
to mobilise,

I am faithful to graffiti
and hands that speak in code
passing hope from house
to house, until
we are stronger than the walls.

The suburbs are rising.
The government cannot sleep

while darkness moves
with such resolve.
In a silent offensive
we burn the police files.
What are laws worth

with prisons inside out
and the army rolling dice
to make a first move.

We gather at the president's door,
ready to invade
his privacy.
How will he govern us

now we have given up looking
for the enemy, and the roads
are ours again.

THE DOCUMENT

An official document arrives in a language
I cannot read. The print
stands to attention, some signatures
crawl beneath it, and a purple stamp
proves its authenticity. A name

resembling mine
balances on a line below
the date, but nothing
makes a familiar sound. Each

letter has its own face.
Each paragraph
is an illiterate army. The syllables
collide when I pronounce them
and I hear

somebody rustling on the other side
of the paper, watching me.
When I hold the paper to the light
the letters are small valleys
too difficult to cross.
With no foothold in the text

I begin my journey
in search of a translator.
Every new border
is hope, as countries fall

silent in my wake.
Nobody knows the language
I carry, or the one
I speak.
Mystics turn to smoke when I address them.

Priests evaporate in prayer.
I bewilder historians

who cannot place me in time.
My only guide
is the paper folded in my hand
like a dove struggling to fly.

THE PICTURE POSTCARDS

Anonymous postcards arrive in the mail,
addressed in the same neat hand
and showing photographs
from a city where somebody
knows my name, and a wide river

flows. Everything there is old
and treasures sparkle
in its darkest vaults. In winter

the city is so pale
it could not bear a colour's weight.
Gothic halls
and painted ceilings fall

into my hands as I collect
messages. I stare
along narrow streets, trying
to find faces on the people walking there
or discover a code

in the leaves
that arrive in October.
There is nothing

to read. The cards
continue for years, while I record
the postmark dates until
I have a file of them

in which to record
and cross reference views
with the days of their sending.
As I search for a pattern

I listen for a hidden voice, so small
it could be trapped beneath a stamp.

THE SUICIDE

Such was the suicide's beauty that she was left untouched for fear of disturbing her classical face or supple, floating limbs. She slipped out of her rope, beside the chair and would not decay. The door was locked, though her fragrance wandered. Unable to resist these arms of rose and incense, I broke into the room to sleep beside her on the floor. We awoke together. As she stood, I pushed my face into my hands, trying to cry her ugliness away.

WEIGHING SOULS

To measure the weight of a soul, the dying are placed on the scale as flesh divides from the ether. The soulweigher watches the last breath drift away and enters in his book the difference between live weight and the dead. In afterlife and silence, our departed are mist without conscience. Back in the world, the scale tips at every passing except when exiles die, for they live far from their souls and the border between Heaven and Hell runs through them. They weigh nothing, having left one life already. The weigher of souls weeps as they evaporate. The sleepless vale is never filled.

RAINCOAT

A brown raincoat hangs in a blizzard
on Old Town Square. The slim
figure of a man with the face of a fox
darts through the squall. He steps
into the coat for shelter

and stills the heart
of the storm. Raising a hand,
he releases a stream of ravens
from his cuff, then runs

a finger inside his collar.
The starch cracks. Flakes
of paper float
through the frozen air, settling
around him, over
his sparkling shoes, and rising

above the hem of his coat.
The square is quickly
covered. The weather ends.
The man pulls a flame

from his tongue, and lets it fall.
It runs in all directions,
scorching the ground and turning
buildings into sepia shadows
that peel away, leaving

only the scent of the fire
and an empty raincoat
with smoke licking the edges of its sleeves.

THE DISSIDENT

'And there's no longer enough of me left for myself.'
— Osip Mandelstam

My doors are breathing.
The curtains are transparent
and the floorboards listen
when I think aloud. I spend the nights

pressing my thoughts to the window
while I memorise lines
before I burn them. Manuscripts

disintegrate as bootsteps rhyme
on the stairs.
My voice hides under my tongue
when I answer the knocking
and nod

after each question from the agents
who come to protect
their country from my words.
They try to read the flakes

in the stove, and arrest my hands
for the black pages
they have written. The rest of me
surrenders. I count the stairs

to the street, and when the door
swings open, I begin
reciting: And there's no longer enough of me,

already I am losing words.
I try to complete the line
but my lips are blank paper.

MARINA TSVETAYEVA

for Joan Silva

Prologue: A Letter to Marina

In your city of white rain and iron
I saw death lying calmly
while winter slid
into the gutters. A spirit climbed

from that pale body, scattering flowers
as I almost touched the face.
It was thirty years
since you had listened to the chimes

and saw the birches
bend outside the Kremlin wall
as you lowered your eyes. The prayers
that blossomed on the lips of old women

could have been for you.
Their language
is of a homeless century.
Another country

grew around them
as they knelt to kiss the old one.
Marina, I have not slept
since then, but wandered

with your bells in my eyes.
In the churches of expatriates
I see that almost breathing face
as if it had been your face

of desperate words.
The trees are waking
in a country of their own.
You carried a branch

to other lives. I have carried nothing.
A spirit dressed in lace
has walked beside me.
In our times

walls are not a home.
We are holding a candle
whose flame rings
a stateless language in our hands.

*

Coming in from the fields
wearing a dress cut for nobility
Marina sits in her mother's Polish chair
which has been finely carved
out of hard wood. One hand

gently loosens
a button at her neck
while the other tears
a crust to feed
her peasant half. Marina stands

her ground through revolution
with her rich hand tracing comets
against a changing sky
and her poor hand
buried in her hair

fingering the faultline
through her mind. She names outcast
as her trade
and breaks her only loaf
like cleaving hope.

*

Stretching her money from beets
to potatoes, Marina
plans a meal of soup
and words. She chews the name Tarusa

tipping it from the spoon
into her appetite
for its graves and trees. In Tarusa

flagellant women ran
themselves into the earth
and lie beneath the fields
with furrows in their backs.
Marina dances

until her table circles her
and she holds the swirling flavour
of birches on her tongue.
She cannot calm her room. The ceiling

crumbles onto her
in a dream of cold black soil.

*

Marina reads white poems
to a red audience.
The royal army advances
from her notebook. It is waist deep
in Russia. Marina

lifts them from the mud
and weeps their losses. These lines
do not retreat. When she cheers
for the Tsar

her Bolshevik listeners
reach for the hand
that opens so bravely
to catch their applause.
How can uniforms understand

this woman is on fire.

*

Sergei is away from her.
Marina warms his place
with another man. Each passion
prepares for the next.
Moscow is a huge lover

too vast in its own sadness
to regret Marina
leaving. The land

falls away like Sergei's arms.
In the condensation
on her carriage window, Marina writes
how faithless

we are to our loves
and how true
to ourselves.

*

Marina's cigarettes in Prague
lie awake on a bed of ash
while Marina weaves
a thread of smoke between
the narrow streets.

Her insomniac shoes
tap small hours on the cobblestones
measuring the lines
she rolls on her tongue, inhaling
words to make

poetry her breath.
She breaks the tension in her lungs
with each new phrase
and her eyelids cannot fall
between her and these nights

in which the Charles Bridge spans
sleeping water and tired gravestones
lean against the shadow
of the synagogue. Marina's dawns
reflect the Moskva River

far to the east. She reenters
the room where light cannot follow
and writes alone
that in a Christian world
every poet wanders like the Jew.

*

Paris cannot read
Marina. A distant alphabet
shapes her manuscript. She speaks

for a land that fights itself
and will not print
her words. A piece of Russia
has been torn away

and blown to France
where Marina is exiled again
among her own. The only side
Marina claims

is that of the lost.
She swallows the news
of Mayakovsky's suicide
and will not spit his name.
She loves her dear enemy

for the ink
running from his temple.
Marina does not bleed

when opinion cuts her.
She looks to the Judgement Day of words
when she will bear no guilt.

*

Marina sinks a hand
into the black mud,
crosses herself with heavy fingers
and kisses her silver rings
to celebrate the thaw
with Moscow's holy bells.

In France she cannot hold the soil.
She shows an empty palm
to exiles' children

telling them not to mourn
an Eden they have never seen
and not to give their love
to countries.
All of them are poor.
A thief

had once invaded the room
where Marina served hunger
at every meal.
He emptied his pockets for her.

She carried his desparate coins abroad.
Prague.
Paris.

Back to a land of bells
whose tongues have been cut out.
Marina buys a rope
in Elabuga. In her poorest room

the weave traps words in her throat.
I say it for her:
Love no country.

SHOSTAKOVICH

I
Stars break open on the tundra.
A conscript fingers his winged lapels
and counts prisoners
wrapped in their bedding.
Drumrolls accompany them
where voices do not reach, where
embraces are chasms
and the train has no brake
to hold it back when the land beneath it
turns to frozen light.

II
Police on the stairs
are stepping to kettledrums
into a paper storm, reciting
the politics of eagles.
It is their season
to peel away words from the page
and patrol errant books.
They arrive
when it is dark,
while the people are dreaming
and talking in their sleep
to the flies on the wall.

III
A joke has escaped
among sweepers clearing platforms
where perspectives of irony
begin their long descent.
A path is made

for the next evacuees
who will replace the laughter
and look ahead, their eyes
crackling as they burn.

IV
The long months are over.
A hero walks to a marsh
where nobody can see him
and throws his medals to the fishes
then hangs his coat on a tree
for its sleeves to stiffen in the wind.

RETURN JOURNEY

I
A ship is waiting
at a field's edge

on red water
with its windows alight

and distant languages
spoken on board. Land

ends with sky
and sea one colour. Shrill

from thick
warm greenery, wooded

calls crack the calm
of the country I am

leaving. At the estuary
a compass

points where all waters
are the Earth's

and the journey
is a one way sleep,

ticket nonrefundable.

II

Copper, lace and linen
out of ancient hands
are for sale between
the tower and canal
at the weekly carnival
of small possessions. Water
alternates in circles
with houses in whose finely
balanced rooms
atlases lie open
at the page least travelled
and shelves are filled
with ceramics too gentle
for use. Each transaction
matches old patinas
with new money.

III

The clock in the Jewish quarter
has stopped. City trams
diverted from their routes

cross the wrong bridges
back and forth across
the river. Nobody knows

how long it will take
to get home
while musicians in the streets

play to the crowd,
keeping up with their times,
one generation behind.

IV

Walking on a long street, I have reached
a year once lived in
without knowing why the walls
of grey apartments were so dark
or sudden noises
shot ice
through rooms.
Fashions were a secret
smuggled in
from other countries.
Food was rationed,
lapels were wide
and the continent divided.
Nothing separates us now.
We are born survivors.

FAMILY REUNION

Our cousins have become strange
living in another country
where they never write
but we send invitations
for a visit. We remind them

about our common flesh
and the ancestors we share
although our land is so wide.
They build a tradition

of privacy, while we insist
on them coming to see
the new house, knowing
that they will not travel far

to be shamed by opulence.
Our shelves are always full,
spare rooms clean, and our letters
describe the welcome
they would receive, the comforts

awaiting them, and the joy
of being united. We remain
convinced that they would never
arrive at our doors

until now. They are driving
cars that barely hold
together, and there are so many
of them. We are finally

one family
with too little to feed

the visitors' eagerness as we sit
at a table that divides us
and remember the vastness of the land
that once held us together.

STATION TO STATION

Quiet wheels on easy steel,
past factory
smoke growing tall in the rain.
Lilacs bloom
beside the tracks.
Weekenders tend
their small green lots

as if the East
had never turned. The border
has been sold for souvenirs
but private walls
take longer to dismantle.
Young passengers love slick
music once forbidden

while an older man explains
how almost saying
what was meant
was enough when everyone listened
beneath the surfaces of words.
Other countries have happy
faces, he says, not like us,
travelling toward a new found sun,

into the spreading radius of fire.
The secret service
with no skills except to listen
is among the unemployed. On Alexanderplatz
a preacher chants religion

from farther east than anyone
imagines. Crosslegged
on concrete he decries

comforts unknown to his audience.
The trains run out of habit

past servicemen asleep,
waiting for connections
on the main line. Names
are being rehabilitated in Prague;
Palach

who ran in flames,
Kafka
whose face juts
from the house in which he wrote,
and students

whose candles
glow between the arches
where they were beaten when
burning was the only freedom.
Early morning, my departure

has vanished from its schedule.
A clerk asks an inspector
whether anything runs south today.
Perhaps. Nobody can say for sure

what happens now. Slow
is fast enough
and time is the sister of place.

AT KAFKA'S GRAVE

The rain's longhand
is written on leaves, new layers
over the old, and the fable
of the sky
grows. Language

hidden might
be remembered by a few
who whisper just
quieter than weather, until lips

moving suffice
to shape meaning in silent years.
Books conceived at night

record wanderings
in the quarters where sleep
is wasted time, and every
sound of shoes
has a story worth preserving.
Among those trees

I come to listen
as if the grave
were a window opening
into the earth.

ARTIST'S STATEMENT

The simple truth
is chosen for its colour.
It comes in shades
with no ambition to be beautiful.

I cannot see it for you,

only guide your eye
along lines of people waiting,
and leave you to guess

the object of their patience.
Pictorial time
is an instant at random.
Turn back the clock
or let it run

ahead, imagine bargains
or rationing. That is your luxury.
This is the spare world

I share with the enduring
travellers, where I study
timetables and meet them
at railway terminals, never asking
where they come from. Their countries
are in tatters

and the moment
is their only hope. Between bright
washed hills, I have hidden

borders. Each direction
is to the other side. We walk
faster than politics
and swear

allegiance to our breath.
I favour revolution
as the way to change

the constant rain, but armed
for nothing headier
than everyday routines, we persevere.
If you prefer

a certain red, or a story
of your own, call a taxi,
read another book. Had I
meant words
I would have used them.

LETTER FROM POLAND

Alma lives in mountains
where air is thin
and food is scarce.
American magazines

show her our tables, while hers
is spread for the inevitable
supper of complaints.
She shares

a gram of pleasure
when bread is fresh,
and walks an hour
to buy it, even when the flavour

betrays her. She writes
to an editor in Washington
that our waste
is her envy,

and laughs
at the wrappings we discard
and the emptiness inside them.
We are a country

that swallows the clouds
and drinks its water fast.
Relaxation is an industry
here, as we watch

the sky corrode
while our money burns.
Alma says her people
want to be like us;

to drown in choices
and inherit a future
that will be brief.

THE SCROLL

High in the silk mountains
water is the dry stroke
of a Chinese brush, twisting

between blank weave
where clouds have gathered
and the land beneath them
is a long thin line. Where men appear,

they fit between the hills
like rock, or lead

their beasts of burden through
a narrow cleft, over
wooden bridges to inspect
the fences at the outposts

where water, trees
making knots in the mist,
and disappearing reeds

mark the edge of their country
and the beginnings of one
which spreads to the fraying extremes
of the scroll, where balance

is no longer an art
and rain burns leaves away
until the bones of a forest
reach for green in the darkening air.

CROSSTOWN FREEWAY

We drive over bones.
Fifty five miles per hour.
Across the remains
of the soil, across sacred
and deserted sites
we ride at the speed
of a century

expiring. We do not stop
to worship, not for rest
or to drink. We live

moving. Our wheels
grind history beneath them.
Our shadows
are burnt at the edges.
Those who lived here
before us are ground
fine as corn, while

their descendants inherit
land already foreign
where nothing can be still.

We are told how fast
to move, where
to turn, and when to stop.
We are a people of directions
straining to break
order, hard down
on the pedal again and back

into the stream, imagining
a country so vast we could race
time itself and never
escape it.

LEAVING THE CITY

Our ruins glitter as none
before them. We shall leave this city
for another and begin again
with nothing to forget
and nobody to remember us. Our migrations
scar the land for others
to follow while hornets
nest in the skulls of our gods.
The air we have used cannot
be used again, and hangs
in many colours
over spaces
where water used to be.
We arrived here thirsty
for the future, burning
time as it happened
until the hours were so short
they fell through cracks in the earth.
No ancestors
weigh us down. We built
avenues of light, bridges of glass,
but when prayers to the paper clouds
bring no rain
and the stars we consult
are rust in the sky,
those who bought the land cannot
afford its water. No foundations
hold us. We can become
anyone now. We cross
deserts, naming prices for everything
we see, and stopping
where dividends are the biggest crop.
Once we lived in a city
that soared

but could not send its roots
deep enough into the ground to hold.
Archaeology won't discover us
who lived so quickly
in the eye of the sun.

THE OFFENSIVE

Throw a handful of fire into the Tigris.
Fill the Euphrates with sand.

Turn all blazing waters
back to their source. Haul down the sky

and rinse darkness away.
Illuminate valleys with flares

while the land is shivering.
Pour oil

into the seas, and let the tide
burn. Beat history

into submission, then clear
a path through the clouds

and raise
the victor's flag on a thorn.

FUGUE

The stars ignite. The monuments
of Eden barely fill
a vase kept underground, to be unearthed

in another age. The sea
burns away until
it would fit inside a child's heart.
The stars of Eden fall like nails
onto the ground. A flame

runs along a dead man's lips.
He will be unearthed in another age.
His heart rattles

as if it were full of seeds.
The monuments of Eden lie beside him.
His pockets are lined
with soot, and in his open hand
is his ration

of black flour. In another age
he would have seen his enemy's eye.
Eden's rivers rattle in their banks

and run into a sea
without tides. At night
the stars come down to Eden and the ground
tears open. A flame
runs along a dead child's fingers

and solders them together.
At the heart of a loaf a mother breaks
is a pool of fire. The racing stars

leave trails of coloured light
behind them as they strip the earth
to its bones. Seabirds cannot lift
their feathers. Their eyes
rattle as they try

to shake the weight from their wings,
but their sea
has no tides. Where the ground

breaks open it reveals
the monuments of Eden and the hearts
of its children. In another age
someone will peel the layers back,
discovering an Eden

too vast for their eyes, and the sea
will run across a dead man's lips
begging him to speak.

DUBROVNIK

Approach Dubrovnik from the coastal road
where traffic takes a narrow
course beside the sea, below mountains
that have you believe

the mainland is stone and charred calcium.
Offshore are islands
barely inhabitable, but a living
is possible for some, regardless

of the bleak ascents
or smooth acres that are their inherited
countries. Ignore
the temptation to stop

between cypresses to watch
the sun go down, or eavesdrop
on the fishermen in any
of the ports along your way. Sleep

if you must, with a family that opens
up to strangers, trusting
them but speaking
no language you could know. Living

on the edge of their country, they have words
for little more than water
and the rock overshadowing them.
Leave them to their plain rooms

and continue until
the battlements are visible.
Walk along them, looking down
into yards where chairs

are set for solitude,
through the back doors
of houses left open for the air inside
to clear, and across

tiled roofs without weight
in the sunlight. Take the steps
into the streets and mingle
with shoppers until you are one of them. You have

come to buy rations for a siege.
Someone has cut the road you arrived on
with scissors. Dubrovnik
is your city now, to defend.

SIBENIK

Buy meagre rations at the market stalls
where strong women sell

radishes and bacon, salt
and bread, vinegar and plums; enough

for you to taste their lives
with their walls appearing suddenly

so thin the wind
passes through them. Not long

ago, visitors posed
on the cathedral steps in summer clothes

with no ambition but to be
pieces of a memory floating

by. They were here for the sun
and the age of the buildings. They liked

how the women stood, smelling
of their crops and black

dresses. You will find none
of this, but a sky

welded to the ends of rifles
as they are raised, and once you take up

a position it is yours. It will be
too late then for choosing sides.

SARAJEVO

Follow the river, where Serbs
are washing their shirts, surrounded
by buzzing trees. When you reach a town
with green and yellow buses

rattling with exhaust
in clouds behind them, overflowing
passengers and staying
loosely to their route, take one
to the hotel on the square

which you will know by the ballroom speakers
playing louder than you can hear.
Sleep.
The rest is a long journey

and once you reach Sarajevo
the final stretch is a backwards ride
along the stony boulevard

to a street of coppersmiths.
This is the past.
Go underground.
Away from the light

is a sale of carpets, sweets and shade.
When your century catches up with you,
stay in that deep country of silks

while the war goes on above you,
growing slowly obsolete.

This book is dedicated to my wife, Brittani. Without your support this would have never been possible.

PROLOGUE

John reached into the cupboard and pulled out two glasses. "Normally, I'm more of a beer guy, but I've got a nice Merlot that I was planning to save for a special occasion. I'd say this counts." His round, clean-shaven face broke out into a boyish grin as he poured the wine. John didn't have an ounce of fat on him, but his large, broad-shouldered frame complimented his chubby face quite nicely.

This was his second date with Kayla, and it was going well. She was a short brunette with an athletic build who lived two floors up in the building he had moved into recently.

The bottle had been a housewarming gift from his best friend, Derek, who was always trying to play matchmaker for him. Ever since Derek and Emily'd had their baby, they'd been pushing extra hard, even by their standards, for him to get out there and meet the right girl.

Although it was difficult to watch his two best friends take steps forward in life while he was still living the bachelor life, John liked where he was at. It wasn't that he didn't want to eventually settle down and have a family of his own, but at the moment, he was making the most of his youthful years while he had them.

Kayla seemed to be just what he needed. She was fun to be around, smart, and understood that he wasn't looking for a big commitment.

With a cup in each hand, John made his way over to the couch. "One glass of red wine. Aged over one thousand years."

"Oh, my. One thousand years, huh?" Kayla chuckled as she grabbed the glass by the stem. She swirled it and pretended to give it a pretentious sniff—her impression of a wine connoisseur.

John smirked as he took a seat on the couch next to her. "Yes. Poured directly from a wineskin passed down in my family through generations."

They both burst out laughing. He wondered how he was lucky enough to meet such a wonderful girl who understood his silly humor.

"So... what should we do now?" John asked when the laughter died down. "I spy?" The condo had a studio layout and he had yet to fully furnish it. Besides the couch they were sitting on, the only other 'spy-able' items in view were a coffee table and a few stacks of cardboard boxes that had yet to be unpacked.

"Hmm." Kayla thought for a moment as she set her drink down. "How about two truths and a lie?" she suggested through a smile.

"Okay. You first." John took another sip.

Just then, there was a knock at the door. "Hold that thought. I'll be right back." John got up to answer it.

He opened the door to see his best friend, rainwater dripping from his shaggy black hair down onto his black leather jacket, out of breath and clearly distraught. "What's up? You okay, man?"

"I don't have a lot of time." Derek was still attempting to catch his breath between his words. "I need you to take Caleb."

John hadn't noticed the car seat on the ground next to Derek at first. He could see the three-month-old baby sleeping soundly inside.

Derek continued, "I need you to raise him. We have to go—"

"Wait. Slow down. What are you talking about?" John noticed the rising tension in his voice and tried to calm his tone. "Just tell me what's going on. What do you mean, *raise* him?" John had agreed to be Caleb's next of kin before he was born, but this was all so sudden.

"I don't have time to explain. Our lives are at risk, and we have to go off the grid. I *need* you to take Caleb. You're the only person I can trust."

John had known Derek his whole life. He had never seen him this rattled. Still confused—but confident he could trust the word of his lifelong friend—he picked up the car seat. "I hope there's some kind of manual on how to take care of him in here." He was sure that now wasn't the time for humor, but he was only half joking.

"John, please. I need to go. I want you to raise him as if he were yours. I trust you completely. I only ask that you don't let them implant a brain drive. They'll send him right to OASIS. We never wanted that for him."

"You have my word. Should I expect to hear from you?"

"No. But take this." Derek pulled a small red memory stick out of his jacket pocket and held it out in his palm. "If Caleb is ever forced to get a brain drive, give this to him. It'll explain all of this." John took it.

Derek bent down, kissed Caleb on the forehead, and whispered something to him. He looked up at John through watery eyes. "He's *your* son now," he choked out.

John nodded, fighting back tears of his own.

Derek exhaled, wiped his eyes, and began nodding rhythmically while staring down at the car seat as if he was trying to convince his body to do something his mind had already decided. Without another word, he darted off, sprinting down the hall and into the stairwell, never looking back.

The reality didn't set in until the following morning when

John received a phone call with the news. He was informed that his best friends, Derek and Emily Foster, had been killed in a fiery car crash, along with their three-month-old son.

CHAPTER ONE

Seventeen years later

Caleb exhaled slowly, lining the sights of his bow up with his prey. It seemed that fate had smiled on him that day. It was rare to see a deer in these woods, let alone one this large.

While Caleb was usually a sure shot with his compound bow, the pressure of going home empty-handed again weighed heavily on his mind. It had been a month since they'd had meat in their freezer. This deer alone could feed him and his father through the entire winter. When he'd left his house that morning, he'd had no idea he'd be faced with such an important shot.

As he stared down the sights of his bow, memories of his recent hunting trip flashed through his mind.

During his last hunt, he'd managed to miss *every* shot he took.

When he'd lined up the shot on his first target—a large snowshoe hare—it felt right. He'd accounted for the wind and elevation relative to the animal, a skill that had been honed over years of hunting in these woods. Despite that, the arrow had landed short of the target by six inches, and the hare scurried away in a startled panic.

Shortly after having missed the hare, Caleb was mid-stride when he spotted a ring-necked pheasant through a clearing in the white birch trees littering the woods. Afraid he would scare the unsuspecting bird away with any movement, he'd decided to shoot from the awkward stance he found himself in. He had been certain he could land the shot, even without proper footing, so he readied his bow and carefully raised it to his eye line.

No sooner had the arrow escaped his bowstring than he closed his eyes in disappointment. The arrow had fallen short, burying itself in the dirt and sending the frightened bird into flight.

Clenching his jaw in frustration, he'd reached down and collected his arrow, wiping the dirt off of the stainless-steel arrowhead and shaft before returning it to his quiver.

A while later, Caleb had picked up on a fresh set of tracks. Another hare—a chance for redemption. After having tracked the animal for a solid ten minutes, he spotted the hare twenty yards away, feeding on berries that had fallen from a bush.

He couldn't count how many times he had hit a shot just like this. Without hesitation, he'd taken aim at the hare and let the arrow fly. Again, the arrow had landed short of his intended target.

That was the last time he had fired his bow.

Ordinarily, Caleb would have realigned his sights before going out for another hunt, but he'd gotten a late start this morning, and it'd slipped his mind entirely. Although he possessed a photographic memory, that didn't mean he remembered *everything*. As natural as it was for Caleb to recall memories in vivid detail as though he was experiencing them again, forgetting mundane tasks came just as naturally.

Caleb adjusted his aim to account for his recent misses. He visualized the last three shots in his mind and mentally overlaid them onto his current target. As a result, he was now aiming near the top of the doe's shoulder blade. If the arrow flew straight, he would miss the kill-shot, but if the arrow instead traveled along the same path as his previous shots, the doe was as good as dead.

Before he could think, his body acted. Caleb's fingers released the bowstring, and the arrow sliced through the cool air like a knife through butter, hitting the deer directly in the heart. The deer ran fifteen feet before collapsing face-first in the rust-colored foliage carpeting the forest floor. Caleb let out an audible sigh of relief.

Caleb's father would, without a doubt, echo the sentiment. Between working long hours to keep food on the table and spending his days off chopping wood to prepare for the coming winter, John didn't have time for hunting, leaving that responsibility solely to Caleb.

When John had first taught Caleb to hunt at the age of twelve, the boy relished every moment in the woods. He'd even spent the bulk of his time at home preparing for his next hunt.

Now it felt more like a never-ending chore. No matter how much time he devoted to hunting, he could never get ahead. The recent unprecedented spike in the number of hunters, driven by necessity rather than sport, made his trips into the woods far less fruitful than ever.

Ten years ago, the local manufacturing plant had been forced to close its doors. It had been the lifeblood of Amahl, the small city where Caleb grew up. In its heyday, the plant had provided work to nearly half of the city. After it shut down, Amahl's population had dwindled down as more and more people fled to find work elsewhere.

Those who stuck around were only faced with further hardships as more and more businesses met the same fate. The desperation of the people of Amahl was palpable. Jobless and hungry, those who were able-bodied took up hunting. It was simply a matter of time before the local deer population dwindled down to a dangerously low level.

According to John, the struggles Amahl faced were merely symptoms of a larger problem plaguing the entire nation of

Materra: technology had advanced to the point of displacing a large amount of the workforce, and the government had done nothing to remedy the issue.

Recently it had become a nightly ritual for John to rant to Caleb at the dinner table about how the president had no idea what he was doing and how his lack of action was obliterating the middle class, effectively eroding the economy.

As Caleb approached the dead deer, he reached to his side and unholstered his hunting knife.

Gutting the deer here in the woods would allow the meat to begin cooling while he dragged it home, and it had the added benefit of reducing the carry weight. There was always the risk of a pack of wolves catching the scent of the gutted animal, but it was a small one, and the benefits far outweighed the risks.

After field-dressing the doe, Caleb reached into his backpack for a harness, attaching one end to the deer carcass and the other to his shoulders before beginning the mile and a half trek home.

It was times like this when Caleb wished he was as big as his father. He wasn't scrawny by any means. He stood six feet tall with broad shoulders, his muscular frame chiseled and lean. But John was truly a mountain of a man, standing a full four inches taller than Caleb, with bulkier shoulders and hands like catcher's mitts.

Aside from his shaggy black hair, Caleb took after his mother in appearance. His eyes were a deeper, darker blue than John's and his jaw was squared rather than rounded.

John had always told Caleb he had his mother's eyes, and though Caleb had no memories of his mother, the few pictures of her he had seen suggested he did, in fact, inherit them from her.

Growing up, Caleb had always been curious about his mother, Emily. He desperately craved information about her, wondering how else he might be like her, or how his parents met in the first place. John always seemed to avoid the topic, so Caleb eventually stopped asking. He figured it was too painful for his father to talk about her. The only time Caleb had seen his father cry was when he told the story of her death. She had died during childbirth due to excessive blood loss during what was considered a routine c-section. Caleb could still recall the agony in John's voice when he uttered the word "routine" as a single tear rolled down his cheek.

Knowing more about his mother wouldn't change anything. It wouldn't bring her back. But understanding that didn't make it any easier for Caleb to ignore his desire to learn more about her. He went as far as looking through boxes in the attic for her old things, but his efforts didn't pay off. His father had gotten rid of everything of hers. So Caleb tried to focus on what he did have: his father.

The last half mile was brutal. Caleb's legs were burning, screaming at him to stop, and his shoulders were aching where the straps had dug into his clavicles. Each breath came heavier than the last. He kept his head up and his eyes fixed on the smoke rising from the treetops in the distance as he hiked forward, one agonizing step at a time.

It was approaching noon when Caleb reached home. Their house was a small, two-bedroom cedar log cabin with a stone chimney and wrap-around porch. Some might've considered it more of a "cottage" than a house, but it was the only home Caleb had ever known. Smoke billowing from the chimney leant it a cozy and welcoming feel.

A red wooden shed accompanied the house. Freshly chopped wood bridged the gap between the two, stacked neatly in three rows. Five full rows of logs would be enough to heat the house for the duration of the winter.

Inside the shed, Caleb lifted and removed the punching bag hanging from the rafters. John would have to live without his stress reliever for a few days. He strung the deer up in the punching bag's place and put a wide bucket underneath to catch the blood. The deer would need to hang and cool for a couple of days before being butchered. Luckily, the weather this time of the year was cold enough to permit storing the deer in the shed.

After washing up at the water pump, Caleb headed inside. He chucked a couple logs into the wood stove before making his way into the kitchen for a quick lunch.

The interior of the house matched the exterior. Stacked red cedar logs made up the walls. Sheltered from the elements, the stones that made up the indoor portion of the chimney retained more of their natural colors, so a mixture of vibrant blue, white, and brown rocks crawled up to the ceiling. The entire living space was confined to one level, and each room was furnished with cedar furniture, adding to the overall charm of the place. Even the cupboards and countertops throughout the house were made of sturdy cedar.

Following lunch, Caleb made his way back outside to chop wood. He knew John was planning to split logs after work, but Caleb had other plans.

It was tradition for them to celebrate getting a deer by going out to dinner. It had been over two years since they'd last eaten at a restaurant, and Caleb longed for a burger from his favorite place, Marv's Diner.

John was aiming to get the last two rows of logs filled in before the first snow. Caleb wielded an axe and got to work. If he could make progress on the firewood, John would be more likely to enjoy a night out at Marv's.

Filled with excitement, Caleb was reenergized, almost like he hadn't dragged a deer carcass over a mile earlier that day. Each swing of his axe felt like a step closer to tasting one of those deluxe bacon cheeseburgers.

Caleb thought back to the first time he'd eaten at Marv's.

"Dad, are you sure about this place?" an apprehensive ten-year-old Caleb had whispered just loudly enough for his father to hear over the chatter of a dinner rush.

"Trust me, bud. This is where my father took me when I turned ten."

The air was thick with the smell of greasy food. The wallpaper was yellow, but it looked like it should have been white, almost as if the *smell* had soaked into the walls. *Can a smell stain walls?* he'd wondered to himself.

A friendly waitress had seated them at a cushiony red booth and gathered drink orders. "Two waters please," John answered with a smile. "I'm excited for you to try the burgers here." He was oozing enthusiasm as he slid the menus aside. "I know you wanted pizza, but this is sort of a family tradition. If my father did one thing right, it was bringing me here on my birthday every year."

Something had Caleb's attention. His face scrunched as he'd stared across the restaurant.

"You okay, bud?"

Caleb had shifted in his seat and manufactured a half-smile. "Yeah, Dad, I'm fine. I just feel like the waitress should have washed her hands before taking that lady her plate."

"You've got to get over that obsession with germs. I love that you're reading those books. You're learning a lot. And you're a smart kid, much smarter than I ever was. But knowledge without context is useless. You're going to learn as you grow up that the real world is different than it is in books. In fact, some germs are good for us. Do your books tell you about those ones?"

"Yeah, Dad, they do. Do we have to eat here?"

John had let out a sigh. "I'll tell you what, bud. I'm going to order us a couple burgers and fries. If you don't like—no, if you don't *love* the burger, I promise you I'll take you wherever you want to get another meal. Okay?"

"Deal." Caleb knew a good deal when he heard one. At the time, he didn't realize which end of the deal was better.

Caleb powered through the remainder of the logs, filling in the third row and getting a good start on the fourth before going back inside to wash up. A warm, refreshing shower would do his muscles good.

After his shower, Caleb went to get dressed. His room was small, barely big enough to fit a bed, dresser and desk, but he kept it tidy and never felt like he needed more space.

He pulled open a drawer on his cedar dresser, reaching past the books that weighed down the front of the drawer to grab clothes out.

One summer day when Caleb was six years old, John had come home with the bed of his truck nearly overflowing with books. Apparently, a local library was undergoing renovations, and in the process, they needed to get rid of books that had been archived. They were simply giving them away. Caleb was ecstatic—he loved to read. John had always embraced Caleb's love for books, maxing out his own library card every month to ensure the boy always had new books to read. Still, Caleb had never seen so many books in one place before. Between the bookshelf in the living room, the top of the hall closet, and the attic, they were only just able to fit all of the books in the house.

Over the years, Caleb started keeping his favorite books in his dresser drawers, which were now half-full of them. He'd read every one at least a dozen times and regarded them as his prized possessions.

Fully-clothed, Caleb headed into the living room, hoping to have time to read a book or two before John returned home from work.

On top of the bookshelf sat a handbook John had brought home from work for Caleb: *The Complete Guide to Small Machine Repair*. He was going to be eighteen soon, and John was encouraging him to follow in his footsteps as a repairman. If Caleb was honest with himself, he wasn't sure what he wanted to do with his life, but he knew fixing machines for a living wasn't for him. He would never tell his father this, but he wanted *more*. Living paycheck to paycheck wasn't something he was interested in.

He moved his attention past the handbook and plucked another off of the shelf: *The Great War: A World Divided* by Alfred

Donovan. He made himself comfortable on the couch, the only piece of furniture in the house not made of cedar. Caleb enjoyed reading anything, but he found non-fiction books far more interesting.

Two hours later, Caleb was nearly half-way through the book. It was all information he had read before, only presented through a new perspective—the author had served in the war as a general.

Long after the world had been fully explored and every land was claimed by its inhabitants, it was divided neatly into four nations, each occupying its own continent. They lived peacefully together, trading freely and sharing resources with one another.

Each nation specialized in different exports. Materra, the largest and northernmost nation, specialized in manufacturing. Agriculture was the chief export of Feraxia, the southernmost nation. Aridor, a relatively small nation to the west, led the world in technology. The nation confined to the eastern continent, Crayna, contributed precious metals and fine jewels to the world through the process of mining.

When it was discovered that Aridor was withholding information regarding its nuclear weapons arsenal—in an attempt to gain power over the rest of the world—the other three nations united in a preemptive strike against Aridor. The short conflict, which led to the destruction of Aridor's capital city and the eventual downfall of its civilization altogether, would forever be known as the Great War.

After the war, a peace treaty was formed between the three remaining nations in an attempt to stabilize the world and prevent future conflict. Included within the agreement were plans for each country to accept refugees from Aridor, as well as stipulations that barred all trade with the fallen nation. It was believed these measures would help ensure that Aridor could never rise to power again.

Following the signing of the peace treaty, there came a forty-eight-year period of technological advancement and worldwide prosperity. Although it was short-lived, Materra, Feraxia and Crayna remained peaceful neighbors ever since. Aridor remained a desolate relic of a nation.

Caleb closed the book, opting to take a nap instead. John was due home in about an hour and he couldn't wait to tell him the good news.

~*~

After a long day of fixing machines all around the city, John pulled into his driveway to a nice surprise. Caleb had chopped up all of the logs he had pulled out of the woods. What a relief. He could finally get some rest.

John didn't grow up aspiring to be a machine repairman, but fate had a funny way of working things out. At one point, he was the heavyweight boxing champion of the world. But when Caleb came into his life, he understood he needed to make some changes. He gave his best friend his word that he would look after the boy, and that's what he did.

Being a freelance repairman offered John benefits that fit his current situation nicely. He was able to make his own hours, which had allowed him to school Caleb at home. Getting paid under the table allowed him to report a lower income to the government, helping him keep a low profile.

But as the years went by and brain drive technology continued to advance, he found he had to lower his rates to stay competitive, which forced him to work longer hours to keep up with his bills. And it didn't help that his brain drive didn't work anymore—yet another sacrifice he'd made in the name of boxing.

John entered the house to find Caleb perched up on the couch, grinning at him. "Hey bud, thanks for chopping up the wood. Why are you looking at me like you're going to try to eat me?"

"I have a surprise for you. C'mon." Caleb got up and started for the door.

"You mind if I change first?" John wore coveralls to work every day and, as usual, he was covered in dirt and oil.

"It'll be quick," Caleb replied, the smile on his face seeming permanent.

He pried open the shed door and stepped inside. John followed. His mouth dropped open when he saw the large doe suspended from the rafters.

"Wow. Good work, Caleb. She's a big one!"

Caleb beamed, pride stretching his smile even further than before.

"Wow..." he said again, staring at the deer as he tried to estimate how much meat they would get from it. He guessed they could make it through the winter with this alone.

After John washed up, he made his way to the kitchen and opened the fridge, giving his scruffy beard a stroke as he took stock.

"What sounds good for dinner, bud? Leftover meatloaf or soup?" he called out to Caleb.

He was met with a confused look. "Are you forgetting about our tradition? I know it's been a while since we got a deer, but you're not *that* old."

The truth was, he hadn't forgotten, but he'd hoped Caleb had. He was working his tail off, but he couldn't seem to get ahead of his bills. It wasn't the house—it was paid for. He was at risk of falling behind on the utility payments on his other property, and he couldn't let that happen.

"I haven't forgotten bud, we just can't... we can't afford it. I know I've been working a lot, but I had to lower my rates again."

Caleb sank down into the couch. "Oh. I guess I thought the deer would take some stress off of the grocery budget."

"That will certainly help, and I really appreciate you working so hard around here. I hate to buck tradition. I'm just worried, bud."

John was underselling how much the deer was worth to them.

Having enough meat for the next six months was huge. But he wouldn't feel comfortable until he was ahead on bills. Until then, he would need to crack down on extra spending.

"I understand, Dad." Caleb picked up a book and leaned back onto the couch, cracking it open. "Soup."

John grabbed a can of soup out of the cupboard and then paused, glancing over at Caleb. The defeated look on his face cut through John and tugged at his heart. Even though John's responsibilities were weighing on him, he never intended for Caleb to have to deal with that pressure. The decisions that led to this situation were his and his alone. Caleb was an innocent bystander caught in the crossfire of John's questionable choices.

"You know what? One dinner out isn't going to be what puts us out on the street. Grab your coat, bud."

Caleb shot up from his seat and had his shoes on before John could set the can down on the counter.

"Don't forget your hat." He felt silly still reminding Caleb to grab a hat after all these years, but the fact remained: he couldn't be seen without one. If anyone saw him without a brain drive implant, all of this—everything he was working for—would be for nothing.

"I know, Dad." Caleb replied in a tone that suggested he'd heard the same reminder a thousand times before. He slipped his winter cap on and they were out the door.

A night out at Marv's was just what they both needed. They ordered two deluxe bacon cheeseburgers with fries and had a great time catching up.

Caleb recounted the story of his hunting trip earlier that day and John listened intently, impressed by Caleb's ability to adjust his aim on the fly like that. His gift was truly incredible. For a moment, John felt like he was looking at himself when he was seventeen. That night reminded him of better times and gave him hope for the future.

The hope was short-lived.

~*~

The following morning, John and Caleb were getting ready to go for a hike when there was a knock at the door.

John answered. "Hey, Officer Garrison, what brings you out this way? You need to search the property again for another lost hiker?"

Officer Garrison was a regular at their house. Since their property backed up to a popular trail, hikers occasionally strayed off the path and ended up lost in the dense woods.

"I'm afraid not, Mr. Shaw." The officer glanced over at Caleb and then back at John. "Can we talk outside?"

Caleb watched through the window as the officer spoke with his father. He couldn't hear what was being said, but he got the impression something was horribly wrong.

The stout officer looked up at John, his slightly wrinkled face very businesslike as he spoke. Caleb had never seen Officer Garrison so serious. He normally wore a smile like a uniform.

Meanwhile, John was growing frantic. He began waving his arms around as he yelled into Officer Garrison's emotionless face.

Officer Garrison repeatedly attempted to calm him down, his expression remaining stoic. At one point, he even pointed to an unmarked car in the driveway as if it held the answer to all of John's concerns.

After a moment of silence from both men, John faced away from the officer and put his hands behind his back. Garrison started slipping handcuffs on his wrists.

Caleb's eyes grew wide and he sprang to his feet, bursting through the front door.

"Johnathan Shaw, you are under arrest for neglect of a minor."

John looked back at Caleb, his face wrought with regret, tears forming at the corners of his eyes. "I'm sorry," he muttered before turning around and walking toward the police car.

It was the second time Caleb had ever seen his father cry.

CHAPTER TWO

Before Caleb had time to process what was happening, a short woman with wavy black hair and dressed in a black pantsuit appeared, seemingly out of nowhere. In reality, she had emerged from the unmarked sedan in the driveway as Caleb watched the cop car haul his father away.

"Hi, Caleb. My name is Kimberly Lynn. I'm with the Child Protection Agency. I know this is all a lot to take in—"

"Where are they taking my dad?" Caleb talked over her in a panic-stricken voice. "What's going on?"

"Your father will be fine. In these cases, the police typically hold the parents overnight and they are released the next morning. He should be back home tomorrow."

"These cases? What are you talking about? Neglect of a minor? What does that even mean?" He kept looking past the woman, toward the driveway, as if the police car was going to pull back in any second.

"I'd be happy to fill you in on all of the details in the car." Kimberly spoke in a calm, reassuring tone. "However, right now I need you to go inside and pack a change of clothes. You'll be coming with me for the night. I'll go wait in my car. When you're done packing, come outside and join me. I'll explain everything."

Frustrated and at a loss for words, Caleb reluctantly followed her orders.

"Looks like a cozy place," Kimberly said through a cheery smile as Caleb got settled into the passenger seat. She was clearly trying to break the ice with a lighter topic, but Caleb saw through the tactic and decided to cut right to the chase.

"Care to tell me what's going on or where you're taking me?" he asked, his words sharp and unapologetic.

"Certainly, let's start there," she said as she pulled out of the driveway and onto the road. "My orders were to bring you directly to the hospital."

"The hospital? Do they think my father hits me or something? Because I can assure you, he—"

"No, no, no," Kimberly interjected. "That's not what this is about. Someone called to report a child without a brain drive implant at a local diner last night, and the tip led us to your house."

Caleb thought back to the previous night. He had only taken his hat off briefly in the bathroom to scratch an itch on the back of his head. He thought he was alone in the bathroom. Had someone seen him? Who would have reported him?

"Did your father ever tell you about the brain drive?"

"Yeah, he told me about it. It's that thing on the back of people's heads that the government uses to track people. He didn't want me to have one, and I agree with him. So what?" Caleb could feel anger starting to rise in his chest. All of this was over a tracking chip?

"Ah, I see." Kimberly arched her eyebrows, looking both understanding and sympathetic. "Well, the brain drive is *not* a tracking device. It's much more than that."

Caleb shot her a skeptical look. They must be talking about two different things, he decided—his father wouldn't lie about something like that.

"I'm probably not the best person to describe it since I don't actually know how it works, but it's essentially a storage device for memories. Your brain can then read the information from saved files and interpret them as if they're your own experiences."

Caleb's head was spinning. If that was true, why would his father keep it from him? Kimberly must have seen the confusion on his face, because she went on.

"So for example, if you wanted to know how to make zucchini bread you could upload a recipe onto your brain drive and then, just like that"—she snapped her fingers for effect—"you'd *know* how to make it."

Caleb's mind was already flooding with the possibilities of such technology. He noticed his mouth was hanging open and quickly shut it. He still couldn't make sense of his father hiding this from him. There had to be a downside.

"Why? Why wouldn't my father have told me that? I really don't understand how any of that could be true."

"That, I'm afraid, I couldn't tell you. It's amazing technology. I don't know how I would function without mine. I'm honestly surprised you made it this long without anyone noticing. Children typically have a brain drive implanted at age six, right before beginning formal schooling. Did you... go to school?" Kimberly asked gingerly, as though trying not to offend him.

"I was homeschooled," Caleb answered plainly. *Was this why?* he wondered. John had always told him it was so he would be able to learn at his own pace. What other lies had John told to cover all of this up? He felt sick to his stomach thinking about it.

"Well, even though you're seventeen now, you'll still need to have a brain drive implanted."

That got Caleb's attention. He snapped his head to the side to look directly at Kimberly.

"Don't worry, it's a simple procedure." Her voice sounded reassuring, but it didn't make him feel any better.

"What if I refuse? And don't you need my father's permission?"

"Technically, while you're under my care, I am acting as your guardian on behalf of the government, so we don't need your father's consent. Aside from that, brain drive implant surgeries are *different*—they're government mandated for all minors. But trust me when I tell you they're a *good* thing."

Caleb didn't respond. Instead he stared blankly out the window. Even though John had kept all of this from him, he still wished he was here. He'd know what to do.

"Listen, I know today has been... weird, to say the least, but we should be at the hospital in about twenty minutes. They'll be able to explain all of this much better than I can. I'll give you some time to process all of this."

They spent the rest of the ride in complete silence.

~*~

Aside from the day he was born, this was the first time Caleb had ever been in a hospital. It didn't seem at all like he would have imagined. Nurses and doctors wearing loose-fitting clothes resembling pajamas walked leisurely through the halls, casually chatting with one another. There was no urgency whatsoever. The walls and floor tiles were both a creamy white color, only in slightly different shades. The ceiling was stark white and fluorescent bulbs illuminated the bland halls in an almost unnatural glow. If the hospital's interior was designed with the intention of making the most boring-looking building imaginable, they succeeded by a mile.

Shortly after completing paperwork, a nurse came to the waiting room, took Caleb to an exam room and asked him a few general questions before leaving.

The exam room looked equally as dull as the hallway. Nearly everything in the room, including the bed Caleb was seated on, was some variation of an off-white color that didn't quite match the floor or the walls.

The door handle turned and a tall skeleton of a man wearing a white lab coat entered. He was bald except for the white hair on the sides and back of his head. Bushy white-gray eyebrows sat above his deep-set eyes and long, pointed nose. His leathery skin reminded Caleb of tree bark.

"Hi, Caleb," the man said as he sat down on a black stool, one of the few non-white objects in the room. "I'm Dr. Parks. I understand you're here to receive a brain drive implant. I spoke with your case worker and she informed me of your circumstances. How are you feeling about all this?"

"Confused," replied Caleb. "My dad was arrested and now this lady is telling me I need surgery to get an implant in my brain. What is going on?"

"To be honest, I was also a little confused when I saw your chart. You're a fair bit older than typical for this procedure. I'm not sure how you managed to slip through the cracks, but the law dictates every minor is to receive a brain drive implant."

"Yeah, that's what Kimberly told me," Caleb said, his chest tightening as the inevitability of surgery became more apparent. "How does it work?" he asked through the lump forming in his throat.

"The brain drive is merely a storage device that holds memories in the form of electronic data. The true technological miracle is contained within the wiring that connects the brain drive to the brain." The doctor spoke in a way that suggested he had said these exact words, in the same exact way, countless times. "These wires have specialized feet that connect to the brain and mimic synapses. This connection allows the brain access to the data contained within the device, and it interprets these stored memories no differently than those native to the brain. Practically speaking, it is used to access information you never had to invest time into learning. It really is a great piece of technology, and I'm certain you'll be happy to have one."

Caleb flashed a cautious smile and nodded. So his father really *had* lied to him. He felt like he should be more upset about such a big lie, but for some reason he wasn't angry, only shocked.

"And the surgery?"

"We start by drilling a small hole near the base of your occipital bone." Dr. Parks put his hand on the back of his head to demonstrate. "This is where your brain drive will sit. Once the hole is drilled, we insert four wires through. Two wires for each side of the brain, one for each of your temporal and occipital lobes. After the wires are attached, the brain drive device is placed over the opening and a small part of it goes inside to plug the hole. The outer edges are then sealed to your skull."

Dr. Parks pulled a model unit of a brain drive out of his coat pocket and held it up, showing Caleb the different parts. It looked like a small metal hockey puck about the size of a bottle cap with a small hole on one end and four short wires coming from the other. "There is a port on the top that's used for transferring memories to and from the brain drive."

Caleb was looking at the model with apprehension, like he was afraid the device could leap out of the man's bony hand at any time and attach itself to him. "I'm not a doctor, but this seems like an unnecessarily risky procedure. I've been fine without this thing and I don't want to have surgery on my skull just to have it. Can't I deny it? I'm almost an adult."

He was sure that wouldn't work, but he had to try. Although he was intrigued by the technology, this all felt wrong. If he was going to have something like this done, he wanted John to be there. Besides, there *had* to be a reason John sheltered him from this. He was sure of it.

"I'm afraid that's not up to me. My hands are tied. I'm required by law to do the surgery. But this technology has been around for almost fifty years now and the complication rate is extremely low. I know it seems like a risky procedure, but in reality, it takes less than an hour and you will be able to go home as early as tomorrow."

Overwhelmed from information and feeling defeated, Caleb looked down at the floor and nodded.

Dr. Parks stood up. "Okay," he said, his voice rising an octave. "I'll have a nurse come and prep you for surgery as soon as an operating room is available." Then he left the room.

Caleb laid back on the examination table, lacing his fingers together and putting his hands over his eyes in an attempt to block out the world and be alone with his thoughts.

He thought back to the first time his father told him about the brain drive. He was five years old at the time.

"Dad, what's that thing on the back of your head?"

John sighed as he'd pulled the truck to a stop at the grocery store, pausing as if he was trying to find the right words. "It's a… tracking chip. The government uses it to find people. So it would tell them where I was if they needed me."

"Why would they need you?" Caleb had asked.

"Well, it could be for any reason, bud. Like, if I broke a law or something, they might need to track me down."

"Why would you break a law?" His face was now scrunched into a puzzled look.

"I wouldn't."

Before he could ask his father what would happen if he broke the law, John spoke again.

"You know what, bud? Let's go get some groceries. We can get any cereal you want!"

"Yes! One more question, Dad. Do I have to get one of those tracker things on my head?"

"No, you don't. Some parents choose to have their kids get one so they can track their kids, but you don't need one. If I can't find you, I'll just assume the wolves got you."

Caleb had looked up with wide eyes. John cracked a smile and ruffled his hair. "I'm just messing with you bud. Now let's go inside."

Thinking back on that day felt strange. Thanks to his photographic memory, Caleb remembered that conversation in vivid detail. But now that he knew the truth about the brain drive, it made the memory feel *tainted*, like John had never really said those things. Why would he have lied? Maybe his five-year-old brain had interpreted it wrong. Doubting his near-flawless memory was uncharted territory for Caleb. It felt like a vital limb had betrayed him. As though he had tried to pick something up only to find his arm no longer moved the way it was supposed to.

A short while later, a nurse came in to ready Caleb for surgery, which included shaving a small part of the back of his head, drawing a vial of blood, and explaining the procedure once more. He changed into the hospital gown he was given and sat down in the wheelchair as instructed, waiting to be transferred.

In the center of the operating room there was a seat that resembled a dentist's chair, save for the hole in the back of the U-shaped headrest. Caleb climbed up into it and sat down at the request of the nurse. The chair was fairly comfortable, but unexpectedly cold.

Two more nurses entered and they all began buzzing around the room gathering tools and supplies, readying them for the doctor. Then one of the nurses placed an IV and hooked Caleb up to a vitals monitor while another nurse began explaining the anesthesia. This was more like the chaotic environment that came to Caleb's mind when he imagined a hospital.

"All right, Caleb," the nurse said, "I'm going to put this mask up to you, and I want you to count backward from ten."

"Ten… nine… eight…"

~*~

Caleb woke up and found himself back in the room he was prepped in. Dr. Parks was standing next to his bed, holding a tablet computer.

"Hey, Caleb, welcome back. Surgery went well; no

complications whatsoever. I want you to try to get some rest right now. In a couple of hours, a nurse will come in to check on you and have you get up and walk around a little bit."

Still groggy from the anesthesia, Caleb had no problem drifting back to sleep.

When Caleb woke again, he felt fairly refreshed. He wasn't sure how much time had passed, but it felt like he had slept an entire night.

He bent his neck forward and reached his hand up to feel the back of his head. There was a large bandage covering the surgery site. He was unsure of what he should be expecting, but so far nothing *felt* different about having a brain drive. Now that the procedure was over, he was actually sort of excited to see how it worked.

While Caleb was still examining the gauze wrapped over the implant, the nurse came in.

"Hey, you're awake. How are you feeling?" she asked cheerfully.

"Good, actually." Caleb was startled by the raspiness of his voice. "Maybe a little thirsty."

"I'll get you some water. It's normal to feel a little hoarse after the surgery. The doctor will be in soon. Is there anything else you need from me?"

Caleb shook his head and smiled.

Almost as soon as the nurse left, Dr. Parks joined Caleb. He wasn't wearing his lab coat, but everything else about the bony man appeared the same.

"I hear you're feeling pretty well," Dr. Parks said, sounding pleased. "Are you feeling up to taking that brain drive for a spin and answering a few questions to make sure it's working correctly?"

"Absolutely," Caleb croaked.

"All right, splendid," Dr. Parks said as he took a seat. "Every brain drive comes preinstalled with information that allows you to answer all of these questions. The questions are meant to test the functionality of the brain drive, so the answers are designed to be fairly obscure. Before we get started, I need to make sure that you're in the right frame of mind. Please state your full name, date of birth, and today's date."

"Caleb Johnathan Shaw. July thirteenth, 1268. Today is Saturday, December third, 1285."

"Wonderful. First Question. What is the scientific name for a muskrat?"

"Ondatra zibethicus," Caleb answered without hesitation and a stunned look grew across his face. He definitely hadn't known that before.

"Good. Question number two. What was the highest recorded temperature during the week of August twenty-third to August twenty-ninth in the year 1245 in the city of Mullerton?"

Caleb gave Dr. Parks a blank stare. How was he supposed to know that? He wasn't even alive then.

"I know it sounds crazy. But remember, your brain thinks of these memories as your own. I want you to *try* to remember."

He thought back to that week and wondered what the temperature was in Mullerton. To Caleb's surprise, he could recall the temperature for each day in perfect detail. In his mind, he sorted through the data.

"The highest temperature recorded that week was seventy-two degrees and it was recorded on August twenty-fifth."

"That is correct. Now, what is the result of subtracting the number of protons in a lithium atom from the total number of thoracic vertebrae in a typical adult human skeleton?"

"Nine," Caleb replied after thinking for a couple seconds.

"Excellent," Dr. Parks responded. "Moving on to question four. If you were in the city of Novi and you walked out of the front door of the Fifth Street Hotel and took a left, then proceeded to the end of the block and took a right, then continued two more blocks before taking a left and walking three blocks before coming to a stop, what crossroad would you be at?"

"Smith and Grand Street," Caleb said immediately. To his amazement, he had been able to follow the directions in his mind as if he was staring at a map laid out in front of him.

"Very good. The next is a two-part question that is designed to test the brain drive's ability to override your native memories. It should not have the capability to alter long-term memory, but it can often affect short-term memory. For the first part, what is your father's name?"

"John," Caleb answered. The name Seth had also popped into his head, but he knew it was wrong.

"Okay, now what is my name?"

Immediately, Caleb's mind went to the name Dr. Goodwin. That seemed right, as if he knew with certainty. But before answering, Caleb thought back to when he first met the doctor. He visualized him walking into the room. He had a name embroidered on his lab coat. It read *Dr. Parks*. This memory *felt* real and Caleb trusted it more.

"Dr. Parks," Caleb replied.

Dr. Parks looked up from his tablet, his bushy eyebrows furrowed.

"Hmm. Did you happen to think of any other names?"

"Yes. At first I came up with Dr. Goodwin, but in the end I didn't trust that memory as much."

"Interesting," he said, rubbing his leathery chin with one hand and staring off as though he was in deep thought. "Well, the important thing is that the device is working well. That particular memory must have simply been too strong to override, despite it being so recent. Final question," Dr. Parks said, looking back at his handheld computer. "It's easiest if you close your eyes during this one."

Caleb gave a slight nod and closed his eyes.

"Now, think back to your apartment when you used to live in Hurley. What smell resonates with that place?"

At this point, Caleb understood it didn't matter that he never actually resided in Hurley. His brain would think he did. He tried to remember the apartment, and the memory came with very little effort. It almost felt like he was there now.

"I can see it," Caleb said. "I like the grain of the wood floors. I remember the cool feeling of stepping on them in the morning. It smells like cinnamon. It's from the bakery downstairs."

"Good," replied Dr. Parks in a soothing voice. "Now do you hear anything? Are you reminded of any particular taste or food?"

"Yes. I can hear the faint sounds of traffic and people walking by on the sidewalk. I can't taste anything, but I have the sudden urge to make peppermint tea."

"Perfect!"

Caleb opened his eyes. That was incredible. Just yesterday, he wouldn't have believed that was possible.

"Everything seems to be in order. The brain drive is functioning as intended and your vitals are looking good. I'm going to remove the bandage from your implant now." Dr. Parks rolled his stool next to Caleb's bed and began removing the medical adhesive.

"You should be clear to return home tomorrow morning. I've already spoken to your caseworker and she will be here early in the morning to pick you up."

"My caseworker?" replied Caleb. His face scrunched up as a few hairs got plucked by the tape. "What about my dad? Why can't he pick me up?"

"I'm not sure what's going on with all of that. I am only telling you what I was told by Kimberly, who is acting as your guardian at the moment. I know today has been a strange day, but you'll be home soon enough."

Caleb's mind drifted back to his father. All of a sudden, he began to feel guilty for being excited about his brain drive. John was probably sitting in a jail cell, all because of Caleb's decision to disobey the strict rule about leaving his hat on in public at all times. He wasn't sure if he could handle sitting in this bed all night with his thoughts nagging at him.

"So, am I allowed to walk around the hospital? I'd love to get up and stretch my legs."

"Of course. You can roam freely. I just ask that you stick to this floor only. We do have sick people here, and I'd prefer not to have to keep you longer than we need to."

Dr. Parks started for the door, but stopped and raised his hand with a finger up. "Oh, and one more thing. Your brain drive was also preloaded with a couple of useful modules. One of them contains our patient policy manual and a map of the hospital. So if you get hungry or need to know where something is, you should already know. The other module is a user manual for the brain drive. It contains everything you need to know about operating it, as well as brain drive terminals."

Before Caleb could begin to wonder what a module or brain drive terminal was, he already knew. *Module* was the term used to describe a folder of files that contained memories that were available for others to upload. A brain drive terminal was a computer used to manage modules on the brain drive.

"Our terminal contains only standard information. While there's nothing particularly special on it, you may find it fun to give it a go."

"Thank you," Caleb said, itching to find out what sort of information was considered standard.

Shortly after Dr. Parks left, Caleb got out of bed and made his way into the hallway, his hospital gown flowing behind him like a sail. As broad as his muscular frame was, the gown still fit him like a dress that was much too large for him.

Thanks to his brain drive, he already knew exactly where the terminal on the third floor was. Halfway down the pale corridor, on the right side, there was a recess that contained various vending machines as well as a drinking fountain.

Next to the vending machines stood a glossy white terminal that resembled a podium. It came up to Caleb's waist and had a large computer screen on the top.

He had seen one of these before. A few years ago, right before

Amahl's library closed for good, Caleb took a trip there one last time. During that visit, he'd noticed this very same machine. At the time, he assumed it was a device that could be used to search through the library's database—something he had no use for since he knew the place like the back of his hand. He never gave it a second glance. *Was this why the library was closed down?* he wondered.

Caleb approached the screen and tapped on it, waking it up from a low-powered state. There were three large buttons front-and-center on the touchscreen: *Browse, Upload,* and *Manage Storage.*

Tapping the *Browse* button brought up a new window with a search bar at the top and an alphabetically-arranged list of available memory modules.

Caleb scrolled through looking for anything that seemed interesting. *Agriculture: The Basics...Anatomy of the Human Body: An Overview...Bike Riding: A Complete Beginner's Guide...*

Most of what he was seeing was either useless or information he already knew. Instead of continuing to browse, he clicked on the search bar and typed in *Hunting.* The list was narrowed down to a few modules and there was one that immediately caught Caleb's eye. *Materra's Complete Guide to Tracking.* Caleb tapped on it and read over the description.

Materra's Complete Guide to Tracking is a comprehensive guide on identifying tracks, droppings and markings associated with the animals native to Materra. Also contained within this guide is information on identifying animals, tracking, animal movement patterns, hibernation, and more. Over thirty years of experience went into carefully crafting this guide.

Caleb was sold. He pulled out the brain drive terminal's interface cable—a sturdy white retractable cord with a single prong on its end—and plugged it into the back of his head.

Here goes nothing, he thought as he tapped the *Upload* button.

CHAPTER THREE

The screen flashed with the words *Upload Complete*. It had only taken a couple seconds at most and the process was uneventful. Caleb felt silly for assuming there would be some sort of physical sensation that accompanied the upload.

Eager to test out the knowledge he'd gained from his new memory module, Caleb thought back to a set of tracks he'd seen in the woods a few weeks ago. At the time, he wasn't able to identify them. They looked like badger tracks, only different. Thanks to his photographic memory he could still remember them as clear as day. As soon as he pictured them in his mind, he knew with certainty they were the tracks of a striped skunk.

A jolt of excitement shot through Caleb, forcing a smile across his face and lighting his mind ablaze with possibilities. The benefits he would gain from this knowledge were endless. Using this information, which took him seconds to gain, would forever change the way he hunted.

Then it hit him. *This*. This was why he'd had such a difficult time finding deer over the last few years. Every other hunter had access to this module at the drop of a hat, zero training needed. Putting him at a severe disadvantage. He was competing with a city full of expert-level hunters.

His excitement soured, turning instead to anger and disbelief. He couldn't imagine why John was keeping this technology from him. This could have helped put meat on their table. There were probably other modules that could have helped them as well.

The anger felt unnatural to Caleb. He'd never been able to hold a grudge against his father. But then again, John had never lied to Caleb. Or so he thought. A knot formed in his stomach as he imagined confronting John. He didn't know what he would say, but he wanted answers.

Caleb turned his attention back to the large touchscreen in front of him. While he had access to the terminal, he might as well find out as much as he could about his brain drive.

Tapping on the *Manage Storage* button brought up a list of file folders contained on Caleb's brain drive. The list had module names next to the amount of storage they were taking up, as well as a color-coded bar graph showing the relative space each module occupied on the brain drive. Sitting at the top of the list was the tracking guide he had just uploaded, with a file size of 10.2 gigabytes. Next on the list was *Mullerton Hospital Policy Manual & Building Layout*—4.8 gigabytes. Following that were two modules called *Factory Preload* and *System*, sitting at 2.4 gigabytes and 1.8 gigabytes, respectively. The wording on the *System* module folder was grayed out, most likely indicating it couldn't be altered.

On the right side of the screen there was a pie chart displaying the percentage of total space each module consumed. The colors on the chart matched those on the bar graphs on the left side of the screen. Near the bottom of the screen it read *Available Space: 980.8 GB*.

That was a lot of free storage. Again, Caleb started imagining what he could gain from this device. He could store so much information on his brain drive. Knowing this, he wondered why everyone he ever met wasn't a wealth of knowledge.

Caleb tapped on the *Factory Preload* module folder. It

expanded, revealing subfolders and options, accompanied by a warning message:

Caution: Deleting one or more subfolders in this module may affect the overall module performance in unpredictable ways.

He deleted the entire module.

Curious as to how this would affect his memory, he tried to recall the apartment details from Dr. Parks's last question but he failed to do so. On the surface, that made sense; without the module installed, he shouldn't be able to recall data that came from it. The thing that struck Caleb as odd was that he couldn't even remember what he had told Dr. Parks when he gave his answer. It was as if he had never known the information at all. Not being able to remember details from a conversation he had so recently felt foreign to him. He made a mental note to ask Dr. Parks about it later.

After browsing through the brain drive terminal a little while longer and uploading a couple more modules that he was interested in—*Trees of Materra* and *Survival: The Ultimate Guide to Mastering the Wilderness*—Caleb decided to return to his room and test out his new modules.

A couple of hours later, Dr. Parks stopped by Caleb's room to check on him. "You know this thing works, right?" Dr. Parks said as he pointed at the television and smirked.

"I assumed so," Caleb replied, returning a smile for the man's sake. "I'm not a big fan of television though. We don't even have one at home." While he wasn't lying—he did prefer to read over watching television—really, he was preoccupied with exploring his new memory modules.

For the last two hours, he had been mentally reviewing and identifying every tree, bush, and wildflower that he had ever seen on their property. He had been able to recognize the majority of them before, but the amount of information he now knew about each species was far greater than he ever could have imagined learning on his own.

"Ah, I see," Dr. Parks said as the lanky man plopped down on his stool. "Well, I wanted to stop by and see you before I finished my shift. Dr. Carter is on call tonight, and she will be overseeing your case until I return early tomorrow. You'll be in good hands with her. Although I don't anticipate any issues arising between now and your discharge in the morning. Did you happen to make a trip down to the terminal yet?"

"Yeah, actually I did. It's all… pretty cool."

"It is," Dr. Parks said through a grin.

"I did have a question though. I deleted the preloaded memories you quizzed me on and now I can't even clearly remember our conversations regarding them. Why don't I remember anything relating to those memories? I figured I'd at least recall what I'd learned while I had access to them."

Dr. Parks thought for a moment before he began to speak. "The brain interprets what is stored on the brain drive as long-term memories. This means your brain does not feel the need to form additional synapses—or connections—in order to store this information in your actual, physiological long-term memory. So when you were referencing the information on your brain drive to answer my questions, you were simply recalling information. Not *learning* anything new. And when the memory modules were removed from your brain drive, you were right back where you started before they were uploaded. We call this the phantom memory phenomenon."

That sounded reasonable, but for some reason Caleb felt unsatisfied with the answer.

Dr. Parks must have interpreted the look on his face as confusion. "Does that make sense?"

Caleb met Dr. Parks's gaze. "Yeah, it does. I guess I was hoping I was missing something. One more question. Does this brain drive have a tracking chip in it?" He had to know if there was any truth to what John had told him.

Dr. Parks let out a brief chuckle. "No, there's no tracking chip. That was a big conspiracy theory that floated around when the brain drive was first brought into the public eye, but it's been debunked numerous times by independent agencies. I apologize for laughing. I haven't gotten that question in about twenty years."

"That's okay. Thanks," Caleb responded as he forced a smile.

For the remainder of his stay at the hospital, Caleb alternated between exploring his new memory modules, resting, and browsing the brain drive terminal. He didn't find any other modules there that piqued his interest, so he opted not to upload any more. Most of those on the hospital's terminal contained basic information that Caleb had already learned naturally over the course of his homeschooling. Furthermore, most of the useful modules were for niche hobbies and crafts that he had no interest in, such as *Hooked: The Art of Crochet*, which seemed to be some variant of knitting based on the module's description.

He did what he could to keep his mind busy, trying to keep himself from dwelling on the fact that his father was probably sitting in a jail cell. Tomorrow he would be home, and things would be normal again.

~*~

"So, how'd it all go?" Kimberly asked as she buckled her seat belt and flicked her wavy black hair behind her shoulders.

"Good. At least that's what the doctor said," Caleb replied as he made himself comfortable in the passenger seat. He wasn't sure if the cramp in his neck was from the surgery or from the nearly sleepless night in a hospital bed, but either way he would be happy to be sleeping in his own bed again.

"What's going on with my dad? Is he home now?"

"Your father should be home any minute now. I got a call from my boss right before I pulled into the parking lot, and she told me your father was released this morning. I was also told he was relieved to hear you'll be home soon." Kimberly was using the same upbeat voice as yesterday. It was more effective today.

She smiled and looked over at Caleb. "Well. What do you

think of the brain drive? Great, huh?"

"Yeah. It seems pretty great so far, I'm just waiting for the catch."

"The catch?" she asked as she chuckled. "Why does there have to be a catch?"

"I guess I'm still trying to figure out why my father held me back from this. I think I'd feel better if I knew there was a big downside that he was protecting me from."

Kimberly smiled sympathetically at Caleb. "That makes sense. It's natural to want to assume the best intentions out of those you love. But I've had my brain drive since I was a kid, and I've yet to see a downside."

"How old were you?"

"I was six years old when I had it done, like most kids. I remember it was right before I started school. I lost my first tooth and got my brain drive implant in the same week. I'm not sure how school was before the brain drive, or how it was for you at home for that matter, but it's hard for me to imagine a world where I would have been able to learn *all* of the information we were given access to on our brain drives. Teachers actually spent more time teaching us what was on our memory modules, and how to use them, than they did teaching us subject matter themselves."

"Huh," Caleb remarked. "That actually makes a lot of sense based on what I saw on the brain drive terminal at the hospital. Most of the modules seemed to be basic educational materials."

Kimberly let out a sarcastic laugh. "The free memory modules available to the general public are lacking, to say the least. Those terminals come in handy in cases where people accidentally delete crucial modules, like those needed to read or write, but are fairly useless otherwise."

Caleb looked at Kimberly as if she just told him she was from another planet. "You... never learned how to read or write?"

"Well, technically I still had to *practice* reading and writing. But we didn't start from scratch. There's no need. It's all been done before. We were taught writing mechanics, language structure and how to properly construct essays and such, but the building blocks were all given to us through modules."

Caleb was still unable to wipe the shocked expression off his face. Up to this point, he had been thinking about all of the possibilities his new brain drive would bring him. He had never considered the implications of kids using the brain drive to learn fundamentals like reading and writing.

Kimberly noticed Caleb was lost in thoughts and she continued. "I know it seems weird to imagine how different things could have been for you, but I wouldn't dwell on that. Your father is all you have, and even though he lied about the brain drive, I would hate for that to come between you guys. I'm sure he had his reasons."

Offended, Caleb's face turned from shocked to a mixture of angry and confused in an instant. Why had she assumed he was thinking that he missed out? Plus, she didn't even know his father! How could she speak for him?

"I'm not thinking about what I missed out on. I'm wondering how the rest of the world is okay with relying on technology to do basic things like read and write. If that thing in your head malfunctions, are you just going to crash this car because you don't know how to drive? I think I can understand why my father didn't want me to be another mindless drone."

Caleb immediately regretted that last sentence. Kimberly raised her eyebrows and turned her full attention to the road ahead of her.

"I'm sorry," Caleb said after a few seconds of silence, "I didn't mean to imply that you're a mindless drone. The last twenty-four hours have been stressful and crazy. I'm still having a hard time making sense of all of this. I know you say my father must have had a good reason, but I'm honestly not so sure."

"It's okay," Kimberly said, her voice full of empathy. "There is some truth to what you said. The brain drive does make us more reliant on technology in some ways, but I'd never really put much thought into it. The way I see it, technology is here to stay. If we don't adapt to it and embrace it for what it is, we risk leaving it only to those who will abuse it and use it for evil."

Now Caleb felt bad for her. How could everyone just accept this as normal? In his opinion, humans shouldn't have to adapt to technology. He thought technology should be considered a tool to solve problems, not create new ones. Caleb decided to change the subject in an effort to salvage the conversation.

"Going back to what you were saying earlier, about the brain drive terminals containing mostly basic modules. How do you get other, more useful memory modules?"

"Most useful memory modules are sold, either by the government or by private businesses. Either way, you pay for it. It's unfortunate, really. This technology is amazing, but the only way to unlock its full potential is to have the money. That's why the rich stay rich and the poor stay poor."

That sounded a lot like what John always said during his nightly rants about the government. "What do you mean?" Caleb asked, wondering if John had always secretly believed that the brain drive had to do with the poverty issues the nation faced.

"Well, rich parents can afford to send their kids to prestigious schools that have access to top-grade modules. Or simply buy whatever modules they need to learn a skill or trade. On the other hand, poor families have a difficult time making ends meet, let alone earning enough credits to buy their children modules that would allow them to get a decent paying job."

"So better modules are more expensive?"

"Yes. The modules that are required for higher-paying careers are often much more costly than those for lower-paying careers."

"Why? If the government has the ability to sell the modules at whatever price they want, why not make them all the same price and allow people to choose their career based on interests alone?"

"It's not that simple," she said, sighing heavily. "The module prices increase proportionally with the amount of experience and cost that goes into developing them. Higher grade modules will always be more expensive. In turn, the careers that require investment into higher education or expensive modules ultimately pay more than those that don't. Sadly, this problem is compounded by the fact that those with abundant resources can buy modules and do work themselves, instead of hiring someone to do it for them, which makes it even more difficult for low entry positions to thrive in this economy."

"Hmm," Caleb said, wondering if what John had said two days ago about having to lower his rates again was the result of this issue.

Kimberly went on. "As a member of the social services wing of the government, I'd like to say we've done a good job keeping up with the needs of our people, but the reality is there just isn't enough work for people anymore, and we haven't figured out how to remedy that. Giving poor people more money directly allows them to afford more necessities, but it also has the unintended consequence of increasing access to low-grade memory modules. That means more people can enter the jobs those modules are used for, essentially making low-income fields far more competitive and driving the cost of their labor down even more."

Wheels were turning in Caleb's head. All of those dinnertime conversations where his father would rag on the president for ruining the middle class felt more significant now. Is this why John was against him getting a brain drive implant? He decided he would find out soon enough.

~*~

John sat at his kitchen table, sipping another cup of coffee in an attempt to calm his nerves. It wasn't working.

Caleb would be home any minute and he would be forced to explain everything he was trying to shelter him from. There weren't many things that could make John feel as uncomfortable as being unprepared. And despite rehearsing this conversation thousands of times in his head over the years, he still felt completely unready for it.

He had gotten too used to Caleb's complacency regarding the topic. Caleb trusted John's word more than John felt he deserved, and now he wasn't sure what his son would think. He couldn't afford to lose his trust now. He had to lay it all out there.

A car pulled into the driveway and Caleb got out, making his way toward the house. John got up and met Caleb on the front porch. Caleb looked at him with apprehension in his eyes.

"Why?" he muttered.

John sighed. "Let's go inside and sit down, bud. I'll tell you everything."

The truth was, John couldn't tell him *everything*, but he would tell him what he needed to know to make sense of all this.

Caleb followed John into the living room and sank down into the couch. John snagged his coffee and a wooden chair from the kitchen and sat across from Caleb.

"I know you probably have a ton of questions, but I am going to start off by saying that I was only trying to protect you in all of this." John took a sip before continuing. "Did you get a chance to upload any modules yet?"

"Yeah," Caleb replied, leaning forward and clasping his hands together. "A few. Why?"

"Those memories you can upload to your brain drive, they have to be created somehow, whether that's by an expert in that particular field, or someone who takes the time to learn the information."

"I gathered as much," Caleb said flatly.

"Well, when the brain drive was invented, it didn't take long for our government to realize that people with photographic memories, like you, create better quality memories than other people. Caleb, your exceptional memory makes you a valuable asset to our government. So valuable, in fact, that they genetically test all children for a photographic memory when they get their brain drives installed. I guess technically it's called an eidetic memory, but that's beside the point. Kids who test positive are taken from their families to a classified facility to work for the government, creating memory modules."

Caleb shifted in his seat, remaining quiet.

John carried on. "I didn't want that life for you. Your mother was forced into that facility at a young age, and I know she wouldn't have wanted that for you either. That's why I sheltered you from the truth, and that's why I homeschooled you."

Curiosity flared in Caleb's eyes as he leaned forward further. "My mother had an eidetic memory too?"

"Yes. I wasn't sure you'd inherited the gene until you were about four or five years old. But after I knew you had an eidetic memory, it became clear to me that I had to do what I could to protect you. You're all I have…" John's voice was beginning to strain and crack. "I hope you can understand that I was only trying to do right by you and your mother."

"I can understand why you wanted to keep me from being sent to that facility," Caleb said sincerely. "But what I'm having a hard time making sense of is why you had to lie to me about this. You could have told me the truth. Why didn't you?"

"It was just easier that way." Strictly speaking, he wasn't lying. At first, that was the only reason he didn't tell Caleb. Explaining all of it to a six-year-old would have been far more difficult than lying about it. As Caleb got older though, John had considered telling him the truth on multiple occasions. But the older he got, the more John began to understand that Caleb was too curious to just accept it and move on. He would have done research on the brain drive and the facility, and John was afraid of what he might find if he went looking.

"I'm sorry, bud. I really am."

Caleb was quiet for a moment, staring into his clasped hands, before he nodded his head and stood up abruptly.

"I need to get some air. I'm going to go for a walk through the woods and clear my head."

"Okay, bud," John said. "I'll be here. I'm taking the day off of work today."

Caleb grabbed his jacket and slipped out the front door. John watched as he walked down the porch and disappeared into the woods. As a father, he had failed him. He knew that. He hoped Caleb would be able to forgive him.

He'd need to. When Caleb got back from his walk, they would need to pack up and leave immediately. He couldn't risk staying here anymore. If they tested Caleb for an eidetic memory at the hospital, they'd be back for him eventually.

~*~

Caleb took in a deep breath of the fresh morning air like a large gulp of ice-cold water on a hot summer day. His shoes crunched against the fallen leaves as he walked slowly through the woods, taking it all in like never before. Birds were singing over the subtle whistling of wind through the bare treetops.

Every tree, wildflower, and animal track along the way provided an opportunity to test out his new brain drive modules.

His attention was drawn to a pile of small animal droppings near a red maple tree. They appeared to be deer droppings at first glance. As he knelt down to study them closer, he noticed they were slightly longer and skinnier. *Porcupine.* Thanks to his newly attained knowledge, he understood that during the winter, porcupines fed on dry plant materials, which tended to make their droppings more pellet-shaped.

Caleb smirked and stood back up, pleased with his new abilities.

Being back in the woods—back home—felt amazing. Exploring their property with his new modules was a unique and refreshing experience. It reminded Caleb of the feeling he would get when rereading a book and picking up on little details he hadn't noticed on the first read-through.

The solitude also gave Caleb time to reflect on the things his father had told him. He found it easier to think out here.

Knowing what he knew now, he didn't blame his father for keeping the brain drive a secret. He didn't agree with his reasoning for lying, but he could accept it. And his father seemed genuinely apologetic. It would take some time for him to fully forgive John, but he knew in time he would.

Instead, the one detail Caleb's mind kept being drawn to was that his mother also had an eidetic memory. For some reason, knowing his mother was like him made Caleb feel closer to her, almost like he knew her in some way. He wondered if John would be open to talking about her more later.

As Caleb headed back for the house, he came up with a few follow-up questions he could ask John that might get him talking more about his mother. If there ever was a good time to ask about her, it would be now.

What he really wanted to know was what she was like when she was alive. He wanted to know if John ever saw his mother in him beyond their matching blue eyes. But he knew he couldn't ask those questions outright. He'd start by asking more about the facility she was sent to and see what John was willing to share.

When Caleb was nearing the edge of the woods behind his house, he saw two police cruisers parked in his driveway. Being careful so as not to be seen, he crept close enough to listen in on the conversation before deciding if it was safe to approach. At first, it was difficult to hear anything they were saying, but then John began to raise his voice.

"You can't do this! He's my son!" John yelled down into the face of the much shorter police officer standing on their porch.

The officer raised one hand and placed it on John's chest in an attempt to create space between the two men without giving up ground. His other hand was on his weapon holster. It was about as useful as pushing against a brick wall. John didn't budge an inch.

"He's *not* your son," the police officer shouted back firmly. "And this is *not* your call, Mr. Shaw. He's coming with us. Now call him out here or we are going in."

The floor fell out of Caleb's stomach. He turned back around and ran as fast as he could.

CHAPTER FOUR

Sprinting through the woods at full speed was nearly impossible, but Caleb was doing his best to run as fast as he could, ducking under branches and jumping over fallen trees as he weaved his way through the thick forest. Occasionally, he would sneak a peek back over his shoulder to see if someone was following him, but he had yet to see or hear anyone.

His destination was their old hunting blind.

When Caleb had first started hunting, he did it from the confines of the blind. He would bring books along with him and read until his prey happened to walk out of the trees and into the grass surrounding the wooden shack. Over a year ago, however, he had been forced to abandon the shelter altogether in favor of mobility. The animals no longer came to him—he had to find them instead.

Caleb hadn't visited the place since, but over the years, John had repeatedly made it crystal clear the hunting blind was where he should go in the case of an emergency at the house. The plan was for the two of them to meet up there if the house was ever unsafe—a fire was the example John always used. Caleb never put too much thought into it. He understood it was in John's nature to be prepared, sometimes much more than necessary. At the present moment, Caleb was thankful for that.

While the majority of his attention was focused on staying alert and pushing his legs to keep up the pace, he couldn't help replaying in his mind what he overheard the officer say. *He's not your son.* Those words echoed through his head, nagging at him with every step like a splinter in his foot. But he couldn't afford to dwell on them. Not yet. He had to get to safety.

Noticing his pace was beginning to slow, he pushed those thoughts to the back of his mind. He could ask John about that later, and until then he'd only be able to speculate anyway.

The hunting outpost sat in a wide clearing, its brown wooden exterior sticking out like a sore thumb among the long green grass and scattered shrubs. As far as blinds go, it was a decent size, able to house two full-grown men comfortably, each with their own window for view and shooting from.

When Caleb reached it, he entered through the only door. Aside from the thin layer of dust coating everything, it looked exactly as he remembered. Two countertops ran along the walls, serving as both windowsills and shelves, each accompanied by a wooden folding chair. The back wall housed an empty gun rack and a few hooks that were also bare save for one, where a green backpack hung.

Dust was sent airborne as Caleb dashed across the wooden floor of the blind and skidded to a stop, ripping open the drawer under the counter and immediately finding what he was looking for. He pulled out a black walkie-talkie and held down the power button. Nothing happened—the batteries were dead. He began frantically sifting through the contents of the drawers in search of new ones. Luckily, he was able to find a pair of nine-volts, and after fumbling to insert them, he powered the device up and tuned it to channel sixteen.

Now, he'd wait. As difficult as it was, that was the plan. If John couldn't get to the blind, which Caleb suspected was the case, Caleb was to wait until he was contacted on the walkie-talkie. Still, every minute Caleb spent staring at the thing seemed to stretch on, testing his resolve against the urge to pick up the two-way radio and run.

After a long ten minutes, his father's voice cut through the static. "Caleb, bud. Are you there?"

He clutched the small black device tight. "I'm here, Dad. What's going on?"

"I need you to listen to me carefully. The hospital found out about your eidetic memory, and now the government wants to take you to that facility. As we speak, the police are searching the property for you. They even called in a K-9 unit. You need to move quickly if you're going to escape. Take the emergency survival backpack from the blind and go east to Yersaw. Don't hitchhike on the interstate, it's too risky. When you get there, head straight to the Fifth Street Market and ask for Don. He's the owner and an old friend of mine. He will let you stay there until it's safe for me to come get to you. Did you get all that?"

"Yeah. East to Yersaw. Fifth Street Market. Stay there."

"And no hitchhiking!"

"No hitchhiking," Caleb repeated. "Before I go though, why did that officer say you weren't my dad?"

"I'm sorry, bud. We don't—there's not enough time to explain. But before you leave the blind, look under the drawers. I taped a memory stick to the bottom of one of them. When you reach safety, find a brain drive terminal and transfer the memory modules onto your brain drive. It will explain everything you need to know about your parents."

Caleb froze for a moment, unsure if he had heard his father correctly. My *parents*? Was the police officer right? Was John not his real father? Was that even his mother in those pictures?

"Caleb, did you hear me?"

He snapped back to reality. "Yeah, I did… *John*."

"I'm sorry. For all of this." Caleb could hear the pain in John's voice. "I promise you'll understand. Now go!"

Caleb was beginning to grow tired of trying to make sense of the lies that were unraveling before him. Was John's promise even worth anything at this point?

He turned the radio off and began running his hand over the bottom of the drawers until he felt something. It was glossy red, rectangular in shape, and about the size of a pack of chewing gum.

With the memory stick safely tucked away in the pocket of his jeans, he pulled the backpack from the wall and stashed the walkie-talkie in its side pocket. Caleb resolved to take stock of the bag's contents when he had a chance. After ensuring the sleeping bag was properly secured to the bottom of the sack, he hoisted it over his broad shoulders and started for the cabin door.

Wind whipped Caleb's messy black hair back and forth as he jogged east. The extra weight slowed him down a little, but he was sure he could outrun the police if he kept up his current pace.

The eastern border of their property butted up against a steep hill. As he approached the bottom of it, the distant sound of a dog barking rang out behind him. His heart rate climbed, and then he did too, picking up the pace and running even faster up the hill. Nearing the top, Caleb looked over the crest and saw two police officers closing in on his location from the other side.

Swiftly, he ducked back down. His breathing grew more rapid as his throat tightened. He needed to find a different route. He worked his way back down the hill a little and followed it north, fighting for footing along the steep hillside as he ran. When he felt he was far enough away, he peeked back over the hill to find nothing but trees between him and the interstate.

But the barking was growing closer.

Caleb took his chance, setting off down the hill in a dead sprint. If he could just make it across the interstate and into the woods on the other side, he would be free.

At this point, the weight of the backpack was starting to wear on Caleb. He swallowed air in jagged gasps. Even with the downhill momentum on his side, it still felt like he was running through sand. He pushed through the pain, staying focused only on his goal as he continued to close the gap between him and the road.

It wouldn't be enough. As he came to the base of the hill, the K-9 unit reached the top, barking wildly in his direction. But he couldn't give up. He was too close.

Continuing in a full-on sprint, Caleb began sorting through options. John said not to hitchhike, but it could be his only chance at this point. Maybe he could flag down a car in time.

He shed his backpack. Sure, it would be helpful to have, but what good was it if he never made it in the first place?

It was too late. Roughly two hundred meters from freedom, Caleb collapsed face-first into the dirt as a searing pain shot up from his ankle. He glanced down to see a dog clamped onto his leg, growling a warning at him as if to tell him he wasn't going anywhere.

Instinctively, Caleb tried to pull his leg away to free himself, but the dog bit down harder and snarled.

An officer eventually caught up with them. He doubled over with his hands on his knees, gulping in air. His long black hair hung down over his face like wrinkled drapes as he bent over. After a few seconds he stood up, choking words out between gasps. "You're a fast kid."

Then he looked down at the dog. "Heel!" It let go of Caleb's leg, trotted over to the officer and sat next to him, panting. "Good boy," the officer said as he reached down and ruffled the fur on the top of his furry companion's head. Caleb could have been imagining it, but it looked like the dog was smiling. Could dogs smile? Either way, it certainly appeared much more friendly than it had a moment ago.

"You can get up now," the officer said to Caleb, although it sounded more like an order. "I won't cuff you, but please don't run. I don't want to have to send Archie after you again."

Caleb stood up and brushed himself off.

"Sorry about that. I thought you'd get away if I didn't let him loose on you. He's usually pretty gentle, though. How's your ankle?"

Caleb lifted his pant leg to inspect his ankle. The dog hadn't broken his skin, leaving only a few surface scratches. "Fine. Am I being arrested?"

"Oh no, nothing like that," the officer replied, stroking the long wispy hair flowing from the bottom of his goatee. "But I do have to search you for weapons. Spread your legs a little wider and stick your arms out to your sides."

Caleb complied and the officer began patting him down.

"The sheriff said to bring you in on account of you being one of those gifted kids. I'm not sure how you managed to skirt the system for so long, but the law states that you gifted kids get sent over to Barton to work at some government facility."

The officer spoke into the radio affixed to the front of his navy-blue uniform. "Dispatch, this is Officer Clemons. I've got the boy. Our position is near the southbound side of interstate five, approximately two miles south of the Hanlin ranch."

"Copy that, Clemons," replied a voice on the other end of the radio. "I'll send a cruiser your way. ETA is five minutes."

"Copy," Officer Clemons replied. "Let's go, kid," he said after clipping a dog leash onto Archie's collar and starting toward the road.

While walking in-step with Officer Clemons, Caleb briefly considered running for it. Archie was restrained now. Maybe he could get across the street and into the brush before he was unleashed. He glanced down at the dog and locked eyes with him, and in that moment, he felt like Archie could read his mind. He thought better of running. Instead, he would try to get some information from the officer.

"So... back at my house I overheard one of the cops tell my father that I wasn't his son. Do you happen to know what that's all about?"

"Not a clue. Sorry, kid."

A police cruiser slowed to a stop in front of them and the

window rolled down. "Someone call for backup?" the uniformed man inside asked with a grin.

No one else found humor in his joke. Officer Clemons let out a heavy sigh. "Thanks, Jim." He opened the rear door of the car and the dog jumped in. "All right, kid, you sit in the back with Archie."

Caleb hesitated, looking from Clemons to Archie, who had his tongue hanging from the side of his mouth.

"Don't worry, he won't bite you. You can even pet him if you want. Just don't make any sudden movements toward his head."

Caleb reluctantly ducked down and took a seat, staying as far away from Archie as he could. As friendly as he looked, he didn't intend on petting him.

~*~

Upon arriving at the police station, Caleb was escorted inside and directly to a small room he assumed was used for interrogation, because of the bare walls and two-way mirror. When Caleb entered, he was surprised to see a familiar face.

Seated at the wooden table in the middle of the room, papers scattered about in front of her, was Kimberly Lynn. "Caleb! It's great to see you. I'll admit, I didn't expect to ever see you again, but I understand they have identified you as gifted. That's exciting!"

Kimberly's excitement was genuine, but Caleb didn't share her enthusiasm. He simply stared at her, his face twisted to convey his confusion. Why would he possibly be excited about any of this?

Her smile faded and her eyes darted down to the paperwork in front of her, searching for something among the mess. "I was just finishing up. I'll get all this picked up and we can get on the road. I brought this for you."

Kimberly handed a folder to Caleb. "This is what we usually

give to parents whose gifted children are being taken to OASIS."

"OASIS?" Caleb asked as he took it and gazed at the cover—a picture of a sprawling public square with kids of various ages walking together, smiling. Large buildings that looked like they belonged in a resort formed a border around the public square.

"It stands for Organization for Advancement of Strategies for International Security. OASIS for short." The excitement returned to her voice. "It's a government-run facility where gifted individuals, such as yourself, are able to learn new skills, all while helping our country. I'll let you look that information over while I get this mess cleaned up."

Caleb opened it up and began browsing through the contents. The first pamphlet went over housing. It stated every gifted individual got their own spacious room contained within a large dormitory that included a cafeteria, state-of-the-art gym, round-the-clock security, and in-house teaching aides.

The second packet covered early childhood education. Caleb skimmed it over, but found it irrelevant to his situation, so he moved onto the third, which discussed visitation. Family members were able to visit OASIS every weekend during a six-hour window. Access was restricted to residential common areas, but supervised tours of the dormitories could be arranged.

The fourth pamphlet contained details about the work gifted individuals would be responsible for while at OASIS. The information was vague, but if Caleb understood it correctly, gifted individuals were responsible for learning information utilizing the most up-to-date resources, and then downloading it in the form of memory modules. That confirmed what John had told him.

The final brochure pertained to benefits for gifted individuals and their families. One such benefit was that over the course of learning to create modules, gifted individuals gained expertise in a field that could then be utilized to build a career. In addition, they were provided with free room and board, healthcare, retirement, and results-based pay. The family of gifted individuals also received healthcare and something called a *gifted family stipend.*

He wondered how much the stipend was. Would it be enough to help John out with the bills? If he could somehow provide for John while at OASIS, he thought it could all be worth it. That was followed by the painful realization that John probably wasn't his real father and therefore likely wouldn't receive benefits. For a brief moment he'd forgotten John had been lying to him his entire life. About the brain drive. About being his father. *What else was he hiding?* Caleb questioned.

He brushed those questions aside and returned his focus to the booklet in his hands. It went on to describe how each gifted individual and their family were all heroes in the eyes of the country and they would forever be held in high esteem.

Caleb looked up from the folder as Kimberly was tucking the last of her paperwork into a black leather briefcase. "So this is something most parents actually *want* for their kids?"

"Oh, absolutely. Most people would kill for their child to be labeled as gifted. Working at OASIS opens so many doors for these children and their families. It can single-handedly take a family from poverty to among the most wealthy in the country. And on top of that, the lifelong benefits are amazing. I know it doesn't seem like it right now, but you're very lucky, Caleb." She beamed at him like a proud mother.

"Yeah. Lucky," Caleb muttered as he closed the folder. "Is there *anything* I can do to get out of going to this place? I'm almost an adult. Can't you make an exception?"

Kimberly looked at Caleb sympathetically. "Unfortunately, it's not up to me. I'm merely acting on the behalf of the government."

"How long do I have to be there? Until I turn eighteen?" If he only had to be there for a few months, he felt he could do that.

"The minimum requirement is eighteen years, which typically

allows people to leave around age twenty-four. For you, however..."

Caleb nodded, swallowing hard. He would be thirty-five before being eligible to leave OASIS.

"But hey," she continued in her normal cheerful tone, "maybe you could look at this as more of an opportunity. You know, try to make the most of it?"

"Yeah," he said, looking again at the smiling kids on the front of the folder. He tried to picture himself being happy there, but his imagination came up empty. Up to this point he'd spent his whole life in one house, eating meals at the same kitchen table every day and sleeping in the same bed every night. He couldn't bring himself to see beyond the front porch.

Kimberly slid out of her chair and grabbed her coat. "Are you ready to hit the road?"

"As ready as I'll ever be," he said, closing his hand tightly around the memory stick in his pocket.

CHAPTER FIVE

Five hours later, they arrived at Barton, a sparse city home to the government facility called OASIS.

During the quiet trip, Caleb used his time to reflect on his predicament. The pamphlets made OASIS sound amazing, and a big part of him wanted to believe it. But every positive thought was shrouded in doubt. If it was truly that great, why wouldn't his mother have wanted him to go there? After all, she would know better than most—she spent her childhood there.

One hope Caleb clung to, more than any other, was that experiencing OASIS would somehow bring him closer to knowing his mother. He would never be able to look his mother in her eyes, but at least he had the chance to walk in her footsteps.

In a blink, they had passed through the entire city of Barton. OASIS was located in the outskirts east of the city proper, in the middle of a dense forest.

Thick concrete walls, at least twenty feet in height and lined with barbed wire at the top, surrounded the compound. As they approached the entrance, Caleb's mouth fell open in awe as he tried and failed to see how far the walls stretched.

A quick conversation with an armed guard led them through

the front gate and to the first building on the other side of the wall—the registration office. The nondescript, slate-gray brick structure was the size of a typical single-story home and had large windows flanking the front entrance on both sides.

Once inside, Kimberly approached the counter. "I have a new gifted individual for you. His name is Caleb Shaw. You should have gotten a call earlier to preregister him. Here's the paperwork." Kimberly pulled out what she had been working on back at the police station and placed it on the counter.

"Yes, we've been expecting Caleb," the woman behind the counter said through a bright smile aimed at him. "I'll get this all filed away and in order. You two can take a seat and someone from residential will arrive shortly to show Caleb to his room."

After a brief wait, a short woman with fair skin and blonde hair tied into a tight bun, wearing a uniform that consisted of navy pants and a matching navy polo shirt, entered the office.

"Hi, Caleb," she said in a voice that reminded Caleb of a chipmunk. That, in turn, made him realize her face *also* reminded him of a chipmunk. "My name is Melanie. I am the GI residence coordinator. I'll be helping you get your security clearances and taking you to your dormitory."

She turned to face Kimberly. "Are you interested in touring the dorms, Mom?"

"I'm not his mother. I'm his caseworker—"

"Oh, I'm so sorry," Melanie interrupted, shifting her gaze back and forth from Caleb to Kimberly as though she wasn't sure who she should be apologizing to.

Caleb could feel his cheeks flush, embarrassed for Kimberly. She didn't look nearly old enough to be his mother.

"No worries." Kimberly reached her hand out for a handshake. "Thank you. It looks like Caleb will be in good hands." She turned to Caleb and gave him a reassuring smile. "Good luck!"

Caleb mustered a half smile.

Melanie clapped her hands together. "Okay, let's get started."

The security building was next door to the registration building, and aside from the lack of windows along the front, the exterior looked identical.

After fingerprints, hand prints, and a photograph, Caleb received an identification badge. On the front, there was a picture of Caleb with his name and title underneath. *Caleb Shaw, Gifted Individual.* On the right side of the badge was the OASIS logo: a silhouette of a large, blocky building bearing the Materra flag waving atop, enclosed in a circle of text that spelled out *Organization for Advancement of Strategies for International Security.*

"Don't lose that," the security officer said as he handed the badge to Caleb. The badge was attached to a clip with a retractable string mechanism inside it. "Before I cut you loose, I need to search your person for contraband. Place both hands on the countertop."

Caleb sighed, complying with the man. Never had he thought he would be searched twice in one day. The officer pulled the memory stick from Caleb's pocket.

"Wait, that's my—"

"This will need to be screened for malware before it's returned to you."

Caleb's shoulders slumped as he watched his only hope of learning the truth about his parents get stuck in a bin on a shelf behind the counter. He felt like he had gotten punched in the gut.

"How long does that usually take?"

"Not long. Maybe a week at the most. After it's screened, it will be delivered to your mailbox in your dormitory."

Caleb nodded. Although he didn't feel comfortable trusting strangers with the safety of his memory stick, he didn't see another option.

Melanie led Caleb to a brain drive terminal located in the corner of the waiting area of the security office. It looked different than the one he'd used at the hospital. Instead of a glossy white podium, it was a matte chrome device that extended from the wall like a permanent fixture. Melanie directed him to upload two modules, one called *Navigating OASIS: A General Reference Guide* and another titled *OASIS Code of Conduct*.

"These two modules will help you get around and know the rules," she explained. "After you receive your assignment, you'll get another module specific to it."

Their next destination was the dormitories, located on the east side of the compound, within the residential area for gifted individuals—or GIs, as Caleb now knew they were regularly called. As Caleb hopped into the passenger seat of a motorized utility vehicle that was similar to a golf cart, he instinctively clipped his new ID badge to his shirt. It was against the code of conduct for GIs to be out of their dorm room without ID properly displayed, a rule he was now familiar with courtesy of his new modules.

With the exception of the armed officers and countless security cameras, the compound resembled an ordinary city. The streets were paved and marked with appropriate traffic signs and lights. Every building was made of the same slate-gray brick, giving the compound a clean, modern appearance, especially considering none of the buildings bore any signage to indicate their function. Busses hauled groups of people around as others traveled along sidewalks on foot, talking and laughing. At first glance, it looked a lot like the front of the folder Kimberly had given him. Could this place really live up to the promises in those pamphlets?

On the drive to the dorms, Caleb was attempting to make sense of the feeling that overcame him while looking around at his surroundings. He was familiar with the route they were taking thanks to his new module and he knew what every building was before he even had the chance to wonder, but he also felt as if he was taking it all in for the first time. It was a strange sensation, similar to déjà vu.

Another observation Caleb made was that these memories were not as *full* as his normal ones. Due to the nature of his eidetic memory, his recollections were typically loaded with vivid imagery. In contrast, the modules seemed merely informational, as if they had been created by someone who had studied a map rather than visiting the physical locations. Not a hint of personal experience was detectable in them—or if it was, Caleb couldn't tell.

While traveling through the GI residential area, they passed an empty park, an arcade, an indoor pool, and a shopping center, all within walking distance of the dormitories. Maybe he would like it here after all.

Caleb's dormitory, a three-story variant of the smaller slate-gray buildings with far more windows, was located on the north end of the GI residential area.

Melanie led the way past the lobby and up to the third floor. Despite its uninspired exterior, the dorm's interior was decorated elegantly with Materra's national colors in mind. Navy blue carpet with sprawling gold lacing lined the floor, complimenting the shiny, gold light fixtures, and gold-framed paintings decorating the muted gray walls.

"Here we are," Melanie said as she came to a stop next to room 312. "Your badge should work." She pointed to the card scanner next to the door. Caleb scanned it. A bright green light blinked along with a chime of approval. He turned the handle and pushed his way inside.

Growing up in a small, two-bedroom cabin had conditioned Caleb to expect nothing more than a cramped bedroom on the other side of the door. Instead, he entered to find himself standing in a foyer that led into a kitchen over twice the size of the one in his childhood home. With his eyes wide, he carried forward into a spacious living room furnished with plush leather couches and solid oak tables.

"Welcome to your new home," Melanie said, sweeping her arm forward like a gameshow host. "This will be your room until you turn eighteen and are transferred to the eighteen and over dorms."

Room? It was an entire apartment.

Caleb walked into the bedroom, immediately taking notice of the towering wooden bookshelf along the wall opposite the bed. His legs carried him to it as though he was being drawn by an invisible force. He ran his fingers along the spines of the books, admiring the collection. They looked brand new.

"I was told you love to read, so I had someone stock the shelf for you," Melanie said, beaming at Caleb.

He pulled himself away from the bookshelf and into the closet. It was stocked with GI uniforms: pants, cargo shorts, T-shirts, sweaters, jackets and coats—all gray in color.

"We had to guess your size. If they don't fit, let the front desk know and they'll bring you the right sizes. I know gray isn't the flashiest color, but we prefer GIs to stand out for their work, not their fashion-sense."

That was fine with Caleb. He was used to trying to blend in anyway.

"Oh, I almost forgot." Melanie pulled a black box out of her jacket pocket and handed it to Caleb. "We don't allow personal computing devices at OASIS, but if you need it, this watch will help you stay on time."

Caleb opened the container and lifted a bulky black timepiece from it, strapping it to his wrist. It was surprisingly comfortable and lightweight.

As he admired his new watch, an uneasy feeling crept over Caleb. Over the years, John had taught him that success was only achievable through hard work. It had been ingrained in him from a young age. Having things dumped into his lap for simply being labeled gifted felt *wrong*.

But why should he feel bad? If he really was as valuable to the nation as everyone was telling him, maybe he deserved it all. Maybe John was wrong. He obviously didn't always tell him the truth. Caleb started to wonder how his mother felt about all of the perks at OASIS. If only he had known her, then he'd know how to feel. He was certain of it.

"We should probably get going now," Melanie said. "We still need to swing by the testing center for your assignment placement. You'll have plenty of time to explore the rest of your room over the next couple days."

Caleb's door clicked shut behind them as they turned and started toward the elevator. Suddenly, the next room down the hall burst open. Out popped a wiry boy with black glasses and short blond hair wound in tight locks. He came to a halt next to them and stood no taller than Caleb's shoulders.

"This must be the newest gifted individual. Is he loud?" He was addressing Melanie, but his hazel eyes seemed to avoid both of them while he talked, instead pointing up toward the top of his square, thick-rimmed glasses. "Because you know I can't sleep when people are loud, and—"

"Dusty, we've talked about this," Melanie interrupted. "If you have any noise complaints, please report them to the front desk and we will address them as they arise."

She turned to Caleb. "Caleb, this is Dusty Harding. He will be your new neighbor, and as you can tell, he's particular about noise."

"*Loud* noise," Dusty clarified, pushing on the bridge of his spectacles.

Melanie sighed. "I'm sure you two will get along just fine."

Caleb reached out for a handshake. "It's nice to meet you, Dusty."

Dusty looked down at Caleb's hand and shook his head, his blond curls bouncing back and forth. "I don't shake hands. While handshakes are acceptable social formalities, they are highly unsanitary. In fact, you're statistically more likely—"

"All right," Melanie cut in with a hand clap. "I'm glad you two had a chance to meet, but we must be going so we can get Caleb his assignment."

With the elevator door shut behind them, Melanie turned to

face Caleb. "I'm sorry about Dusty. He can be a bit *much*. He's autistic, which has allowed him to develop into a mathematical savant, but unfortunately can make him quite annoying."

"Oh, there's no need to apologize. He seemed interesting."

She scoffed. "Yeah, he's *interesting*, all right."

Caleb furrowed his brow and went to speak, but his glare went unnoticed and his voice failed him. He wanted to tell Melanie how wrong she was for putting Dusty down like that, but he couldn't bring himself to.

His mind flashed back to a memory of when John had forced him to train his fighting technique. Frustrated by his apparent lack of progress, Caleb had thrown his boxing gloves to the ground as he mean-mugged the swaying punching bag hanging from the shed rafters. "I don't get why you're making me do this. Boxing clearly isn't my thing."

"You *need* to know how to fight, bud. You're fourteen now, and before you know it, you'll be a man. There may come a day when you need to fight to protect those you love, or to defend someone who can't defend themselves, or maybe even to survive. Now put the gloves back on."

Caleb had rolled his eyes, but slipped his hands back into his gloves.

He felt that same frustration as he stood silently in the elevator next to Melanie. He knew this wasn't what John was referring to when he told him he may have to defend someone, but he still felt like he'd let John down by failing to speak up for Dusty. It's what he would have done.

The disappointment in himself faded quickly as Caleb was reminded of the lies John had told him: about the brain drive, about being his *father*. Why should he feel the need to live up to the standards of someone who couldn't even live up to his own?

John was a liar.

Caleb was left wondering, *Who am I?*

~*~

The main complex—better known as the Hub by the OASIS residents—stood at the center of OASIS. Waving high above each of the corners of the cubic four-story building was the Materra flag, bearing the image of a golden sun against a navy-blue background. The reflective sun shone bright like a beacon, as though to remind those who looked upon it of OASIS's chief purpose: to advance the nation of Materra.

Each floor of the Hub had a similar layout: a cafeteria at the center, wrapped in two layers of rooms separated by a hallway that stretched around the building to form a perfect square.

Caleb followed Melanie through the quiet hallway that wound around the first floor of the Hub, glancing into rooms as he passed by. They appeared to be classrooms. Children were working diligently at desks, some in groups, while others studied alone, or one-on-one with a teacher. Caleb only had his own experience as a homeschooled child to compare it to, but the classrooms looked much calmer than he would have expected.

"The Hub is where you'll spend most of your time here at OASIS," Melanie said as she led the way. "You won't usually be on the first floor, since this is primarily where early childhood education takes place, but we need to swing by the testing center for an aptitude test to get you an assignment. While everyone here is gifted, some are more talented in certain areas than others, and we use the results of the aptitude test for placement."

"When do kids typically take this test?" Caleb asked.

"Most are ready around age ten."

Melanie looked back at Caleb and raised a finger to her lips as she opened a door and ushered Caleb inside.

At the front of the room was a desk occupied by an old woman in a navy uniform. She tipped her head forward, looking at them over her reading glasses with raised eyebrows and tightly-pursed lips. The wrinkles on her face told Caleb this expression was common for her.

Melanie handed her a slip of paper. The lady read it before she turned to her computer and began typing. "Room six," she said to Melanie, her voice just above a whisper.

Caleb looked up to see six numbered doors along the wall opposite where they entered. Testing rooms, he imagined. Six was the only one open at the moment.

Melanie waved Caleb forward to the terminal at the end of the room. "Before taking the test," she whispered, "we need to remove everything from your brain drive and load it with the testing module, which will include the instructions along with fundamental learning modules. This allows us to level the playing field for all subjects. Afterward, any modules you came in with will be restored."

Caleb felt his shoulders loosen in relief, which took him by surprise. He hadn't realized he cared so much about his modules. Of course, they would be easy to reacquire if he ever lost them, but for some reason the thought of them being removed made him uneasy. Maybe it was because he was growing tired of having things taken from him. Whatever the reason, he was happy to hear he'd get them back.

After the upload, Caleb was given noise-cancelling headphones and showed to a cramped room with bare walls, where he was seated at a computer to begin.

The test seemed to have no rhyme or reason. Some questions were timed, others were not. Some seemed impossible, others simple. Bouncing from subject to subject left Caleb feeling mentally nauseated by the end. He couldn't have imagined taking this test when he was ten.

Following his completion, Melanie accessed a computer to view Caleb's results. She squinted at the screen and slouched forward as she read the report.

He was actually kind of excited to see which areas he excelled in.

"This is odd. It says you don't have aptitude in *any* subjects. You didn't make it far enough in any path for a definite assignment."

Those words stung Caleb. While he never considered himself gifted, he always thought of himself as intelligent. Maybe he wasn't even that.

"Diving further into your results, the only subsection that you consistently performed above average on was in regards to visual recollection. Let me check the assignment database."

A knot was forming in Caleb's stomach. How had he performed so poorly on a test designed for *ten-year-olds*? At least if they didn't want him here, he could go back home. Or would they put him in foster care instead?

"Here we go," Melanie said, perking up in her chair but keeping her voice quiet. "We have openings in cartography and film studies. Normally your assignment is chosen for you, but under the circumstances, I'll allow you to choose. Take your pick!"

CHAPTER SIX

"What do you mean I can't come visit?" John barked into the receiver of his phone, his frustration spilling over more and more into every word as he spoke. "Yes, I have the brochure right in front of me."

John had been trying to get through to someone at OASIS who could give him answers for over an hour. This was the closest he'd gotten so far.

"It says right here." John pushed his finger down on the pamphlet as if someone was standing in front of him. "Family members are allowed to visit during a three-hour period every weekend. I just want to know when I can see my son! How are you going to tell me he isn't mine? I raised that boy since he was three months old!"

John slammed the corded phone down on its base, cracking it in half. He let out a primal roar, venting his anger. Typically, John didn't let his emotions get the best of him, but the sheer absurdity of this whole situation was making it difficult at the moment. Caleb was his son, and no one was going to tell him otherwise. One thing John despised more than Materra's corrupt government were those who blindly followed its orders without regard for common sense or human decency. He'd have to take matters into his own hands.

In one swift rehearsed motion he snagged his keys off the countertop, grabbed his coat off the rack, and opened the front door.

His father didn't teach him much, but during his drunken ramblings he always found a way to slip in what he thought was profound wisdom through boxing idioms. *You'll never know your true strength until your back's against the ropes.* John could hear his father's voice echoing through his mind as he started up his truck. He was determined to find out if those drunken words held any weight.

~*~

A nervous excitement filled Caleb's stomach, leaving no room for breakfast. It was the first day of his assignment. After two uneventful days off, he was looking forward to learning more about the place where his mother spent her childhood.

Melanie had explained that GIs were given their first two days off to explore the compound and to get to know others. Instead, Caleb spent most of his time in his room, enjoying his new books.

As the elevator was closing to take Caleb down to the lobby of his dorm, a skinny arm shot through and the door slid back open. In walked his new neighbor, Dusty.

"Good morning, Caleb. Is today your first day?" Dusty asked, pushing his glasses up on his nose, eyes glued to the wall as he spoke.

"Yup. Got any tips for me?"

"I have one suggestion. Two suggestions, actually. Firstly, formulate a plan and stick to it. Approximately eighty-seven percent of all project failures are the result of poor preparation. Lack of proper vision can derail a module before you've even started. Secondly, be patient. Module creation is difficult, and most GIs fail their first few attempts. But these aren't earth-shattering tips by any measure. Your supervisor should tell you all of that anyway."

"I appreciate the heads-up." Caleb said as the elevator doors opened. They made their way outside, where a shuttle bus was waiting.

"What assignment were you given?" Dusty asked as they boarded.

The sounds of a rumbling engine and chatter filled the air as they searched for an open seat. "Cartography," Caleb said as he slid into one near the back of the bus. "I know nothing about maps, but I guess former knowledge isn't a requirement."

Dusty plopped down next to him. "Knowledge in your assigned area of expertise is less of a prerequisite and more the nature of your work. You will initially spend all of your time researching and learning about your field. Once you are able to exhibit mastery in that subject, that's when your real work starts."

"You mean downloading modules?" Caleb asked, looking over at Dusty, who was staring into his own lap.

"Exactly. Perfecting module creation is why we're all here. It's vital to the strength of our nation. Speaking of which, how is it you have just been sent here *now*? Is there something wrong with you? Were you in jail? Because I've heard that if a gifted individual is sentenced to jail as a child, they're still required to come here after their sentence."

Caleb couldn't help but laugh. "No, nothing like that."

"Well, what's the reason then?"

"It's… complicated." He wasn't ready to share his life story with someone he'd just met. Plus, he suspected this would only be the beginning of the questions if he started down that road. "But what about you? What's your assignment?"

"Statistics and probability are my areas of expertise." Dusty said matter-of-factly as he leaned over to look down the bus aisle. "Oh, great. Here comes Ricky." Dusty put his head down even further, his blond curls hanging over his glasses and covering his eyes.

Before he could ask who Ricky was, Caleb spotted a stout boy who looked to be about his age, dressed in an all-black security officer uniform and making his way toward them, looking every passenger up and down with an air of superiority as he passed by. His brown hair was buzzed short, and his round head sat atop a short, thick neck.

When his eyes met Caleb's, he stopped.

"And who might we have here?" Ricky reached his pudgy hand down to Caleb's badge and pulled it closer to his face, squinting.

"Caleb Shaw," he said, exaggerating the consonants. Then he dropped the card, allowing it to pull back to Caleb's chest with a smack.

"Well, I'm not sure if mister autistic here told you or not," Ricky said as he ruffled Dusty's hair, "but my name is Ricky Gunther. I'm a GI that specializes in security operations. Looks like we'll be seeing each other around. If you see anything suspicious, feel free to stop by. I'm on the first floor here. Room 110."

Ricky carried on down the aisle, continuing to scan people before finally taking a seat in the last row.

"His father, George Gunther, is the head of security here." Dusty muttered so his voice wouldn't carry. "He's not even gifted. They allow him to stay in our dorm, practicing his inevitable authority over us, just because of who his father is."

"So he's technically not a security officer?" Caleb asked as he glanced back at Ricky again.

"Nope. He has, however, been known to report things to his father, which has gotten GIs in trouble in the past. He thinks he's a big deal because they gave him his own little security shack where he can play pretend."

Taking notice of Dusty's fists clenching up as he spoke, Caleb decided to change the subject. "So, statistics, huh? What are the chances our bus crashes on the way to the Hub?"

"Well... taking into account the weather, the bus driver's driving record, average traffic flow at this hour, and of course..."

The diversion tactic worked. With his mind focused on statistical probability, Dusty's shoulders began to sag and his hands relaxed.

Though he had no interest in the answers, Caleb listened intently as Dusty answered one random statistical question after another, never growing annoyed by Caleb's endless queries.

Upon arriving at the Hub, the passengers disembarked and filed into the building, forming a line at the security checkpoint. Ricky cut to the front, passing through the checkpoint as a pair of security officers were busy checking in a group of small children who looked to be about six or seven years old.

The children stood in a tidy row wearing the standard gray GI uniforms, following the directions of their chaperone to the letter. Caleb was impressed by their calm behavior. Instead of watches, they all wore silver bracelets on their wrists. He wondered about their function—his memory modules had no information on them, which was startling, considering how complete they'd been so far. Before long, the security officers waved the children through what looked like a metal detector. They followed their chaperone in a single-file line into the Hub.

Once inside, Caleb took an elevator to the second floor, where he was to report to his supervisor to officially receive his assignment. Dusty continued on up to the third floor.

The second and third floors of the Hub were designated for GI research, housing numerous study rooms as well as a vast library that spanned both floors. It was there where GIs researched and studied their assignments, preparing themselves to eventually create memory modules.

At any given time, most GIs in the Hub were located on the second and third floor, and that day it was as true as ever. Caleb pushed his way through the bustling hallway in search of a supervisor, squeezing between groups of GIs talking and laughing.

Eventually, Caleb found his floor supervisor's office and ducked in, escaping the chaos of the hallway. A young man with a red untamed chinstrap beard that encircled his face like a lion's mane looked up from his computer at Caleb.

His badge read: *Jeremy Rigs.*

"Hello," Caleb said, standing at the edge of his desk. "I'm a new GI, and I'm here for my assignment."

The man's orange eyebrows furrowed. Caleb couldn't read his expression. He seemed either upset or confused.

"Name?" he asked in an unexpectedly deep and raspy voice.

Caleb answered and a few keystrokes later he was given a brief overview of his assignment and loaded up with a module containing the necessary information to perform his duties.

The instructions seemed simple enough: create updated, detailed maps of Materra's cities. Although map modules of nearly every city already existed, they were severely outdated. Most of them had been created using maps that were drawn over a hundred years prior. Since then, houses and roads had been built, businesses had gone under and new ones had sprouted up.

What his assignment didn't specify was how map module creation was to be done. No stranger to self-learning, Caleb dove right in.

~*~

It was approaching noon and Dusty had one thing on his mind: tacos. He collected his notebooks and pencils, stuffing them haphazardly into his bag. His backpack was a mess, but he liked to think of it as an *organized* mess. It didn't matter where he put things; he'd remember where each item was the next time he needed it.

Tacos were Dusty's favorite food, though he imagined the world at large offered a much wider array of choices than those served at OASIS, and maybe there was a mystery food out there that would be his new favorite if he ever had the chance to try it. Most likely that was the case.

On his way to the cafeteria, he wondered how his friend Caleb was doing on his first day at the Hub. Was he technically a friend? Maybe he could ask Caleb later, make it official or something. Dusty had never been able to figure out what it meant to be friends. Over the course of his eleven years at OASIS, he'd met many kids he'd considered friends—but it always seemed like the more time he spent with them, the less they wanted to be around him, making up excuse after excuse to avoid his invitations. It was exhausting.

This time would be different. Maybe he'd try not to talk about birds as much. For as long as he could remember, Dusty had always been fascinated by them. However, not everyone shared in his passion for the winged animals, which baffled him. They could *fly*. That alone should have been incredible to anyone with an ounce of curiosity, he thought.

What if Caleb liked them though? He'd have to think of a small comment he could make about birds to see how he felt about the topic. If Caleb seemed interested, maybe then he could share an interesting fact or two.

Now at the front of the lunch line, Dusty grabbed a tray and glanced down at the food. He saw only hamburgers. His chest tightened and his heart began to race. Today was taco day, he was sure of it.

"Where are the tacos?" he said to the man behind the counter in a navy uniform, although his eyes never left the food. Looking the man in the eyes would only make him more uncomfortable.

"They were moved next week. Our shipment of taco seasoning was delayed. Sorry, it's burgers today."

Dusty clenched his teeth. That wasn't possible. Tacos were on the menu, clear as day. "No, today is taco day. It's on the schedule. Look behind you." Dusty was pointing to the large calendar on the wall with the meal schedules written on it.

"Listen, kid," the man said, his voice stern, "I don't have taco seasoning. We're serving hamburgers today. Or you can help yourself to a salad instead if you'd like."

"No!" Dusty yelled. "You people promised me tacos. It's lunchtime. Lunch today was tacos. I planned for this, and I *need* tacos!"

Dusty could feel the eyes on him as the cafeteria fell silent. He didn't care. This wasn't fair, and everyone else should agree. They were all lied to, just like he was.

"Calm down," the man said, holding his hands up in a disarming gesture as though it would provide Dusty with some sort of comfort. It didn't.

Dusty felt a hand grip his shoulder and squeeze tightly. He didn't have to look to know who it was.

"Is he causing you trouble?" Ricky Gunther asked the man behind the counter.

"Stay out of this, Ricky," Dusty said, rolling his shoulder to free it from his grip. "It's none of your business."

Ricky was always looking for ways to stick his nose where it didn't belong. If he was a bird, Dusty imagined he'd be a vulture —always swooping in to prey on the vulnerable.

"Oh, it's very much my business. As a security officer in training, I couldn't stand by while you make a scene in the cafeteria and hold up the line just because your simple brain can't understand a change in the menu. You're not five years old."

Dusty's knuckles were beginning to turn white from clenching his fists so tight, and he could feel his eyes welling up. He'd had enough of Ricky today.

Ricky reached for the radio on his uniform and began talking into it. Dusty took the opening and unleashed on Ricky, pushing him and pounding on his chest with his fists.

He didn't budge.

Ricky and Dusty were the same height, but Ricky was somehow looking down on Dusty like he was a toddler throwing a temper tantrum.

Then, all of a sudden, Dusty felt a pudgy fist connect with his nose and he fell backward, clutching his face. He pulled his hands away and saw nothing but red.

~*~

As the sun was setting over the trees, casting long shadows over the OASIS compound, John was placing his binoculars and spiral-bound notebook into a camouflage bag, preparing to head back to his hotel room. After spending most of his day perched in a tree studying the operations of OASIS, he needed to wash up and get some rest. This wasn't going to be an overnight extraction. If he was really going to break his son out of this place, he needed more information.

From what he could gather so far, the compound had four entrances, with the main entrance located on the south end. That would be the hardest to sneak into, since it had the heaviest presence of security personnel.

The west entrance led into a residential area, where staff members and their families lived. Infiltrating through there would be somewhat difficult, because even if he managed to successfully slip in with an unassuming family, he would have to go unnoticed through another security checkpoint before even making it into the main compound.

Entering through the east entrance would also prove to be tough, as it seemed to be closed the entire day. Although it was the closest entrance to the dormitories, John suspected it was only accessible during visitation hours. On top of that, there was a security office nearby that was manned even when the gate was closed.

John had also taken notice of what looked like a small stout security officer that seemed to roam aimlessly around the dormitories and surrounding areas, making occasional stops at an outpost. So far, he had not been able to make sense of the man's patrol; he'd have to continue studying his routines.

At this point, the north gate seemed to be the best potential point of entry. That end of the compound housed nothing but staff buildings. The entrance was guarded, but they rarely searched the contents of the delivery vehicles, usually only stopping drivers to check credentials. If he could manage to hide in a delivery truck, he'd have a puncher's chance at getting inside the compound without having to face security.

In order for a plan like that to work, John would need more time to learn the delivery schedules. He'd need to know when a given truck would arrive, where it would eventually end up, and how he was going to get from there to the dorms. On top of that, anticipating where anyone would be at any given time on the north end of the compound would be next to impossible. Staff were constantly going in and out of buildings for supplies. He'd need to find a way to blend in.

John began his hike back to the access road where he'd parked his truck, mentally preparing for another long day of surveillance the next day. It would be a while before he could fully realize a rescue operation on a facility of this size. John was a patient man, but he would need every bit of patience he could muster if he wanted this plan to succeed. It had to be perfect.

CHAPTER SEVEN

Stepping out of the elevator onto the fourth floor of the Hub—the floor reserved solely for module design and creation—Caleb couldn't shake the feeling that he was somewhere he wasn't supposed to be. The early morning chatter that filled the halls of the second and third floors was nowhere to be found here. In fact, aside from the distant sound of a door opening and closing down the hall, it was completely silent.

It was Caleb's first trip to the fourth floor. Over the last two weeks, he'd been working diligently to create the foundation for his first memory module: an updated top-down general reference map of the city of Abicar.

Fortunately, Caleb's assignment module contained what had to amount to a lifetime of experience in cartography. Equipped with it, he could read general reference and topographical maps with ease. Symbols that were commonly used in map design had a certain familiarity to them that was similar to recognizing text on a page as his own handwriting. It was like he'd lived an entire life as a cartographer and was reincarnated into a new body. The feeling was unique, but oddly refreshing.

Despite being given all of the resources he needed to create updated map modules, it didn't take Caleb long to realize that in order to create immersive maps utilizing the full potential of his eidetic memory he would need to visit the cities in person. The experience of traveling down the streets and taking in the sights would give him far more information than he could possibly gather here at OASIS.

However, every time he brought up the idea with his supervisor, it was immediately shot down. After multiple denied requests, he settled for creating new top-down general reference maps of Materra's cities, starting in alphabetical order. It wouldn't be his best work, but it was a start.

Caleb brushed aside the uneasy feeling brought on by the eerie silence and started down the hall. It took him no time at all to find an open module architecture room, and he made his way inside, taking a seat at the large table. He pulled out his hand-drawn maps, spreading them across the large computer screen built into the tabletop.

The main purpose of these rooms was to provide a space to prepare outlines for module creation. They served as a guide, breaking down complicated, information-dense subjects into smaller subsections to be downloaded into subfolders within the module. By breaking them up into smaller, more digestible pieces, module creation became easier and the end result was a better-quality memory for the user.

Caleb related the outlines to books. Books, he reasoned, are separated into chapters, and furthermore into paragraphs. When these paragraphs are arranged in the correct order, he thought, they combine to form a story that is greater than the sum of their individual parts.

According to Supervisor Rigs, developing a good outline was critical to creating top-grade memory modules. However, unlike most assignments, cartography didn't require one. The maps themselves served as an adequate guideline for module creation.

Looking over his hand-drawn maps one last time, he felt a sense of pride. They were perfect—the culmination of weeks of research.

For the first time in Caleb's life, he felt like he had a purpose. In no way at all was he enthusiastic about cartography, but there was something incredibly fulfilling about the idea of using his eidetic memory to *create*. It was as if this was his fate all along. He wondered if this was how his mother felt when she was here.

As quickly as Caleb's feeling of satisfaction came, it was gone, replaced with shame. All of a sudden his face grew hot and he gathered his belongings, returning them to his backpack. Even though he was hundreds of miles away, it still felt as if John was standing over his shoulder watching everything he did, and he knew what he'd say: *Finish the job, and then you can be proud.*

Caleb scooped his bag up, throwing it over his shoulder before leaving to find an open download room across the hall, slipping inside and locking the door behind him.

Immediately, he noticed the walls—they were lined from floor to ceiling with white foam panels. Even the door was completely covered in the plain square panels—for soundproofing, he assumed. He took a seat at the small desk, pulling his maps out. Like the room he came from, the desk had a computer screen built into it, though it was much smaller and clearly designed for one person. Above the desk, attached to the wall, was a brain drive terminal.

Although Caleb had no experience downloading memory modules, his assignment contained the necessary instructions.

Moving with the grace of someone who had done this numerous times before, he scanned his ID badge on the brain drive terminal, hooked himself up with the interface cable, and added a new project folder, complete with subfolders for each map.

As he stared down at his first map, he could feel his heart picking up the pace. Why did he feel nervous? There was no one watching him, and if he messed up, he could start over. Caleb took a deep breath and exhaled.

Then he tapped the *Download* button.

Devoting all of his attention to the map he'd created and studied over the last two weeks, his mind slowly combed through every street, intersection and address. It wasn't enough to just look at the map and think about what was on it. It was really only there to serve as a constant reminder of what his mind should be focused on. He was downloading his *memories*. There had to be long-term memories of the information for the process to be successful and, equally as important, he needed to be accessing those memories while the download was occurring.

Caleb actually found it easier to keep his eyes closed, relying on his eidetic memory to recall the map. The process was tedious, and at times he wasn't sure if he was thinking *too* much.

Six hours later, Caleb emerged from the confines of the tiny white-paneled room. He had completed his first memory module: a complete, updated map of the city of Abicar. His stomach grumbled, begging him for food, and the sudden weight of his eyelids threatened to close his eyes against his will. His thoughts were sluggish as well.

After a quick bite at the cafeteria, he boarded the shuttle bus back to his dorm. He glanced around at the other passengers before taking a seat. There was no sign of Dusty. He hadn't seen his neighbor since his first day on the job, but he was the closest thing Caleb had to a friend right now and he wanted to share his accomplishment with him.

For the first time since starting his assignment, Caleb didn't have work to distract him. He was alone with his thoughts. He wondered how John was doing. After the first visitation day came and went without any sign of him, he had assumed that John was not permitted to visit since he wasn't technically family. When John failed to show on visitation day, Caleb had been surprised to feel a sense of relief. He'd be lying to himself if he said he didn't miss John at all, but he wasn't sure he was ready to face him. He still didn't know what was on that memory stick, and he was having a hard time sorting out his feelings.

His gut reaction was to forgive John, to put his hurt in the past and move on. Yet, he found that every time he thought of the man, anger would creep back to the surface. He felt betrayed by the only person he'd ever fully trusted.

With a headache beginning to form from attempting to hold back tears, Caleb closed his eyes and leaned his head back to rest on the seat behind him, trying to switch his exhausted mind off.

Caleb had grown up in a house with one parent who worked most of the time. He was used to being alone. What he realized that night was that *being* alone and *feeling* alone were two completely different things.

~*~

John settled into his favorite branch of the tall pine tree he had chosen as a vantage point over OASIS, preparing for another long night of surveillance. After more than a week of observing the compound's operations during daylight hours, he was convinced even further that the north gateway was the optimal entrance point. Since then, he had flipped his schedule, sleeping during the day and monitoring the facility at night.

While he did miss catching glimpses of Caleb going to and from his dorm every day, he knew his best chance of success would be a nighttime infiltration. He could sneak around under the cover of darkness and it would be easier to predict where Caleb was, since he always returned to his dorm in the evening. Now, he needed to learn the routine of the night shift.

Thus far, John had identified two delivery trucks as potential targets. Neither of them were routinely searched at the gate and both always made deliveries at night. One of the trucks delivered household items and the other food.

With less than a week's worth of notes on the night shift, John still had plenty of research ahead of him. He planned to log the truck arrivals over time in an attempt to observe a pattern that would allow him to accurately predict days and times of deliveries along with destinations and the habits of the OASIS staff during those time frames.

That night, he'd share a tree with a noisy owl, both of them wide awake and surveying the terrain below for answers to their problems.

~*~

Awoken by the buzzing of his wristwatch, Caleb rolled out of bed, nearly toppling over as he stood. He steadied himself with his hand on the wall, waiting for the feeling of disorientation to pass. Although he'd gotten a full night of rest, he felt as though he hadn't slept a wink. *Was this normal after a long day of downloading modules?* he wondered.

Guiding himself, one careful step after another, he eventually managed to get dressed. By the time he needed to leave, he seemed to have regained his balance. He gathered his backpack and headed out into the hallway, making his way toward the elevator.

Just then, Dusty emerged from the elevator. He was being guided to his room by a security officer who held him firmly by the arm. Dried blood painted his lips and chin red. The front of his gray shirt was stained a dark crimson around the collar while the rest of his GI uniform was riddled with sweat stains and urine. His typically bouncy blond curls were matted to his head, and his glasses were bent out of shape, sitting down on the end of his freckled nose.

"Dusty!" Caleb said enthusiastically, attempting to mask the concern on his face. "I haven't seen you in two weeks. What— happened to you?"

Dusty stared through Caleb, his face lacking expression, as he continued to shuffle his feet forward slowly under the guidance of the officer.

"Excuse me," the man said as they passed Caleb.

Caleb watched as his unresponsive neighbor was escorted to his room. He waited for the security officer to come back down the hall.

"What happened to him?" Caleb didn't bother hiding the worry in his voice this time. "Is he okay?"

The security officer looked at Caleb like he just asked them what planet they were on. "He'll be fine. He just finished his two weeks in solitary. You new here or something?" The question was rhetorical—he had already disappeared into the elevator.

Solitary? Caleb knew solitary confinement was a potential punishment, but as hard as he tried, he couldn't recall *what* it was. The code of conduct manual module must not have gone into detail on the actual punishment.

Dusty didn't look like he had been in any sort of solitary confinement Caleb could imagine. He looked like he'd been beaten and tortured.

Caleb hurried to Dusty's door and rapped his knuckles against it. After a few minutes of knocking with no response, he continued on to the Hub.

Worried about Dusty's well-being, Caleb had a hard time focusing on his work. Fortunately, the first step in creating a map—collecting resources—required the least amount of attention. Still, he got very little done over the course of the morning.

The afternoon started much the same. Coming to the realization that he wasn't going to get anything productive done until he had some answers, he decided to find another GI to ask about solitary.

He spotted a GI studying alone in a room nearby. Caleb entered and took a seat at the conference table across from an olive-skinned girl with long black hair that was tied back in a single braid. Her badge read *Rava Garza*.

Her amber eyes flicked up from her textbook, piercing Caleb. "Can I help you?" she asked flatly.

"I hope so. My friend just came back from two weeks in solitary confinement and he looked rough, to say the least. I was hoping you could help me make sense of it. Have you ever been to solitary?"

"You must be the new guy. Are you talking about Dusty?" Caleb was caught off guard. She'd heard of him? "How do you know who I am? And yeah, Dusty. He's my neighbor."

"Listen," Rava said, sounding a tad annoyed, "I don't have time to chit-chat. If I tell you what happened to Dusty, will you leave me alone?"

He nodded.

"I saw him in the cafeteria the day he was sent to solitary. They changed the daily special from tacos to burgers at the last minute. Well, you know Dusty. He doesn't do well with sudden changes, especially when he feels like he's been deceived or lied to. So he caused a big scene in the cafeteria, demanding tacos because he was 'promised tacos.'" Rava used her fingers as air quotes. "He was yelling at the chefs until Ricky Gunther stepped in and called security. Dusty decided to try beating up Ricky, which didn't go so well. And that was when security showed up and hauled him away. I had no idea he got two weeks though. That seems excessive."

Caleb didn't know Dusty well, but he didn't seem like the kind of person to pick fights. He couldn't believe he had really tried to tussle with Ricky.

He leaned forward in his seat, eager for more answers. "So, what is solitary like?"

Rava leaned back and ran her hand down the back of her head, pulling her long braid over her shoulder to rest in front of her, twirling the end of it in her fingers as she spoke. "I don't know from personal experience. I've never been sent there. But I've heard about it from others. First, they empty your brain drive. Then, they fill it up with modules loaded with awful memories. And I mean *awful*. Memories of being assaulted, tortured, starved, you name it."

Caleb looked like he'd just seen a ghost, face pale and mouth hanging open slightly.

"After that, they put you in a padded holding cell for the duration of your punishment. Once your sentence is served, they remove all of the modules containing the dreadful memories and put your old ones back. I've heard it's quite disorienting coming out of there. You're left with a whole lot of emotions that you can't possibly make sense of because you no longer have the memories that created them. It's like experiencing complete pain while being numb at the same time."

After a few seconds of complete silence, questions filling his mind faster than he could possibly put them into words, Caleb finally spoke. "I mean... how is that even legal?"

Unexpectedly, Rava burst into laughter, startling him. "Legal?" She blurted out between chuckles. "The government can do whatever they want. They make the laws. They own *me*. They own *you*. We work for *them*. Once your parents signed that contract, which they were required to by law anyway, you became property of Materra. Welcome to the club." She shot Caleb a cheesy grin and two congratulatory thumbs up for effect. Although it was fake, he thought her smile was cute.

Caleb was surprised by her enthusiastic distrust of the government. It wasn't so much that someone would have that opinion—John was evidence enough there were people with a deep distrust of the government—but every other conversation he'd had with a GI about what they did always ended up with them reciting some sentiment about how OASIS was essential for the success of the nation. Rava's unapologetic authenticity was refreshing.

Overwhelmed by his thoughts, Caleb decided to head back to his room early to get some rest and check on his friend again. "Well, thank you. I won't waste any more of your time."

"No problem," Rava said, her voice softer this time. "And under different circumstances I'd be happy to chat more. But I'm behind schedule, and I need to finish this algorithmic

programming module by the end of the week."
Caleb nodded and reached for the handle.
"And I'm sorry about your friend Dusty. Don't be a stranger
though. Stop by if you see me around the Hub."
Caleb returned a smile before turning to leave. His was
genuine.

There was something about Rava that intrigued Caleb,
and due to the nature of his eidetic memory he was sure he
would be replaying this moment over and over in his mind,
trying to find out what it was.

CHAPTER EIGHT

With thoughts buzzing through his mind like honeybees through a field of flowers in bloom, Caleb found himself lying wide awake in his bed, unable to fall asleep. Every moment of peace and quiet was chased away by a never-ending barrage of questions.

What was solitary confinement like? Was his mother ever sent there? When would he get his memory stick back? What was on it? Why had John felt the need to lie in the first place? Was Dusty going to be okay?

Dusty hadn't answered the door when he'd knocked again earlier. The security officer had assured him that Dusty would be fine, but he was beginning to doubt the man.

Despite the lack of sleep, when Caleb's alarm woke him up the next morning, he felt fairly refreshed. Though he was feeling fine, he decided to take a day off from work to check on Dusty. GIs were permitted one unexcused absence per month, and could earn additional days off through "consistent work performance," whatever that meant. But he knew he wouldn't get much work done until he knew Dusty was okay.

Following a shower and a quick breakfast, Caleb made his way to Dusty's door. He knocked lightly in case he was still asleep. Nothing but silence came from within his apartment. In an attempt to clear his mind and kill some time, Caleb grabbed his coat and headed out for a walk. A biting chill filled the air as snow fell slowly to the ground, melting immediately as it landed. Although today was particularly cold, snow wasn't common this far south.

Normally, the first snow of the season brought Caleb joy. He had so many great memories of snowball fights and building forts with John. Today, each snowflake that graced his skin served as a cold reminder of better days.

Caleb lifted his eyes from the sidewalk to see Ricky exiting his personal security office. He was popping a donut hole into his mouth as he closed the door behind him. For only a second, they locked eyes, and Caleb quickly put his head back down, walking past the boy. He didn't want any trouble and he certainly didn't want to get sent to solitary himself after seeing what it did to Dusty.

"Where are you going so fast, newbie?" Ricky called from around the corner through a mouth full of donuts.

He stopped and turned around as Ricky came around the corner, choking down the remainder of his breakfast. "Taking a day off, huh?" he said as he wiped his hand on his black pants, leaving a streak of white powder behind.

Caleb glared into the stout boy's round face, noticing his facial features all looked too small for the size of his head. "What do you want, Ricky?"

"Whoa, what's with the hostility?"

His innocent tone didn't fool Caleb. The smile forming at the corner of Ricky's mouth told him everything. He was enjoying this.

"Is this about your buddy, Dusty? Yeah, it's true I was the one that recommended the two weeks in solitary, but he deserved it. You can't go around throwing fits like that. I was only doing my job, upholding the code of conduct."

That got Caleb's full attention. "*You* gave him the two

weeks?" His hands curled into fists inside his jacket pockets as his heart began to hammer against his ribcage.

"Yeah. And I know you guys are friends and all, but you should be careful around him. He's unstable."

That was it; he couldn't listen to it anymore. He had failed to stand up for Dusty before and he wasn't going to make the same mistake twice.

Before his mind could talk his body out of it, Caleb shoved Ricky up against the wall of his own security office, using his forearm to pin him against the building by his throat. Judging by the look on Ricky's face, he'd been taken completely by surprise.

"I know you're used to everyone here walking on eggshells around you because of who your father is, but I won't."

He pushed even harder against Ricky's pudgy neck. Ricky's arms were flailing around, grasping at Caleb's, but his grip was firm and the boy struggled to breathe. "If I see you even look in Dusty's direction again, not even your father will be able to save you from what I'll do to you. Understood?"

Ricky made his best attempt at a nod and Caleb released him. He fell to his knees, gasping for air. As he glanced up, the expression on Ricky's face reminded him of the look he saw in the eyes of animals after he shot them and their life was slowly leaving them—a look of pain and regret. At least that's how he imagined they felt. Caleb never took pleasure in killing animals —it was done out of necessity. Similarly, he took no pleasure in Ricky's fear.

With his point made, he continued on his walk as Ricky remained doubled over, panting. Caleb deliberately moved at a normal pace and refrained from looking back. He needed to exude confidence, showing no concern of retaliation. John had always told him to never panic if he came face-to-face with a pack of wolves out in the woods. Though these circumstances were vastly different, he imagined the end result would be the same. Showing weakness would be a mistake he couldn't afford.

About an hour later, Caleb returned to his dorm. On the way through the lobby, he stopped at his mailbox to check for his memory stick and was surprised to find a letter in it. He opened the envelope to find a memory module grading form inside. It was the rating for his first module. He'd received a perfect score —ten out of ten—which came along with a whopping five hundred credits to his personal account.

A rush of conflicting emotions flooded through Caleb all at once. He was ecstatic that he'd gotten a perfect rating, but at the same time disappointed. He felt like he could make even better modules if he had the chance to visit the cities in person. They considered *that* a ten? Nonetheless, he was pleased he did well.

His true excitement came from the monetary reward. Five hundred credits were more than he'd ever earned, and more than he'd ever personally seen at one time.

Caleb swelled with a much greater sense of purpose now. Setting aside the feeling of accomplishment that came along with using his "gift" and his motivation to get to know his mother through experiencing OASIS, he now had another reason to push forward. If he could continue churning out memory modules of this quality, the amount of money he could make would be *life changing*. In no time at all, he could earn enough credits to set him and John up forever. He wondered if there was a way that he could send money to John and made a mental note to ask his supervisor the next chance he got.

He had the urge to rush to the Hub to get back to work right away, but he was reminded of the reason he took the day off in the first place. His thoughts sobered and he remembered tacos were on the menu for lunch that day. He swung by the cafeteria and grabbed a couple before heading up to Dusty's room.

~*~

For the second time that morning, Dusty heard a knock at his door. A shiver ran down his spine, but he suppressed the fear almost instantly.

He was getting better control of his emotions now that it had been a couple days since his release, and he was finally able to get himself washed up and dressed. Recovering from solitary confinement was never easy, but it had only gotten more difficult over the years. According to Dusty's estimation, he had been sent to solitary confinement more than fifty times.

Now, on his second day of recovery, Dusty was eager to get back to work. He had never missed two days in a row before.

Through the peephole, he saw his neighbor holding a pair of tacos.

"Dusty, you okay in there? I grabbed a couple tacos from the cafeteria in case you were hungry."

Why did Caleb care so much about his well-being? They barely knew each other. Still, his persistence was impressive, Dusty thought, like that of a woodpecker crafting a nest into the side of a tree with its beak.

Dusty cracked the door open and poked his head out. "Hi, Caleb. I'm fine, I—" His eyes locked onto the letter in Caleb's hand. "Is that a module rating?" He opened the door and snatched the paper out of his hand. His eyes grew wide. "A ten?" he exclaimed, pushing his glasses up on his nose to make sure his eyes weren't playing tricks on him. A ten was impossible, or so he'd thought.

As a math prodigy, Dusty was an obvious choice for his statistics and probability assignment. In spite of his calculator-like mind, he had never scored above a seven in module creation, and that was only one time.

"How?" he muttered.

Caleb shrugged, as though he wasn't impressed by his perfect score. "Not sure. This was my first one, so I have nothing to compare it to."

A pang of jealousy pierced Dusty's pride. This was the score of his *first* memory module. Dusty had been working for *years* for scores half this good, and Caleb just waltzed into OASIS and created a perfect module on his first try. How was that fair?

"Are you sure you're okay?" Caleb asked.

Now he wasn't. But he couldn't let Caleb know that. That's not what friends did—he'd learned that the hard way. Friends supported each other, and he did want to be Caleb's friend, after all. Maybe if he got closer to Caleb, he could learn how he made such amazing memory modules. If he was able to get a perfect rating, he could send it home to his parents and prove to them he was worth something. Maybe then they'd come and visit him.

"Yeah," Dusty said, forcing a smile.

"You feeling up for some company? I brought you some tacos," Caleb said, holding them up.

"Yeah, come in." He stepped aside and allowed Caleb into his apartment. He took a seat at the kitchen table. "I apologize for the mess. I haven't let housekeeping in over the last few days." Really, Dusty wasn't sorry, and he didn't feel like his apartment was a mess, but he'd heard other people say the phrase enough that he thought it was only appropriate.

"No worries. I'm just happy to see you're doing well. I heard you got two weeks in solitary. I'm not sure if you remember seeing me in the hallway when you came back, but you looked like you were in rough shape."

Dusty glanced at the pile of soiled clothes lying on his bedroom floor and began to understand why Caleb was so worried.

"Unfortunately, I don't remember seeing you that day. My recollection surrounding my solitary confinement is a bit hazy, which is typical." Dusty sat down at the table across from Caleb, taking a bite of his food.

"Typical? Nothing I've heard about that place sounds typical. Another GI, Rava, filled me in on the incident in the cafeteria and what they did to you. That's messed up. Have you ever told your parents about solitary confinement?"

"My parents don't care. They were thrilled to send me here.

You've probably noticed I'm... *different*." Dusty paused. He hated explaining this to people, because they always felt sorry for him, like he was dying of an incurable illness. "I have autism. My parents considered me an embarrassment. Now, the only reminder they have that I exist is the monthly stipend checks they get from the government."

Dusty waited for the inevitable sympathetic response from Caleb, but instead Caleb looked... angry? He couldn't be sure without looking right at him. Caleb was about to speak when Dusty cut him off before he could get a word out. "Wait, did you say *Rava* told you?"

"Yeah, I sort of barged in on her study session and chatted with her a little bit. Why?"

"I'm shocked she talked to you. She's known around here as a loner. Has been ever since she arrived, five years ago."

Dusty felt sort of silly calling someone else a loner, given his horrific track record of failing to maintain friendships, but he wasn't a loner by choice. Rava drove away anyone who so much as attempted a conversation with her.

Caleb leaned forward. "So, what's her story?"

"I wouldn't know," Dusty said, starting in on his second taco. "Like I said, she's a loner. You probably know more about her than I do. The only thing I know about her is she's a native Aridorian."

"Aridorian?"

"She's a refugee from Aridor. She was born there. You couldn't tell?"

"I've never met a refugee from Aridor before." Caleb sounded embarrassed to admit that, so Dusty tried to change the subject.

"What about you? What's *your* story?" Dusty asked. Caleb let out a long sigh and began to unravel his past as Dusty finished his taco.

Dusty did his best to conceal his excitement. He was actually making a friend.

~*~

At the age of ten, Avery Blake had been officially identified as gifted, though his court-ordered therapist had long suspected it. His therapist was relieved, and told him as much. He'd repeatedly referred to the young boy as "troubled."

OASIS had taken him in, cultivating his special mind and giving him a new life. It was there that Avery began to understand how different he was from other kids his age.

His aptitude test had revealed excellence in critical thinking, philosophy, and history, making him a perfect fit for his law assignment. Avery spent his childhood studying justice and the government's responsibility to uphold it, as well as protect it.

When he was twelve, he had experienced OASIS's justice system at work when he earned his first trip to solitary confinement. Rumors about solitary were commonplace. He'd known what to expect, yet he found himself unafraid. Instead, he was merely intrigued.

After twelve hours locked away—a fair punishment for stealing from another GI, he thought—he'd walked out of solitary confinement like nothing had happened.

During his time at OASIS, Avery had utilized every resource available to soak up as much knowledge as possible, but he failed to ever deliver a single memory module. At the age of fifteen, he was discharged from OASIS, an unprecedented decision by the disciplinary board. Gifted children were a precious resource to the nation, meant to be nurtured and harvested like a fruit-bearing tree. Avery was found to be barren.

None of their punishments had worked on him either. He was as unmalleable as they came. Worse yet, Avery was an expert manipulator, often convincing other GIs to do his dirty work for him. In the end, it was easier to just get rid of him altogether.

Unfortunately, the easiest path doesn't always yield the best outcome, as many of those who had occupied seats on the disciplinary board that chose to expel Avery had come to understand better than most.

Now, *they* worked for *him*.

At the young age of twenty-four, Avery Blake had been elected to the office of President of Materra thanks to a campaign that showcased his undeniable charm and quick-wittedness. His youthful energy was a breath of fresh air to Materra's citizens, who were growing tired of electing their elders only to see no tangible improvements to their quality of life. In the eyes of many, he had represented a much-needed change to the status quo.

For the next twenty-two years, he had served as the President of Materra, winning every reelection by a wide margin.

While his advisors were not his biggest fans, President Blake didn't care what they thought of him, only what they could do for him. He wanted results, and they had been falling short of his expectations, which is what brought him back to OASIS. He intended to deal personally with a matter that should have been taken care of long before: Operation Sundown.

The president sat at the end of a long brushed-steel table in an otherwise empty room in the secure bunker beneath OASIS. He was a tall man of average build with sharp facial features and a dark brown comb-over. His demeanor was relaxed as he awaited the arrival of his advisors, one leg resting over the other as he leaned back in his chair with his navy suit jacket unbuttoned.

They wouldn't be expecting him. His advisors were scheduled to convene privately today to discuss their options to veto his planned operation. Their cowardice disgusted him.

As his subordinates began to trickle in, he relished the look on each of their faces, though his facial expression remained cold and distant. None of them said a word, shuffling to their seats and fidgeting with their belongings while they waited for the others to arrive.

In all, there were nine attendees, President Blake and eight of his advisors. With every seat in the room filled, President Blake's senior advisor to OASIS, Craig Polsik, looked to him with unease as though he was waiting for permission to begin the meeting. The bald, bug-eyed man was well into his sixties now, but his wrinkled skin and emaciated build gave him the appearance of someone with one foot in the grave. The stress of overseeing OASIS for the last thirty years had aged him far beyond his years. Truthfully, he was great at his job, and running that facility was no easy task. But his lack of confidence and tendency to shrivel under pressure annoyed President Blake to no end.

After a few minutes of agonizing silence, Senior Advisor Polsik took the initiative to begin the meeting. President Blake didn't so much as look in his direction, but out of the corner of his eye he could see the wrinkled man glancing at him after every few sentences.

Eventually, the subject of Operation Sundown was brought to the forefront of the discussion. President Blake turned his head to meet Senior Advisor Polsik's gaze as he spoke and the man began to stutter.

"So, uh, in conclusion. Due to, uh, a lack of proper resources, I call to a vote the motion to, uh, veto Operation Sundown as proposed."

President Blake stood abruptly, leaning over the table and placing his hands flat on the surface. "Yes, I agree with Craig. Let's take a vote, shall we? All in favor of vetoing Operation Sundown, raise your hand."

"Mr. President, our, uh, protocol states that we are to cast votes anonymously," Senior Advisor Polsik said, his voice trembling.

President Blake spared his words no attention. "Nice and high so I can be sure to count accurately."

A woman in the back, the youngest of the bunch, raised her hand halfway before looking around and realizing she was the only one with her hand up. She lowered it back down.

President Blake's face broke out in a wide grin. "Unanimous decision! Incredible. I'm pleased to see so much... *enthusiasm* for my proposed operation." Like many of his colleagues, Senior Advisor Polsik's eyes were fixed on the papers in front of him.

"Now, if I may be so bold," President Blake continued, "I'd like to *personally* see to it that this operation takes off within the next month."

Polsik's gaze shot up from the desk. "Sir, I'm sorry but that is impossible—not to mention reckless, even if it were."

President Blake's grin faded and he pierced his advisor with an icy glare. "It is entirely possible, and it *will* be done."

Polsik slouched back down in his chair. *Coward*, thought Blake.

President Blake's cheerful grin reformed in an instant and he addressed the room. "Now, find me a GI that can perform to the standards necessary to complete the operation."

CHAPTER NINE

Rava Garza was sitting alone in a quiet study room on the third floor of the Hub. She glanced up from her work and brushed a stray strand of dark hair away from her eyes as she looked through the window on the door.

It had been two days since she had met Caleb, but Rava hadn't stopped thinking about him since. There was something different about that boy. Something *authentic*. He hadn't been brainwashed by OASIS yet. Meeting him had been like taking in a breath of fresh air after holding her breath for far too long, and she wanted more of that. She desperately hoped he'd take her up on that offer to chat more.

She should have been nicer to him, but trusting others didn't come naturally to her. It was easier to push people away. Safer, she told herself. Expecting to stay in one place for long was foolish, she thought. Sure, she'd been at OASIS for five years now, but who knew how long it would last.

Growing up in Aridor—or more accurately, the desolate ruins that remained of the once thriving nation—didn't provide Rava with much of a childhood, leaving her with a jaded outlook on life. Bouncing from one makeshift city to another, constantly on the run from various gangs fighting for territory, she never got used to staying in one place for long. OASIS was no different, she told herself. She was intent on avoiding getting attached.

The longest Rava and her family had ever lived in one place in Aridor was one year. She thought back to that time.

They'd set up camp in a nameless village of tents near the eastern coast of Aridor. Rava, who was nine years old at the time, naively thought this would be their home for good. She'd even stopped carrying all of her toys and books around in a satchel, instead settling them into her "room" in their tent. The warm sun would tire her out during the day, and the sound of waves crashing on the beach would lull her to sleep at night. With every day that passed, she began to feel more and more at home. It was a feeling she hoped she could hold onto.

Her hopes had been shattered when a local gang raided their camp in broad daylight, killing their scouts before they had a chance to warn them. One minute, Rava and her friend were playing soccer, and the next, she was being thrown over her father's shoulder as the makeshift city devolved into complete chaos. Shirtless savages known as the Druids had cut through tents with machetes with no regard to their occupants, sending scraps of fabric flying through the air. Families screamed and ran in every direction, tripping over each other as they fled. Some were captured, and those who fought back were killed. Rava could still picture the look of horror on her friend Tica's face as her father had hauled her away. She hadn't seen the boy since that fateful day.

Another home overrun by violence. Another friendship severed by circumstances out of her control. Another life lesson learned: don't get attached to places or people—it's all subject to change.

Fearing their only chance of survival was to leave Aridor, Rava's family had boarded a refugee ship to Materra. At the time of their escape, Rava was ten years old. By the time she was twelve, Rava's teacher had identified her as gifted. After a genetic test, her teacher's suspicions were confirmed and she was sent off to OASIS. Even refugees were expected to contribute in Materra.

Rava looked back down to her notebook, unclenching her teeth and setting her mind back on her task. In her opinion, dwelling on the past was about as useful as trying to eat soup with a fork.

Then the door opened, and she jerked her head back up.

In walked Dusty Harding, pushing the bridge of his glasses up his nose with his finger. "What are you—" She cut herself off, getting the answer to her question as a boy with shaggy black hair, jagged as if he cut it himself, filed in behind Dusty.

"Hey," Caleb said, lifting a hand from his backpack strap to send a small wave her way. "I hope you don't mind us dropping in. You said it was okay to stop by sometime. Do you mind if we study with you today?"

Now that Caleb was there, she had to fight the urge to tell the two of them she was too busy. For some reason, when she looked Caleb in his eyes, she felt like she could trust him, like she'd known him her whole life. It was as if everyone else was a bland memory module, filled with information that was useful but felt foreign to her, and Caleb was one of her native memories, one she could *feel* was trustworthy. And that vulnerability made her uncomfortable. She fought back the feeling.

"Oh. No, I don't mind. Go ahead, take a seat." She mustered up a smile. She wasn't happy to have Dusty here, but she'd live with it. She doubted he'd stay long—he was as much of a loner as she was. And even if he did, it was a small price to pay for spending more time with Caleb.

The two boys got settled and they all began working on their respective assignments. As Rava dove back into her studies, she couldn't shake the feeling that this was all a mistake. Somehow this would all come back to hurt her. She was sure of it.

~*~

Settling into a groove, Caleb spent the next three weeks creating five new map modules. All of them received perfect ten ratings, which still bothered him. He knew he could do better.

Module creation was becoming second nature. Caleb had his process down to a three-day cycle. The first day was spent gathering resources and researching the currently available maps, the second day creating new maps by hand, and the third day memorizing them and creating the module. Since Caleb was making the maps himself, the process of memorization was far more fluid than if he needed to study someone else's work. Remembering details of something he'd spent hours meticulously crafting proved to be much easier than he'd anticipated.

One day, Caleb was taking a break from his usual routine at the Hub in an attempt to show his supervisor how much better his modules could be if he were to visit the cities as a part of his process. If he could show Mr. Rigs his true potential, he was sure he would cave and allow him supervised trips.

Since he couldn't leave the compound, his plan was to remake the map of OASIS utilizing his eidetic memory.

Unfortunately, this meant he wouldn't be able to spend time with Rava. Having finished a module the day before, that would make two days in a row that he didn't see her. In the grand scheme of things, it wasn't a long time, and it would be worth it, but it felt like an eternity in relation to the short time they'd been getting to know each other.

Over the previous three weeks, Caleb and Rava had spent most days together at the Hub. They worked well together. He enjoyed having someone to talk to, and both of them were able to maintain focus on their projects while keeping each other company.

Growing up in a small house, Caleb had been forced to master the art of tuning out his surroundings. There were days where he would be reading a book while John was listening to the radio in the same room. Needless to say, studying in the same room as someone else was not a distraction for him in the slightest— although he did catch himself, on occasion, stealing a glance at Rava.

Dusty would stop by every once in a while, but he preferred to work alone. Any small distraction could spiral out of control in his mind, starting an avalanche of calculating one statistical probability after another.

Rava, on the other hand, would start and stop conversations abruptly and seemingly out of nowhere. Her ability to compartmentalize was second to none. Caleb was catching on to this, but there were still times where he'd find himself waiting for her to finish her thought before noticing she'd already moved on and was working diligently.

At times, Rava would also listen to music modules on her brain drive. How she was able to focus on her work while thinking about music at the same time was a mystery to Caleb. He had yet to experience music modules, though he had little interest in them.

For the first time in a while, Caleb actually felt at home. OASIS seemed to fit him like a broken-in pair of shoes. For once, he could see a future ahead of him—not just days on a calendar that he would live out, but a *life*. He could create modules for others, using his eidetic memory to help people. Over time, he'd earn enough money to retire young, set John up for life, and raise a family of his own. All of this was made possible by the facility John had tried so hard to keep him from, and he still couldn't understand why. Sure, OASIS wasn't perfect, but there was a lot of upside. Maybe when he got his memory stick back, he would have more clarity, but he was beginning to doubt he would *ever* get it back.

Until then, he had a job to do. The first step in his plan to recreate the map of OASIS was to remove his general reference guide module from this brain drive. This would ensure that all of the memories of the layout were his own. In anticipation of feeling lost after deleting the module that was responsible for navigating the compound, Caleb had sketched a crude map with landmarks and left detailed notes for himself.

The one aspect of his plan that he had yet to work out was how he was going to get inside the staff residential area on the west side of the compound. GIs weren't allowed in that area, and the entrance was manned by security all hours of the day. In the end, if he couldn't gain access, he figured he could map out the rest of the compound to prove his point and add that area later. It would certainly avoid some awkward questions from his supervisor about how he'd gotten in there.

With the general reference guide module removed, he was off to the front desk of his dormitory. For fifty credits, GIs in the sixteen and older dorms could rent out utility vehicles on a first-come, first-served basis. The fee was reasonable, but that didn't make it any easier to spend. Fifty credits would have paid for groceries for an entire *week* back home.

Utility vehicle key in one hand and a map in the other, Caleb was ready to begin.

Starting in the GI residential area, Caleb drove through the compound at a snail's pace, taking in his surroundings more than ever before in an attempt to memorize every detail about the layout. He didn't bother with the interior of any of the buildings, but he did take note of all available entrances to each one.

The process was lengthy. Despite Caleb's incredible memory, it seemed like he noticed new details every time he looped through the area. Following multiple laps over the course of a couple of hours, he felt comfortable enough to move on.

Next, Caleb drove to the north end of the compound to mentally document the layout there. There was no official rule stating GIs couldn't be on that side, but they typically had no business roaming around up there. Unsure of how it would be perceived, Caleb was faced with a decision: try to sneak around undetected, or act like he belonged there. He chose the latter, and to his surprise, it worked. Whenever he drove by someone dressed in a navy-blue OASIS uniform, he made sure to wave like it was a normal occurrence for a GI to be driving a utility vehicle between the staff buildings, studying them intently. Aside from a handful of curious looks, he was ignored. They were either too busy or too indifferent to care.

Next up was the south end. That area housed the registration buildings, administrative offices, and various staff training facilities.

When Caleb drove by the security registration office, he brought the utility vehicle to a stop. A quick detour to check on the status of his memory stick wouldn't slow him down too much. It had been over a month since it was confiscated and it still hadn't arrived in the mail.

He entered the building and walked up to the counter, but the office was dead silent. Behind the counter were five unoccupied desks, each littered with paperwork and coffee cups. Caleb looked past them to a metal shelf where the security officer had stashed his memory stick on his first day. Inside a clear bin labeled *Screen*—the same bin his memory stick had been placed in—was a glossy red rectangular object about the length of a stick of gum. *Has it even been moved since it was put in there?* he wondered.

"Hello?" Caleb called through the office. Hearing no answer, he tried again, this time louder. "Hello!" Still nothing but silence.

While craning his neck over the counter to look around for any indication that someone was there, a realization sank in. If he acted quickly, he could leap over, zig-zag through the desks, and grab his memory stick before anyone was the wiser.

Caleb's eyes locked onto the memory stick as though he was trying to inch it closer using only his mind. That small red stick, no bigger than a cigarette lighter, held the answers about his parents.

And there it was, unguarded, daring him to take it.

Every one of his instincts begged him not to. Stealing it was, unquestionably, a bad idea. According to the code of conduct, if he was caught anywhere behind the security counter, he would be sentenced to a minimum of twenty-four hours in solitary confinement. And even if he wasn't caught immediately, if someone happened to review the security footage, he would inevitably be found out.

On the other hand, what if the memory stick was *never* returned to him? At some point he could, of course, get answers from John, but was he willing to wait that long? Could he even trust what John would tell him?

These thoughts waged war inside Caleb's mind, one side urging him to take action and the other keeping his feet planted firmly on his side of the counter. With every second that passed, Caleb reevaluated the pros and cons of stealing his memory stick, and the fear someone would walk in at any moment steadily built.

John would tell him not to act on impulse, to formulate a plan before taking such a risk. But he wasn't John, and maybe it was time to try doing things his own way.

Faced with the possibility of going additional weeks, or months even, without knowing the truth about his parents, his self-control failed him. With one more glance around the office to confirm the coast was clear, Caleb jumped over the counter and lunged forward to snatch the memory stick off of the shelf.

As he was making his way back to the lobby, a security officer strolled in.

"What are you doing back there?" the black-haired man with a tight buzz cut asked, glancing down at the memory stick in Caleb's hand.

"I..." He tried to answer but he found himself completely distracted by the gruesome scar on the man's face. It ran from his hairline, across his left eye socket—leaving his left eyelid deformed and in a permanent state of being half open—and down to his thick beard. Although he had done nothing threatening and was speaking in a friendly tone, the man's face gave Caleb the impression that he was looking for a confrontation.

Caleb peeled his eyes away from the man's menacing face and looked down at the memory stick in his hand, searching for a logical excuse. "Oh... I just... I didn't know if..."

A second heavy-set security officer with a thick wild brown mustache walked in, taking in the scene before speaking. "What do we have here, Thorington?" He asked, addressing his colleague with a firm, gravelly voice.

The man with the scar cleared his throat. "Well sir, I walked in to find this young man behind the counter of the security office attempting to steal what looks to be a memory stick." He pointed at Caleb's hand. Caleb closed his fingers around it as though concealing it would make his problem go away.

"And as an officer in training, what do you recommend we do with this young man?" The mustached officer asked.

"First, I will confiscate the memory stick." He reached over, holding his hand out with his palm up, curling his fingers in a gesture Caleb interpreted as "hand it over." Reluctantly, Caleb dropped it into his outstretched hand.

"Then, I will escort him to solitary confinement, where he will serve twenty-four hours as a punishment for attempted theft and trespassing."

"Very good, Thorington. However, *I* will escort"—the burly man looked down at Caleb's badge—"Caleb, here, to solitary. I want you to stay here until I return and we will finish our rounds. Good work, though. You're catching on quick."

"Yes, sir. Thank you, sir." Officer Thorington gave a firm nod to his superior.

Following a brief ride, they arrived at a building on the north side of the compound that Caleb was very familiar with, after driving past it multiple times that day. He didn't know what was inside, but he had gathered it was a security office, and there was a single entrance to the building.

Upon entering, Caleb was escorted through a nondescript steel door and down a hallway that led to the back of the building. As they walked down the long hallway, lined with metal doors on both sides, Caleb could hear the gentle hum of the fluorescent bulbs overhead, along with the clanking of instruments on the portly security officer's belt. Caleb looked and noticed he was carrying a gun. He began to wonder if all of the security officers were armed. He hadn't noticed before, but now that he thought about it, his eidetic memory cycled through a blur of images that confirmed most, if not all of them, were.

Caleb nearly walked into the security officer as he stopped abruptly in front of one of the doors. "Place your hands on the wall," he said in a monotone voice, as if it was the hundredth time he had said those words. He patted Caleb down. Then, without warning, he plugged a cable into the back of Caleb's head, causing him to flinch.

"Relax, kid, I'm just getting you ready. Your current modules will be removed and kept safely in this terminal."

Caleb now realized every door had a brain drive terminal next to it, only they were modified to sit flush with the wall. They had no touch screen, only a few tactile buttons.

"After that, I'll load you up with the solitary confinement module and put you in your room. You'll serve twenty-four hours in there, after which you'll get your modules back."

None of this information came as a surprise to Caleb. He understood the procedure, but knowing what would happen certainly wouldn't prepare him for it.

After a brief moment, Caleb was unplugged and shoved into his holding cell. The room was on the small side, about eight feet wide and square. Firm white padding lined the walls and ceiling while glossy white tiles made up the floor. Sitting on the floor on the far side of the room was a white cot and a white pillow, the room's only contents. In the very center of the floor was a drain pipe.

He turned back toward the door and it slammed shut. It was

also covered in white padding, save for the window, which was blocked by a metal shutter, and a wide metal opening that resembled a large mail slot.

An image of Dusty walking down the hall on the day he returned from solitary confinement, seemingly lifeless, flashed through Caleb's mind. He was about to find out firsthand what horrors had traumatized his friend.

~*~

As the sun was creeping up over the horizon, John slipped a key into his motel room door, ready to get some rest after a long night of surveillance.

He was making steady progress on his mission, and after the last night, he had finally settled on a delivery truck to infiltrate. It was the ideal vehicle, but it only made deliveries every other week, which was slowing John's progress more than he'd have liked.

But like his drunken father would always say, "You shouldn't step foot in the ring unless you're prepared to go the full twelve rounds." John was ready to do whatever he needed to bring his son home.

The delivery truck he'd chosen was tasked with delivering dry-cleaned uniforms. Having access to uniforms would be great, and being in a truck full of them would be even better. It would give him plenty of time to change into one on the way.

He'd decided on impersonating a security officer. While a plain navy staff uniform would arouse the least amount of suspicion in his estimation, the authority that came with the black outfit would more than make up for the risk.

After having all of the clean uniforms unloaded inside the compound, the truck was then filled with dirty ones to be taken back for dry-cleaning. The whole process took roughly forty minutes. That gave John a short window to find Caleb and return before his getaway vehicle departed. The dirty clothes would also give them cover to hide in the back of the truck.

John had yet to see that truck searched on arrival, and it always made deliveries around twelve. This lined up well with the midnight shift change, and he thought it should provide him with enough time to sneak out of the truck undetected and blend in with security officers that were coming and going from their posts.

It actually made John uncomfortable how perfect this delivery vehicle was for the job. He had to be overlooking something, but if he was, he would find the flaw. If there was one thing he was good at, it was preparation.

This left only two major problems to solve. The first was locating Caleb. He had already memorized the route from the laundry facility to the dorm, but he didn't have a good way to find out what room he was staying in. He hoped he'd be able to improvise and use the security officer uniform to get this information on the fly.

The second problem involved the truck, and would be much easier to solve. Since the delivery truck was unmarked, John would need to follow the truck after its next delivery to find out where it came from. After that, he would need to observe it before a delivery in order to identify the best time and place to sneak aboard unnoticed.

He was close. He could feel it. His plan was taking shape, becoming as real as the pillow underneath his head as he dozed off to sleep.

CHAPTER TEN

The heavy stench of tobacco smoke filled the room, as if the walls were coated with cigarette ash. Caleb cowered in the corner, covering his head with his hands while he waited for John to return. He'd be back soon, probably on the next commercial break, and he *always* hit him harder the second time. Caleb wasn't sure what he did to upset his father, but it didn't matter. There was no reasoning with him.

But John wouldn't do that. He was sure of it. John was a good man. He used to take him to Marv's diner for his birthday, where they would order burgers and fries.

The smell faded as the dark room melted back to white. Caleb drew in a deep breath. The episode was over, but there would no doubt be more. He wondered how long he'd been in solitary.

His mind stayed fixed on the burger from Marv's as he eyed the untouched food tray that had been slid through the door of his cell. Hungry as he was, he had no plans to eat the slop in that bowl.

Suddenly, his mouth was filled with the taste of rotting meat. Before he had a chance to make sense of what was happening, he bent over and threw up onto the floor. The taste was too disgusting, not to mention the *smell*.

A feeling of panic overwhelmed Caleb as he laid eyes on the mess he'd made. He had to clean it up, and fast. If his mother saw it, she would make him eat it up off the floor, every last bit. She had no tolerance for him not finishing his food. He'd learn to eat it the first time, she'd always say. He would have no trouble eating if she fed him anything other than rotting meat, but he wasn't so lucky. At least he wasn't starved, he reasoned.

He frantically searched the room for a towel or dishrag, but found only a pillow. That would have to do. Caleb took the pillow and wiped up what he could from the pile of puke. He could hear his mother's words echoing in his mind as he cleaned. *You don't like what I made you? How about seconds?* He pictured her face as she would scrape the regurgitated meat off of their table and back onto his plate for his second attempt at eating the rot.

"No," he said just above a whisper, tears running down his face. He couldn't eat it again.

Wait, that wasn't his mother. He shook his head in denial. No, his mother was dead. This was *impossible*.

He broke out of the nightmare, wiping the sweat from his forehead and tears from his eyes before collapsing into a heap on the floor. He was fine. It wasn't real.

How much longer?

~*~

Erin Guibley unplugged herself from her workstation and nearly leapt to her feet. Typically, she found herself exhausted after an eight-hour shift, but not today. *This is it*, she thought. This was going to be her big break.

As one of OASIS's many junior-level module evaluators, Erin was constantly searching for a way to stand out among her peers. Typically, they were promoted solely based on experience. With only five years under her belt, she was nowhere near the top of the list for a senior-level position.

That angered her. Experience wasn't everything. Sure, it was important, but she believed skill was equally important. Erin may not have been good at creating modules, but she *was* among the best at evaluating them. The numerous mistakes she had made as a GI were the same ones she was now able to effortlessly identify in the work of others.

She was amazing at her job. She knew talent when she saw it. Caleb Shaw was an artist. His work was impeccable. Every module he submitted was a masterpiece. It wasn't just his attention to detail that caught her eye—there was something unique about the quality of his memories. She had never seen anything like it, and every perfect rating he had received from her was deserved.

One day, she hoped to shake his hand and personally thank him for providing her with the opportunity he presented her with. But first, she had to get to Senior Advisor Polsik before he selected another GI. She started down the hallway toward his office. Her long brown hair trailed behind her like a flowing gown as her legs carried her forward at a brisk pace. She stopped outside of his door and straightened her navy uniform out before knocking.

"Come in," the man called from the other side of the door. He sounded more tired than usual.

She entered the office to find OASIS's senior advisor, Craig Polsik, hunched over his desk. He glanced up over the top of his reading glasses and then returned to his paperwork without saying a word.

Erin waited, unsure if he was looking to finish something up before addressing her.

"Well, come out with it," he said without looking up. "I haven't got all day. Fate could take me any minute. I'm basically half-dead already." He let out a weak chuckle.

She didn't laugh. He certainly looked half-dead, but she wouldn't dream of acknowledging it.

"Yes, sir," she replied, her pulse picking up as her nerves

spiked. Technically, she should have presented this to a senior-level module evaluator instead. But she couldn't allow them to steal the credit for her find, or she'd never get her promotion. "I wanted to bring to your attention a certain GI that I believe would be a perfect fit for your assignment."

Here it was, the moment of truth. Would he allow her to present her case, or would he be outraged that she'd jumped the chain of command to seek a meeting with him directly?

He pulled his reading glasses off his wrinkled face and folded them up, raising his head to meet her gaze.

"Go on, I'm listening."

~*~

As the door to his cell opened, Caleb shot up from his bed, eager to leave the confines of the padded white room. After twenty-four hours of being locked away with nothing but his thoughts and the horrible memories that were loaded onto his brain drive, he was itching for fresh air.

Rava's description of solitary confinement was accurate, but the reality was worse than he'd imagined when she described it to him. Not only were the memories awful, they were also countless and relentless. And they all had one thing in common; they induced fear. No matter what he tried to think of to distract himself, there was a corresponding horrifying memory that would creep in, turning his thoughts to nightmares in an instant. He spent most of his time in a dizzy frenzy where he continuously attempted to separate the visions from reality.

Worse yet, when Caleb was able to find periods of numbing silence between episodes, they were often interrupted by the faint screams of the children in the neighboring cells.

As Caleb stepped out into the cool, crisp air, he took a deep breath and felt his muscles relax. The sense of relief was quickly swept away by an unease, like something terrible was about to happen. He turned his head back and forth, scanning his environment for threats, but he found none.

This, Caleb decided, must be the disorienting feeling that Rava had referred to. He tried to think back on the last twenty-four hours to see if he could remember what had happened, but much of it was a blur. He had vague memories of being in the padded room and a sense of feeling terrified, but his recollection of events ended there. He was unable to recall any reason for feeling the way he felt. His stomach began to turn and he pushed the thoughts out of his mind.

Making his way over to the Hub to catch a bus back to his dorm, Caleb moved with caution, still unsure why he felt like he was being followed. In the moments of clarity on his anxiety-ridden bus ride home, Caleb had one thing on his mind: he needed to find a way out of this place.

Earning money while experiencing the place where his mother had spent her childhood was enough to keep him going before, but now he wanted no part of OASIS. This was not his fate. He wouldn't allow it to be.

When he entered the lobby of his dorm, the amalgam of navy and gold that he once considered an elegant design now disgusted him. How could he take pride in a nation that rationalized the psychological torture of children for the greater good? He was beginning to understand why John didn't want him to end up here.

"Caleb!" called a vaguely familiar voice from behind him as he crossed the lobby.

He spun around to find himself face-to-face with the security officer who had caught him stealing his memory stick. As Caleb looked at the nasty scar that ran down the left side of his face his hair began to stand on end. The effects of solitary were still wearing off.

"Officer Thorington?" Caleb replied, a puzzled look on his face.

"Call me Chris," he said. "The whole officer title still sounds weird. I won't take up too much of your time. I felt bad about sending you to solitary. It's only my second week on the job. And I *need* this job so... Well anyway, I went ahead and scanned this for you."

The man reached his hand out, holding a red memory stick between his fingers.

For a moment, Caleb stared at it in disbelief. He wondered if it was some sort of hallucination. He took the memory stick and thanked the officer, sounding both grateful and puzzled.

"It's the least I could do," the bearded man said. "It should have been done weeks ago, but the officer responsible for the delay didn't properly document the seizure. I felt a responsibility to try to make it right somehow. If there's anything else I can do..."

Caleb sensed sincerity in the man's eyes, trying his hardest not to shift his gaze to the large scar on his face. He was probably used to people gawking at it, but Caleb didn't want to offend him after he had been kind enough to help him get his memory stick back.

"Thanks again." Caleb began to turn to walk away before stopping halfway as an idea formed in his mind. If he could convince Officer Thorington to sneak him into the staff residential area, he would be able to complete the OASIS map module. That might be enough to convince Mr. Rigs to grant him supervised trips, he thought. If he was allowed outside of the compound's walls, he was sure he could find a way to slip away for an escape. It was a gamble, but he was willing to take it.

He spun back around to face Officer Thorington. "Actually, I do have something you could help me with..."

~*~

Filled with resolve, Caleb rushed out his door the next morning to find Dusty standing in the hall, clutching two breakfast burritos.

"They don't serve tacos this early." He held out the burritos, avoiding eye contact as usual.

The gesture was nice, and most days Caleb would have loved to sit down with Dusty and enjoy breakfast with his friend, but he didn't have time today.

"Thank you. I'll have to take this to go though. I have a lot to do today." He took a breakfast burrito from Dusty and started toward the elevator.

Dusty kept pace with him, "I'm glad to see you're doing well. Listen, Rava was worried about you."

Caleb didn't break his stride, but he glanced over at Dusty. "She told you she was worried about me?"

"I mean, she didn't exactly say it in those words, but I know she was. You should stop by today and let her know you're doing okay."

He stopped at the elevator and began mashing the button. "I'm not sure I'll have time today, but thanks Dusty. You're a good friend."

Dusty smiled at the ground before turning to walk back down to his apartment.

Caleb bit into the breakfast burrito on the elevator ride down. He hadn't eaten since before his solitary confinement and he would need the energy. Fortunately, the anxious feelings he was feeling had faded late last night and he was able to sleep well.

First on his mental checklist was to take his memory stick to the Hub and upload it onto his brain drive. That was the reason he was in such a hurry this morning. He would finally have answers about his parents.

But that wasn't the only thing he was looking forward to. Officer Thorington had agreed to pick him up after lunch and sneak him into the staff residential area so he could finish his map of the compound. Caleb still couldn't believe it. The man was either much nicer than his face gave him credit for, or he really did carry a lot of guilt for sending him to solitary. Caleb didn't care which option was true—he was only grateful for the opportunity. With his map completed, he'd at least have some form of a plan to escape this place.

Following the shuttle ride to the Hub, Caleb once again found himself waiting behind a class of children at the security checkpoint.

While the teacher was talking with the officer, one of the kids in the back strayed away from the group and was running his hand along a conveyor belt. The teacher took notice and pushed a button on her tablet, and the boy sprinted back to the group like a puppy with his tail between his legs, shaking the wrist that had the metal bracelet on it.

Caleb's mouth fell open as he realized the silver rings were actually electric shock bracelets. He didn't understand how the parents of the kids were okay with that. He wondered if they were even aware. At the moment, Caleb didn't just want to escape OASIS, he wanted to burn the place to the ground.

One step at a time, he thought.

As Caleb proceeded casually through the metal detector, the alarm triggered. A security officer pulled him aside and began waving a handheld scanner around him, quickly narrowing the location of whatever tripped the alarm down to Caleb's left jacket pocket. His stomach dropped. That was where his memory stick was.

He reached into Caleb's pocket and pulled it out. "Ah, I see. We don't allow external storage devices. You should know that. I'll have to confiscate this. It will be scanned and returned to you within a couple of weeks."

"What? No," Caleb pleaded through the lump in his throat. "I'll just take it back to my dorm. *Please.* I got this back from being scanned yesterday. You don't need to screen it again. I won't bring it back—"

"Listen," the security officer interrupted, "I don't make the rules. And I'm not about to break them over your memory stick here. Like I said, you'll get it back. There's no need to get all worked up about it." The man pulled him forward and was already looking past him at the next person coming through the metal detector as if the matter was settled.

Begrudgingly, Caleb carried on through the doors into the Hub. His thoughts were clouded with disbelief. He'd lost his memory stick *again*. There was a very real possibility he would have to leave OASIS without it. If John didn't have a backup, he would have to rely on his word. He wasn't sure if he could ever fully trust him again. Caleb believed that if he never knew the truth about his parents, he would never fully discover who he was.

Despite the crushing reality of losing his memory stick again, he couldn't afford to be derailed. If he ever wanted to escape, he had to stay focused.

Caleb spent the rest of his morning on the fourth floor studying the map he'd made and retracing his trip through the compound in his mind, one building at a time. If he was going to make a lifelike map module, he'd need to be able to recall each building as if he were standing right in front of it.

The process reminded Caleb of the stories that John used to tell him about some of the greatest boxers of all time. They would rehearse matches in their mind over and over before a big fight, utilizing their knowledge of their opponent's tendencies to anticipate their actions. They would imagine themselves winning and losing, visualizing the various pathways to both outcomes. For an inexperienced boxer, this could be a dangerous exercise, resulting in reinforcement of poor technique and feeding an over-inflated ego with confirmation bias. But for the best of the best—those truly at the top of the craft—it was invaluable, helping them identify their shortcomings as well as their opponent's weaknesses.

Caleb wasn't defending a title belt, but he did feel like an underdog.

Hours later, he returned to his dorm to find Officer Thorington waiting at the front desk of the lobby. As he walked in, the front desk attendant pointed to Caleb and Thorington nodded before approaching him with a demeanor that suited his naturally threatening face.

"Caleb Shaw, I need you to come with me," he said in a flat voice as he ushered him back outside.

Officer Thorington led Caleb to his truck and opened the door. He slid into the passenger seat of the work-issued white pickup and the door closed behind him.

"Wow, that was amazing," Caleb said with a smile on his face after Officer Thorington took his place in the driver's seat. "You really sold that. Everyone back there definitely thinks I'm in trouble."

Officer Thorington didn't smile back. "Honestly, I'm not sure you aren't," he said while starting the vehicle. Before pulling away, he looked over at Caleb. "Look, I had every intention of helping you out today. But right before I left to come here, I received direct orders to bring you in. I don't know what this is about, but the call is coming from pretty high up."

"Bring me in? To where?" The day was not going at all how Caleb had imagined. First, he'd lost his memory stick and now, this. He didn't understand what someone that important would want with him.

"My orders were to escort you to the Hub. From there, I'm not sure."

"Did they say who sent down the orders?"

"The orders came down from my boss, George Gunther. But if I had to guess, I'd say this is coming from higher up. In my experience, George doesn't usually get involved in small matters."

So this was about his altercation with Ricky, he concluded. He must have told his father and now this, whatever this was, was retaliation.

"He might if you threaten his son."

"You threatened Ricky?" Officer Thorington asked, sounding amused, his teeth flashing through his beard in a grin. "I can't stand that little twerp! I'm glad someone put him in his place."

Caleb couldn't help but return a light chuckle with a smile. "It did feel good. I'm regretting it right about now, though."

"I can't imagine this is about that." Officer Thorington pulled the truck up to the Hub, turning off the engine. "Now, before you go in, I want you to know something. There are very powerful people pulling the strings behind the scenes here. You'd be wise to be careful who you trust."

Caleb nodded, silently considering whether he should trust the advice of a security officer he'd just met a couple days ago. He seemed nice enough, but even by his own logic, Caleb should be skeptical of him.

They got out and entered the Hub. Waiting for them near the security checkpoint was a bald, middle-aged man with a handlebar mustache, his bulky frame threatening to tear his black suit at the seams. *George Gunther* was written across the badge hanging from his chest.

"Thank you, Thorington. I'll take him from here," George said, his voice gruff. Without so much as a glance at Caleb, he turned around and walked inside. "Follow me."

Caleb did as he was told, sticking close to the man and staying quiet. He stood a full head taller than George and as he followed him, he could see the overhead lights being reflected off of the man's shiny smooth head.

George led him to the elevator on the north end of the building and held his badge out over the button panel. The doors closed.

Only instead of going up, the elevator went down.

Caleb wasn't aware the Hub had a basement, but it made sense to him. However, he got the sensation that they went down more than one level. He wondered if all of the elevators went down.

"Target secured. Heading down now," George said.

Caleb looked around to make sure no one else was in the elevator before replying. "What?"

"Wasn't talking to you," he said, still not bothering to look in Caleb's direction.

That was when Caleb noticed the small earpiece in George's ear. *He must be communicating with other security personnel,* Caleb thought. Being referred to as a target made Caleb even more nervous. He wiped the sweat from his palms on his pants.

The elevator doors opened to a wide, long concrete hallway that branched off in three directions. George proceeded straight.

Their footsteps echoed through the empty hallway as the fluorescent lights above their heads flickered on to light the way ahead of them. Caleb searched for context clues in an attempt to figure out where he was being taken, but every one of the solid-steel doors they passed was windowless, and none of them had signage to indicate what was behind them.

Eventually, they turned down a hallway and Caleb saw two men flanking an entrance, both dressed in suits identical to George's. As they approached and George opened the door, neither of the men acknowledged them, continuing to stare straight ahead at the plain concrete wall in front of them.

Inside, six additional security personnel were posted around the perimeter of the spacious concrete-walled room. George took his post next to the door, waving Caleb on with his hand.

Caleb wandered forward, taking in the scene and attempting to make sense of the situation. In the center of the room was a large steel table. Along both of the long sides were four seats, all occupied by people who were old enough to be Caleb's grandparents, and all dressed in formal attire. He didn't recognize any of them.

A clean-shaven man with a chiseled jaw who appeared to be about half of the age of the other attendees sat at the head of the table wearing a perfectly-tailored navy suit. His dark-brown hair was combed to one side. The man looked familiar, but Caleb couldn't place him. He stood up and every eye in the room locked onto him in anticipation.

"Well, it appears my guest has arrived. We'll have to wrap this up later. You're all dismissed," the young man in the suit said, waving his hand as if shooing them away.

An old, balding man wearing silver-rimmed glasses raised his hand in protest. "Sir, if I may, we could finish—"

"You may not," he snapped as he glared at the bald man. "We will finish this *later*."

"My apologies, Mr. President," the old man said as he stood up. The other guests followed his lead, filing out of the room one by one. A few of them glanced in Caleb's direction as they passed by him, looking him up and down before dismissing him with their eyes.

Caleb suddenly remembered where he'd seen the man's face before—in the newspaper John read every week. That was the man John had complained about on an almost nightly basis. He was standing before Materra's sitting president, Avery Blake.

CHAPTER ELEVEN

After the last guest left the room, President Blake asked his security team to step out as well, leaving Caleb alone with him.

A charming smile spread across his face as soon as the door closed. "Caleb Shaw. Welcome! Thank you for joining me today. Please, take a seat." He gestured to the one next to him.

Caleb sat in the cushioned chair, meeting the man's gaze. His eyes were dark brown, almost black. They looked *inhuman*.

"I've heard great things about the work you've been doing for me here at OASIS." He poured a glass of water from a pitcher on the table and placed it in front of Caleb before unbuttoning his blazer and taking a seat. "It's remarkable, really. All tens. I've personally reviewed some of your work and I can say with certainty that the perfect ratings are deserved."

Caleb was unsure of the appropriate response to such a compliment from the president, but he was afraid to offend the man. He mustered a nervous smile in return.

The president leaned back in his chair, crossing his legs. "And I, for one, should know. You may not be aware, but long before I was known as President Blake I was known as GI Blake. Though, it took very little time for me to realize that my skills were more suitable for... *leadership*. You see, Caleb, I am exceptional at getting people to do what I want them to. It's not always glamorous. Despite my best efforts, at times it can be quite... *barbaric*. But I *get* results." He firmly pressed his pointer finger straight down on the table as if he was pushing an invisible button, never breaking eye contact.

A shiver ran up Caleb's spine. There was something strange about the way President Blake spoke. While his speech was eloquent, his charisma felt manufactured, as though he was imitating what he imagined he was supposed to be like. Occasionally, he would stop mid-sentence, like he was pondering his word choice until he landed on the perfect one to illustrate his point.

After a few long seconds, he went on. "And as we've established, you're no stranger to getting results yourself. In fact, I noticed you've even been working on a side project of sorts recently."

Caleb shifted in his seat, unable to look the president in his eyes now. He could feel his throat begin to tighten as his heartbeat reverberated through his ears. President Blake knowing about the OASIS map meant he must have been spying on him.

President Blake stood up and began slowly pacing around the room, one hand in his pocket, the other gesturing in the air as he spoke. "Now, ordinarily I would be upset about a GI disobeying orders. But as I said, I am partial to results. And you've shown a certain...*willingness* to bend the rules to get them." He looked directly at Caleb. "I like that."

The president's words splashed over Caleb like a warm shower, relieving the tension in his muscles and putting him more at ease as his fear of repercussions melted away.

"Which brings me to the reason I asked for your presence here today. I am in need of your particular... *expertise*. As you could imagine, there are calculated risks one must take when leading a nation. One such risk I've deemed necessary for the success of Materra is utilizing espionage operations in order to obtain information on our rivals. These operations will involve the creation of detailed map modules of top-secret facilities from all over the world. That's where you come in."

Caleb leaned forward in his seat, envisioning himself escaping the clutches of his security detail on a top-secret mission. This could be his way out, he imagined. President Blake obviously had some idea of what he was up to with recreating OASIS's map module. He might understand the benefit of Caleb visiting the facilities himself.

President Blake took notice of Caleb's interest, turning to face him again. "I knew you'd be on board! The moment you walked into this room, I had a feeling you were special. The true greats are constantly looking for ways to push the boundaries of their craft beyond where others would have given up long ago. I see that in you. *Greatness.*"

Caleb allowed himself an authentic smile. While he didn't necessarily trust the man standing in front of him, that didn't automatically disqualify everything he said. He knew he had more potential than what he had been able to show thus far, and it was nice to hear someone else acknowledge that.

"Unfortunately, my advisors are... *displeased* with my decision to launch this operation. They're begging me to call it off. They don't think you have what it takes to perform to the standards necessary for success. They believe your inexperience will result in failure and all-out war between us and our adversaries." His dark eyes met Caleb's, his smile replaced with a sneer. "They are wrong, and they are *cowards*. That's why they are advisors, not leaders."

He settled back into the chair at the head of the table. "Unlike my naive advisors, I understand that in today's age of ever-advancing technology, if we are not one step ahead of our rivals, we risk being reduced to nothing more than the next chapter in the history books. I prefer to be the one *writing* the history books."

The uneasy feeling returned to Caleb, driving away what little comfort he'd gained from the president's compliments. If his advisors were right, Caleb's actions could directly result in war. He wasn't sure how he could live with himself if that happened.

"It is imperative I get your agreement to participate in this operation. Can I expect your full cooperation?" He looked at the boy intently, as though studying his response carefully.

Although President Blake had phrased it as a question, Caleb didn't feel like he really had a choice in the matter. His stomach turned at the thought of what might happen if he said no. He was sure his potential was greater than what he'd shown so far, but would it be enough?

He couldn't let his hesitancy show in his response. He had to come off as enthusiastic. "Where am I off to first?"

The president shot him a brief confused glance before replying. "Ah, my apologies, I was unclear. I'm sure you'll be relieved to know you won't have to travel to these locations to fulfill your duties. You're far too important to the operation to put at unnecessary risk. You'll be creating map modules using video recordings of the facilities provided by spies who have already successfully infiltrated the ranks of our adversaries."

Caleb smiled and nodded. "Oh, good."

He swallowed hard as the reality of the situation hit him like an uppercut. Instead of getting closer to an escape plan, he put himself firmly at the center of an operation that had the potential to spark a war.

~*~

As Caleb sat in the empty conference room, tapping his leg, he couldn't help but anticipate the worst. It had been nearly two weeks since he had started his new classified assignment, and he'd spent every possible waking hour creating memory modules of top-secret facilities. Thanks to his hard work, he had already completed three maps.

The overall process for creating them was the same—learn the information, memorize the information, download the information—but there were a few distinct challenges that came along with his new assignment. Instead of researching written documents, the details were provided in video form. Caleb had to watch the films over and over, studying every detail of the facility's layout carefully. While he considered watching the recordings all day unappealing on its own, that wasn't even the worst part. In an attempt to better simulate reality, he was forced to wear a virtual reality headset. Though he was getting used to it, at first, he could only wear it for about an hour at a time before feeling sick and needing a break.

Once familiar with the layout, he would construct a detailed top-down map with accurate scaling. This was Caleb's favorite part of the process by far. The craftsmanship that went into drawing a map by hand was incredible. It gave him an appreciation for whoever left the cartography module behind for him to use. After an initial draft was finished, he would study the videos again, adding any additional details he had missed until he was fully comfortable with the map.

By the time it was complete, he found he had already memorized the building layout enough to begin module creation. This step turned out to be far more time consuming than he had imagined. Downloading a map module of a single compound in excruciating detail required upwards of twelve hours. As he thought back on his desire to make entire city maps of that quality, he finally understood why his requests had been continuously denied by his supervisor. It simply wasn't worth his time.

Caleb had been sure of his work. But when he received an order that morning to report for an impromptu meeting with his supervisor, he lost all confidence. President Blake's advisors were right, he decided. He wasn't ready for this.

The door swung open and his new supervisor entered the conference room, clutching two brown folders. She took a seat across from him, adjusting her oval brown glasses while letting out a heavy sigh.

Caleb got the impression she didn't care for supervising him. He didn't fault her for it, though. As the president's advisor on foreign affairs, he was sure that Mrs. Wanda Bloomfield had aspirations beyond babysitting him. But there she was, overseeing the work of a teenager.

She tried to hide her age with hair dye and makeup, but the gray roots of her shoulder-length brown locks and unconcealable wrinkles gave her away. Caleb placed her well into her sixties.

"Good morning, Mr. Shaw," she grumbled as she placed the files onto the table and opened one up. He felt strange being referred to as Mr. Shaw, but Mrs. Bloomfield refused to call him by his given name.

She continued, her voice devoid of any enthusiasm whatsoever. "President Blake asked me to meet with you today to update you on the progress that's been made so far on Operation Sundown."

She slid a folder across the table to Caleb. "Late last night we were able to neutralize our first target."

A picture was clipped to the top and Caleb's eyes were immediately drawn to it. He recognized the man in the photo from the video recordings of his first map module.

Suddenly, Caleb felt sick to his stomach.

"Thanks in large part to your great work, the first strike was a success. Our elite special operations team was in and out in minutes, and there were no casualties. President Blake requested I deliver this news to you personally so you could form an appreciation for the work you're doing and understand how truly important you are to this operation. On behalf of our great nation, President Blake thanks you."

None of what Senior Advisor Bloomfield said made him feel any better. In fact, being thanked made him feel worse. Caleb wished he had been kept in the dark about all of this. Knowing he had contributed to the death of another person—enemy or not—was an uncomfortable and overwhelming feeling.

"You can expect to see eighteen thousand credits deposited in your personal account within the next two days."

Caleb bent over the edge of his seat, frantically scanning the floor for a trash can before losing his breakfast onto the floor next to him. "I'm sorry," he muttered through his sleeve as he wiped his mouth clean. "I'm not feeling well today."

That was a lie, but he imagined telling her the truth would be worse. Being paid an exorbitant amount of money for contributing to the death of another human being was too much for him.

"I can see that," Mrs. Bloomfield replied flatly. "Just be glad President Blake isn't here. You'd be hearing all about how his mother used to make him eat his vomit back up off the floor. That man had an odd upbringing, to say the least."

Caleb held his breath and covered his mouth in anticipation of another round of vomiting. Fortunately for him, nothing came.

To his surprise, Mrs. Bloomfield apologized. "Oh, I'm sorry. I've been told I'm not the most comforting person in situations like this. Why don't you take the day off today? Get some rest. I expect you bright and early tomorrow to start your next assignment."

Without another word, Caleb bolted for the door. Before he knew it, he was outside the Hub, bending over with his hands on his knees, gasping for air.

He was in too deep now. He had to find a way out of that place, and fast. Not only that, but after he escaped, he wanted nothing to do with his brain drive. His time at OASIS had convinced Caleb that technology was ruining the world, and he wanted nothing to do with it anymore.

~*~

Later that morning, Caleb returned to the Hub. He hadn't seen Rava or Dusty at all since starting his classified assignment and he was hoping to catch up with them. Actually, once he thought about it, he realized he hadn't seen Rava since before his time in solitary.

He felt guilty for dedicating all of his time to his new assignment, and it didn't help that his work was restricted to the classified floor of the Hub. But he would have felt much worse if his lack of results had led to full-on war. The pressure he was under was insane.

Rava was alone in a study room, slouched over a pair of textbooks and a spiral-bound notebook, chewing on the end of her pen like she usually did when she was deep in thought.

Caleb turned the handle and pushed his way inside. Rava looked up from her work at him and he instantly found comfort in her amber eyes—a comfort he hadn't felt in weeks. A relieved smile accompanied it.

She returned her eyes to her notes. "Did you need something?" Her words were sharp.

Blindsided by her reaction, Caleb stumbled over his words. "I...Well...I mean—"

"Spit it out. Can't you see I'm busy?"

"I don't *need* anything. I wanted to stop by to see how you were doing. I've missed you."

"Oh, is that how this works?" she snapped. "You just stop by when you miss me to *bless* me with your presence?"

He had no answer. Caleb just stared at her, stunned.

"You get twenty-four hours in solitary and then you disappear on me for two weeks without a word. And now what? You *miss* me, so you just stroll back in here like we're best friends? I don't think so. I'm not some toy you can pick up and play with when you get bored."

"It's not like that, Rava," he pleaded. "I was reassigned. I'm sorry I didn't stop by sooner. I've been under a lot of pressure."

He wanted to tell her more, to fill her in on what had been going on, to share how he was feeling after the meeting, to let her into his mind. But he couldn't. He was forbidden to share details about his classified work. And even if he could tell her, he wasn't sure she would understand. If Rava knew about his new assignment, if she knew he was doing the bidding of the president, she would surely resent him for taking it.

"We're all under a lot of pressure here, Caleb." She shook her head as though disappointed. "I thought we were friends. I thought you were different. Instead, you just reminded me I'm better off alone."

Rava kept her head down, but Caleb could see her wipe at the corner of her eyes.

"Rava, I—"

"Please leave."

He turned to leave, stopping briefly in the doorway, unable to turn and face her. "I'm sorry."

Caleb gathered himself outside the study room before starting for the elevator. He needed some fresh air and a good book. Just as he reached the elevator, he heard a squeaky voice call to him from behind.

"Caleb! Caleb, wait up!"

He turned around to see his friend Dusty barreling toward him while simultaneously digging through his backpack. His blond curls bounced with every step.

"Check this out." Dusty yanked a paper out of his bag and shoved it toward Caleb. It was a module rating. He'd received a nine.

"I know it's not a ten, but I figured you would share in my excitement!"

He worked up a smile for his friend. "That's really great, Dusty. I'm proud of you."

"Thanks. Hey, do you want to grab some food? I didn't eat this morning, and I'm getting pretty hungry."

Finding himself famished after barfing up his breakfast, Caleb agreed to join Dusty in the cafeteria. Considering Caleb had eaten most of his meals on the go over the last couple of weeks, it was nice to be able to sit down and enjoy a meal.

"How's the world of statistics lately?" Caleb asked through a mouthful of blueberry waffles.

"Good. Did you know that, statistically, waffles have the highest rate of fatal choking accidents of all breakfast foods?"

Caleb nearly spit out his apple juice. "Seriously?"

Dusty broke out into high-pitched laughter. "No, I just made that up."

Caleb didn't think it was funny, taking another swig.

"Are you all right? I was certain you'd find humor in that joke. I know I'm typically awful at picking up on social cues, but I don't have to look into your eyes to see that something is off."

Caleb poked at his food, contemplating where to even begin. At the moment, there was more wrong in his life than right. Ultimately, he decided to discuss the incident with Rava.

"Before I ran into you in the hall, I stopped by to see Rava. I've been so busy that I haven't seen her in a while. Actually, not since before my trip to solitary. Anyway, she was upset, and hurt I think, that I hadn't made it a priority. I messed up."

"I told you!" Dusty said emphatically. "You should have stopped by when I told you she was worried."

"What? When was that?" Caleb looked at Dusty, his brow furrowed. He thought he would have certainly remembered the conversation.

"The morning following your solitary confinement. I talked to you in the hall. You said you were busy. You really don't remember? The breakfast burrito?"

It was all coming back to him. "The memory stick," he muttered. He was so distracted by his own plans that day he had completely forgotten Dusty had stopped him that morning to let him know Rava was worried.

"Memory stick?"

"Never mind that. I'm such an idiot! I've been so wrapped up in myself lately."

"You have to talk to her and try to patch things up. Ninety-two percent of all relationships fail due to breakdowns in communication."

"Another fake statistic? Really?"

"Nope," Dusty said with a grin. "That one is real."

Caleb finally let out a laugh.

~*~

John lay wide awake in his motel bed as light began to pierce the gaps between the window blinds. After a long night of putting the finishing touches on his rescue operation, he was hoping to get some rest. Sleep wasn't coming easy as his mind vibrated with anticipation, begging him to act immediately.

But timing was everything, and he knew he needed to wait. In five days, he would sneak into the delivery truck that was parked outside of a local dry cleaner, where he would wait for the driver to unknowingly smuggle him into the OASIS compound that night.

To his great fortune, the employee responsible for loading and unloading the vehicle had a habit of leaving it unlocked. He couldn't blame him, though; Barton was a small city and if their local paper was any indication, there wasn't much crime. It was possible the presence of a large military base kept the criminals at bay.

Leaving it unlocked also made practical sense, allowing the driver to quickly verify the contents before transport. Clothing wasn't exactly a prime target for theft anyway.

There was a two-hour window of time between when the truck was typically loaded and when the driver arrived. *More than enough time*, John thought.

He tore back the comforter and rolled out of bed. Forcing himself to rest wasn't working, so he'd go for a run to exhaust some of his energy. That would help him settle down.

He was in the habit of jogging three to four times a day to help fill his time and give his mind a break. Even though he hadn't exercised much since Caleb was dropped off on his doorstep, he felt like he hadn't missed a beat. In his estimation, he was almost back in fighting shape. It was satisfying, like putting on an old pair of jeans and having them still fit perfectly.

Although running reminded him of his boxing days, he didn't find himself missing the sport. The only thing he missed was his son.

Every step hitting the pavement felt like a grain of sand slipping through the hourglass.

~*~

Hoping to get a jumpstart to his day, Caleb rolled out of bed an entire two hours earlier than normal. He figured if he could get ahead on his new assignment, he would have enough time to go upstairs and patch things up with Rava over lunch.

After talking it over with Dusty, he had come to realize how selfish he had been lately. Maintaining relationships was never something he had to do as a child, and it was evident he needed more practice. He could only hope she would give him another chance.

His meeting with Senior Advisor Bloomfield the prior day still haunted his thoughts. Unfortunately, he was going to have to continue his assignment until he could formulate an escape plan.

One thing he'd learned during his first two weeks on his new assignment was that even the most secure places on the planet had vulnerabilities. Given enough time, he would eventually find a way out of OASIS. Until then, he'd need to utilize his brain drive to complete his work, which he wasn't happy about, but he saw no other options.

The Hub was a ghost town at this hour, which was for the best. He wouldn't have to worry about someone stepping onto the elevator with him. The elevators on the north end of the building were the best ones to use to get to the classified area due to the lower amount of traffic on that side of the first floor. But this early, he could take his pick.

He slipped into an empty elevator, waving his badge over the buttons. The door closed, and the elevator began to hum, taking him down.

Caleb nicknamed this floor "the bunker" because that's what it reminded him of. What was once a concrete maze of unmarked steel doors was now as familiar as the streets of the city he grew up in. He headed down a dim hallway as the motion-activated lights illuminated the way in front of him.

His first stop was his locker. As typical with any new classified assignment, Mrs. Bloomfield would leave him a folder containing video files and general information about the target facility.

After he reached the row of jet-black metal containers, he placed his thumb against the fingerprint reader on the door of his assigned storage space. An audible click sounded and he opened it up. Inside was a manilla folder labeled *Levanta*.

He pulled the file from his locker and found an unoccupied room to begin the first step in creating his module: learning the information.

With the door locked behind him, he took a seat at a computer desk. Unlike the main floors of the Hub, the rooms in the bunker weren't as neatly separated by function. That one had everything he needed to create a module from start to finish: a computer, writing utensils, a whiteboard, and a brain drive terminal.

Caleb opened the folder and couldn't believe his eyes. The location of the next facility was Aridor.

According to every book he'd ever read on the subject, Aridor's government was dismantled during the Great War. He couldn't imagine who they would even be spying on over there.

He was sure he'd regret this later, but his curiosity forced him to glance at the name of the target of the operation: *Dr. Olivia Birch*.

Intrigued, he loaded the file and strapped on the virtual

reality headset.

The first video was shot from what looked to be chest height. Caleb liked to guess where the camera was hidden, and this time he figured it was disguised as a shirt button.

Based on the feminine hands and voice, he gathered that the spy was likely female. She wore a loose silver bracelet on her left wrist with a heart-shaped ruby pendant dangling from it.

Unlike the previous facilities Caleb had studied, there appeared to be a complete lack of security at this place. Instead of guards, everyone carried their own personal firearm, and rather than uniforms, the personnel wore street clothes.

The concrete walls were lined with boarded-up windows and riddled with cracks. Overall, the building did not appear to be structurally sound.

Caleb was failing to see why this compound was included in the operation. He didn't understand what President Blake could possibly want with the run-down facility, and furthermore, why he needed Caleb to create a map. The place literally had holes in it. He was an hour into the video and he had yet to see anything remotely threatening going on there.

He was considering taking his first break for the day when the spy turned a corner and began following a woman in a white lab coat.

"Dr. Birch!" she called out. "I brought you some coffee."

The woman in the lab coat spun around as a hand shot in from the edge of the frame and extended a mug forward. The small ruby pendant dangled, clanking against the cup.

"Thank you, Judy!" the brunette woman in the lab coat replied with a bright smile.

But the woman in the lab coat wasn't Dr. Olivia Birch—at least not to Caleb. He knew her as Emily Shaw.

Caleb was staring at his mother.

CHAPTER TWELVE

Mesmerized by what he was seeing, Caleb absorbed every second of available footage. He couldn't believe his eyes. His mother was alive. Watching intently, he clung to every word she said, trying to memorize her voice as if he would never hear it again.

He didn't see how this was possible. But there she was, the woman from the photographs John had shown him, alive and well. He could add this to the growing list of secrets John was keeping from him. Again he wondered what, exactly, was on that memory stick.

Not only was his mother alive, but she was also in charge of a team of computer scientists who were developing a top-secret technology under the code name *Project Ariel*.

Caleb didn't understand much of what they were talking about when discussing the project, but he gathered they'd recently hit a wall in development. One of the programmers thought there was something wrong with the spatial awareness algorithm, while another disagreed, saying it was far more likely to be a problem with pattern recognition. Caleb's mother disagreed with both of them, arguing instead that there was a bug in the injection logic. Her suggestion was met with groans, but was immediately followed by her subordinates turning back to their work and digging through the code for the bug. They respected her, and for some reason that made Caleb feel proud of her.

When he finally removed the virtual reality headset from his head, it was approaching dinnertime. Caleb rolled his head counterclockwise, stretching his strained neck muscles before gathering his feet underneath himself and standing, bracing his arms against the desk while his legs were slowly reminded of their purpose.

After finding his balance, Caleb immediately knew what had to be done; he needed to warn his mother. He couldn't afford to wait around for an opportunity to present itself. He had to find a way out of this place, and fast. A special operations team would likely be deployed within two weeks, and this time his mother was the target. Based on how easily they handled the first heavily-guarded compound, he was sure they would make quick work of his mother's makeshift facility.

Back at the dormitory, Caleb stopped short of his apartment, knocking on Dusty's door. When he answered, he looked like he hadn't slept in days. Bags were forming under his eyes, and his curls were flatter than normal, as though he hadn't had time to bathe.

"I really need to talk. Are you busy?" Caleb could see text books strewn about his kitchen table.

"Not at all," Dusty said, rather unconvincingly. "Is this about Rava? Did you take my brilliant advice and patch things up with her?"

"Not exactly… Something came up. Do you mind if I come in?"

"Caleb!" Dusty protested in his high-pitched voice that seemed to get even higher when he was worked up. "This is what you did last time. It can't always be about you—"

"Dusty, Dusty, Dusty!" he interjected until he got his attention. "My mother is *alive*."

Dusty's face froze, his mouth gaping and bloodshot eyes wide.

"Can I come in?" Caleb asked again.

Snapping out of his trance, Dusty stepped aside to let him in. "Of course. My apologies." He shook his head as if trying to wake himself up. "You're *certain* she's alive?"

Twenty minutes later, Dusty was up to speed. Caleb technically wasn't allowed to share information on his classified assignments, but he was past following rules at that point.

"Okay, so the woman in the video is the same as the one in the pictures your father showed you. But how can you be certain it's your mother? John did lie to you about being your father, after all."

"I can't explain it. I just *know*. And even if she isn't, John was obviously close with her. I have to find her before they do, and warn her."

"Find her? You can't possibly mean—"

"Yes. I'm planning to escape OASIS. I've been thinking about it for a while, actually. I don't belong here."

"That's ludicrous, Caleb. If anyone belongs here, it's you. You've scored perfect ratings on every module you've created. And now you've been promoted to work on *classified* assignments, something I didn't even know was possible." Dusty was waving his arms around emphatically as he spoke.

"That's not what I mean. I'm talking about my fate, what I was made to do. Before I came here, I thought OASIS would provide me with an opportunity to get to know my mother, in a sense. It turns out I was right, just in a way I never thought possible. My mother needs me."

Silence fell over the room as Dusty paced back and forth in his kitchen, rubbing his chin like he did when he was performing a complicated mathematical calculation. After chewing on the information for a short while, he pointed his hand in the air as if he'd had an epiphany. "Okay. I've decided I am coming with you."

"What? Why?" Caleb asked. He didn't see a reason Dusty should risk his future to help him.

"Don't be ridiculous. You're going to need assistance if you want to formulate and execute a plan of escape from OASIS, not to mention travel to Aridor. You know it's an entirely separate continent, right?"

Caleb looked at Dusty as if he had asked him if he knew the sky was blue. Of course he knew where Aridor was.

"And more importantly, how could I claim to be a true friend if I was unwilling to help you in your greatest hour of need?"

Caleb mulled over Dusty's words. If things went south and they were caught, he wouldn't just be jeopardizing his own life, but that of his friend as well.

"Fine," he said at last. "But I won't blame you if you change your mind. You have your entire life ahead of you. You don't have to ruin it for me."

Dusty scoffed, turning to face Caleb with his eyes fixed on the floor. "What life? The one where I slave away working inside these walls while my family, who have never come to visit, get paid for it? And then one day, maybe I can retire or request a transfer? Don't you see, Caleb? You're the closest thing I've had to a family in a long time. If you're going, I'm going."

Caleb nodded and smiled. "Okay. Let's get to work."

~*~

Two days later, Caleb and Dusty were slouched over Caleb's kitchen table, ironing out the kinks in their escape plan.

"There are simply too many unknown variables for me to even consider giving this higher than a fifteen percent chance of success," Dusty said with authority, adjusting his glasses.

That wasn't what Caleb wanted to hear. He hoped after two days of planning, Dusty would come around, but it seemed like he would never feel comfortable until success was practically guaranteed. That just wasn't realistic.

Their idea revolved around Caleb's hunch that the locked doors around the perimeter of the bunker under the Hub had emergency escape tunnels behind them. Based on the knowledge he'd gained from studying compounds similar to OASIS, he understood underground bunkers typically had tunnels that led to emergency exits located at least a mile outside the main facility walls. In the event of an attack, these underground passages would be used to evacuate as many people as possible.

The major hang-up was gaining access to the area beyond the bunker. Caleb's clearance allowed him into the classified area, but his badge didn't work on the doors he thought might lead to the tunnels. Since he'd begun working in the bunker, he had only seen a handful of people access them, all of whom were high ranking government officials.

Dusty was apprehensive about attempting to escape from the most secure location in the compound. "And how are we going to get through those doors? And even if we *do* bypass them somehow, there's no guarantee the tunnels even exist, or that they're not swarming with security officers."

"I told you, I have a meeting with Senior Advisor Bloomfield tonight. I'm going to create a distraction and swipe her badge when she's not looking."

Dusty rolled his eyes.

Caleb knew it was a long shot at best, and he hadn't planned what he would do to distract the woman, but it was the only way he could think of to get into that area. He hadn't seen her open those doors, but he'd seen two of President Blake's other advisors use them, which led him to believe they all had access.

"As far as security goes, I have yet to see a single officer use those doors. It's a risk, but I'd say there's a good chance they don't patrol the tunnels. There'd be no need. No one knows about them. Sure, there could be cameras, but we'll be long gone before they can catch up."

"No offense, but I think you should defer to *my* expertise when it comes to predicting chances."

"And you should defer to mine when it comes to what lies beyond those doors."

"That's fair," Dusty said after a moment, but he didn't sound convinced. He leaned forward, burying his head in his hands and threading his fingers through his hair.

"Look, I understand this plan requires a leap of faith. I wouldn't blame you at all if you decide to back out."

"No. That's not an option," he said, straightening up. "Now what about your mother's facility? Did you find any new maps today?"

They still hadn't narrowed down the location of his mother's facility. It wasn't enough to know it was in Aridor. They had to know *where* in Aridor it was located. Since every history book Caleb had ever read referred to the nation as a deserted wasteland, he knew next to nothing about the geography of the continent.

"Yes, actually, I did." Caleb carefully unrolled a pre-war map of Aridor.

At around two million square miles, Aridor was by far the smallest of the world's four continents. But what it lacked in size, it made up for in density. Unlike the rolling hills and open fields one might find when driving from one industrialized city to another in Materra, Aridor was packed with crowded cityscapes interconnected by highways that weaved through vast seas of suburbs. In all, there were few undeveloped areas.

The map gave Caleb an entirely new perspective on the fall of Aridor. He had always wondered how an attack on their capital city brought down the entire nation. After studying the map, he understood. Before being developed, Aridor was nothing but a large desert island, lacking access to the proper natural resources for settlement. Developing large urban centers was necessary to allow their inhabitants access to essentials for living.

Lacking the means to become self-sufficient after the Great War, they were doomed to fail. Without a government to provide structure and reassurance to a society that so heavily relied on international trade for essential goods, their critical infrastructure crumbled. Developing a nuclear arsenal behind the backs of the rest of the world turned out to be a gross miscalculation on the part of their government.

"I have it narrowed down to these three cities." Caleb gestured to the map, pointing out the locations on the map. "When I cross-referenced the map I created of my mother's facility with those of every major city in Aridor, accounting for the dimensions of the facility, I was able to narrow down the potential location to three different buildings in these cities."

There was no way they could check each building, so they had to choose one. Fortunately, Caleb and Dusty both agreed on this: the most likely location was the building near the center of the old capital city of Jorence.

This left one final detail to settle: timing.

"Given more time to prepare, I'm certain we could improve our odds of success," Dusty said, clearly hoping to convince Caleb. Normally, he would agree with Dusty. More preparation would undoubtedly be better. But they didn't have more time.

"I'm already having trouble stalling on my assignment," Caleb said, trying his best to remain calm and rational. He was growing frustrated with Dusty, but Caleb knew his friend wouldn't respond well to an argument based on emotions. "It's probably why my supervisor asked for that meeting tonight. I can only delay giving them results for so long, not to mention the team of elite assassins that are headed my mother's way."

"Point taken," Dusty said. "I'll be ready when you are."

~*~

Much like early in the morning, the Hub was quiet at six o'clock in the afternoon. On occasion, there were a few GIs working late into the night to meet a deadline, but most preferred to have their evenings to themselves.

The bunker was even more dead at that hour. Caleb hadn't

seen a single person until he arrived at the conference room to find Senior Advisor Bloomfield waiting.

"Hello, Mr. Shaw," she said in a bored tone, as if speaking at all was a chore. "Please, take a seat."

Caleb sat across from the grumpy woman. He hadn't prepared what he was going to say to his supervisor about his lack of results on his assignment thus far, and right then he wished he'd prepared some sort of excuse.

"I'm sure you're busy with your new assignment these days, and I hate to divide your attention further, but I have a second job for you. You'll be expected to work both concurrently."

Caleb's eyebrows raised. It was exactly what he needed. It would give him a legitimate excuse for delaying his assignment, granting him more time to plan his escape. Dusty was sure to be thrilled.

"I know, I was as shocked as you are," she said. "I don't agree with the decision, but it's not mine to make. I'm only passing down orders."

Mrs. Bloomfield pulled a folder out of her bag and handed it to him.

"Your second assignment is to create a comprehensive map module of this floor, C1. President Blake feels strongly that we should know this place better than anyone and specifically requested you perform this assignment. You're making quite the name for yourself."

Caleb smiled, but not for the reason Senior Advisor Bloomfield may have thought.

"We understand this may slow your progress on your current task, but this is a priority. In the file you will find schematics of C1 to assist you. Your security clearance has been temporarily increased to allow access to this entire floor. We only ask that you don't let any of those floor plans leave the premises. Any questions?"

Caleb felt like he had to be dreaming. This was too perfect. Not only would the second assignment provide additional planning time, but it would also provide him the resources he needed to formulate a more solid plan of escape. He opened the folder and quickly looked over the blueprints. Afraid to say anything that would jeopardize this opportunity, Caleb avoided asking any questions. "I understand what is expected of me. This will be my top priority."

"*Both* of your assignments will be your priority," she clarified. "Oh, and one more thing. I have something for you." She reached into her pocket and pulled out a small red memory stick, setting it down on the table in front of Caleb. "This came across my desk. Apparently, it was screened for malware and was supposed to be returned to you."

He was certain he was dreaming. Any second now he would wake up to the disappointing reality that he needed a better escape plan and he still didn't have his memory stick.

He scooped the memory stick up off the table and slid it into his jacket. He looked up to see Senior Advisor Bloomfield staring at him through her oval glasses.

"Well," she croaked, "are you going to sit there and make eyes with me or are you going to get to work?"

~*~

Following his meeting with Senior Advisor Bloomfield, Caleb immediately found a room in the bunker with a brain drive terminal and locked himself inside.

After all of the waiting, he was finally going to find out what was on that memory stick.

Steadying his shaky hands, he plugged the memory stick into the terminal. A folder popped up on the screen titled *For Caleb*. Without delay he plugged himself into the machine and uploaded the module to his brain drive. The transfer took seconds.

He didn't notice anything at first. Nothing felt different. He wasn't suddenly overwhelmed with information he hadn't known before. Although Caleb had been training extensively to create modules, he still didn't have a ton of experience using them. He figured he had to trigger the memories somehow, but how would he know what to think about?

Hoping to gain some insight, Caleb turned his attention back to the terminal. He opened the main folder to view the subfolders. The first one was named *The day you were born*.

He thought back to when his son was born. The memory was clear as day. In Caleb's mind's eye, he could picture the hospital again as if he were standing there. A doctor with a smudged face handed his son to Emily, his wife. The look of exhaustion on her face fled instantly and was replaced by a radiating smile as she held her newborn. He had never seen her happier. "You should hold him," she said, looking up at him with her deep-blue eyes. He carefully lifted the baby from her arms and held him close. The joy he felt holding his son for the first time was incomparable. *This is love*, he thought.

The delivery room faded away and Caleb was back in the dimly lit room of the bunker. Somehow, it seemed darker than it had before.

That was, by far, the most vivid memory he had ever experienced from a module. Is that what his were like for other people? The woman from the memory was, without a doubt, the same woman in the pictures John had shown him. His mother was in danger, and it felt even more real now.

Caleb moved onto the next subfolder, labeled *The Assassination Plot*. Assassination plot?

Suddenly his mind took him back to that day. He was standing in his bedroom. Emily was sitting on the bed, biting her nails—a nervous habit of hers. "What do you mean we have to leave?" he said frantically. "We can't take Caleb to Aridor, he won't survive!"

"Well *we* won't survive here, Derek!" Emily shot back, eyes welling up. "My contact says they are planning to ambush us after the charity dinner. We need to go tonight! I've already arranged transport and new identities. They won't be able to find us there."

"Tonight?" he exclaimed. "Are you crazy? What are we going to do with Caleb?"

"Why are you acting like we haven't talked about this?" Emily stood up, wiping her eyes dry. "Our contingency plan has always been to leave him with John. He will be safer with him. John is a good man and he will raise him right. Besides, you and I both know he would have just been taken from us when he was six anyway. Maybe with John, he'll have a chance at a normal life."

He looked down at the baby, sound asleep in his crib. "I'll take him," he muttered through a cracked voice.

The memory ended there and Caleb came back from his daydream. Who would have been trying to assassinate his parents? And why? No memories came to answer his questions. Maybe the answer was in another subfolder.

The final one was titled *The Last Time I Saw You*. He thought back to the last time he saw his son.

The gentle sound of rain falling on the roof filled his ears as the memory came into focus. He was at John's apartment, standing outside of his door, but he couldn't remember what color the walls were. Blue and green swirled and shimmered where the wall should be, as though his brain couldn't decide on a color.

Then he knocked on John's door, only he didn't remember knocking. He just *knew* that he had knocked.

The door opened and he looked up at John, who seemed to be standing in the doorway of a pitch-black room. He couldn't remember anything about the interior of his apartment.

A concerned look overtook John's boyish face. He tried his best to convey to John the gravity of the situation without telling him too much. John couldn't know the plan or he would try to talk them out of it, or worse yet, try to find them. John had a habit of trying to protect those he loved, and that's what he was hoping he would do for Caleb.

He bent down to say goodbye to his son, kissing the sleeping child on the forehead. He tried to hold back his tears, but he couldn't. "I love you more than you'll ever know, CJ."

"He's *your* son now," he choked out, looking up at John. More than anything, he was trying to convince himself. Leaving his son behind was the hardest thing he'd ever had to do.

Caleb snapped back to reality. He brushed the tears from his cheeks, but more followed. It was as if an entire lifetime of emotions were flooding him all at once. He felt empathy for his parents, who were forced to abandon him abruptly. He felt confused as to why they would even risk losing him. He, once again, felt anger towards John for withholding this information from him.

But most of all, he felt sad.

He wondered how things could have been different if he'd had his real parents. Getting a glimpse into the life he could have had left Caleb feeling like an imposter in his own body.

CHAPTER THIRTEEN

The engine of the delivery truck roared to life and John looked down at his watch. Right on time. They would arrive at the compound just before midnight.

Avoiding detection during the driver's inventory check was his first victory. He folded and stuffed himself into a mesh bin and covered himself with clean laundry, leaving a hole to peek through. It wasn't comfortable, but it sure beat sitting on a tree branch for eight hours straight.

To help ease his nerves, he recapped the plan in his mind on the way to the compound. Tonight, weeks of preparation would finally come to fruition. In less than an hour, he would be reunited with his son.

Before long, the truck came to a stop. Seconds later, the back door rattled open. He could hear faint laughter as the driver chatted with an OASIS employee. John watched through his peephole as the employee, dressed in all blue, began unloading the truck.

When the truck was nearly half unloaded, the staff member disappeared into the loading bay. John checked the time. Shift change—time to move.

He carefully climbed out of the laundry bin and exited the

back of the truck. The night air had a biting chill to it and as John took a deep breath, his lungs were filled with cool air, a subtle reminder of the reality of the situation.

Before setting off, he straightened his security officer uniform and made sure it was tucked in. Although he lacked a badge and weapon, he hoped it wouldn't be noticeable under the cover of darkness.

Weaving between various staff buildings as he walked, John made his way to the entrance of the GI residential area. The north end of the compound presented very little challenge to blending in. Most of the people he passed didn't so much as glance in his direction. Some of them appeared to be on their way to their posts while others appeared to be heading home after their shift. Either way, they were too preoccupied to worry about him.

Getting into the enclosed GI residential area without a security officer badge would prove to be more difficult. The best idea he could come up with was to wait for a security officer to leave the checkpoint building and hope they would hold the door for him on his way in. While surveilling the compound he'd witnessed this happen countless times. Once inside, he could travel the length of the office and exit out the other end and into the GI residential area, so long as no one noticed his missing badge and stopped him.

While crossing the street to get closer, a new plan formed in his mind. He acted on it before the opportunity passed.

As a shuttle bus was coming through the checkpoint, he stepped out in front of it and held his palm out, signaling the driver to stop. The bus came to a halt. He walked around to the side of the bus and the driver opened the door.

John spoke in a casual manner. "Evening. I rode on one of these busses earlier, and I seem to have lost my badge. Did one turn up on here?"

The driver, an old man with a bushy gray mustache, glanced down in a cubby under the dash. "Nope. Not unless it got turned in already," he replied. "Check with Franny at the garage. She'll have it if it was left on a bus."

"Well, thanks for checking. I'm hoping I can find it before my supervisor finds out I lost it. Have a good night."

The old man let out a hearty chuckle. "Yeah, George can be a real stickler. Good luck to you!"

John smiled and nodded, taking a step back from the bus. The door closed and it pulled away. He turned and walked right through the checkpoint while the gate arm was still raised in the air.

He looked toward the security checkpoint building and saw two officers studying him through the window. John raised his hand and gave them a quick wave. One of them waved back while the other wandered away.

Despite the cold weather, a bead of sweat ran down his forehead. That had gone much better than he anticipated. He was able to avoid going through the checkpoint building and he doubted the officers in the window noticed his missing badge under the soft glow of the streetlamp.

A few minutes later, John reached Caleb's dormitory. That was where his plan would require a bit of improvisation. He wiped the sweat from his forehead and entered the lobby, approaching the front desk with purpose.

"I need the room number for Caleb Shaw," he demanded, following it up with a confident smile. He then looked around, pretending to admire the gold-bordered paintings hanging behind the desk.

"I'm sorry, sir," the woman behind the desk said. "Do you have your ID?"

"Unfortunately, I do not. I'm actually hoping Mr. Shaw can tell me where it is. I have a sneaking suspicion he stole it from me earlier today. I know it's late, but I'm afraid it can't wait."

"I understand, sir. If you just give me your badge number, I can get you that information right away."

"Honestly, ma'am, I don't remember my badge number. I was

hoping to resolve this issue without getting my supervisor involved. You know how it is. Kids do dumb things. I was going to give him a chance to make it right on his own."

She stared at him blankly for a few seconds. Just as she was about to speak again, he cut her off.

"I don't think George would appreciate being woken up at this hour, but if you'd rather I call him…"

"No, that won't be necessary." She flashed a nervous smile. "Room 312. Would you like me to call him down?"

"That's all right. I'll go up. Thank you." John gave the woman a firm nod, and he turned to the elevator.

As the doors closed, he let out a deep sigh. He'd practiced that exact conversation in his mind at least twenty times, contemplating which excuse would be best to use and developing answers to potential questions he might be asked. None of his rehearsed conversations went *that* well.

The elevator came to a stop and before it opened fully John had already slid through and into the hallway, making haste to room 312. He wasn't necessarily running late. In his estimation, he still had plenty of time to make it back to the delivery truck with Caleb. It was his excitement that was rushing him forward.

John stopped at Caleb's apartment and firmly rapped his knuckles against the wooden door. No answer came. At this hour, Caleb was probably sleeping. He knocked again, a little louder and for a longer duration. Still no answer. John glanced back and forth to make sure none of the neighbors were poking their heads out. He banged even louder but heard nothing inside the room. He tried the knob, but it was locked.

Suddenly, an alarm sounded, blaring through the hallway and drowning out all hope he had for a clean escape.

John began frantically banging on the door and yelling for his son.

"Caleb!"

~*~

Six hours earlier

Caleb tapped his leg as he waited for Dusty in a study room on the second floor of the Hub. He was supposed to be there already to run through their escape plan one final time.

Caleb's last two days had been spent memorizing the layout and schematic of floor C1. His hunch was right. The doors on the periphery of C1 did, in fact, lead to exit tunnels. There were also peripheral access points that connected above-ground buildings, such as security offices, with the tunnels. In the event of an emergency that required evacuating, these hidden hatches would save precious time, allowing OASIS residents to enter the bunker without needing to travel all the way to the Hub. Based on Caleb's knowledge of the above-ground compound, he had a fairly good idea of which buildings had access points, but the blueprints didn't make it apparent.

The door to the study room opened and Dusty walked in, his head hanging low. But he wasn't the only one there. Walking behind him was Rava, her dark-black hair tied back in two braids instead of her usual one.

"Are you insane?" she barked at Caleb immediately.

"What?" Caleb shifted his gaze to Dusty. "Dusty, what's going on here?"

"I thought that—"

"What's going on here," she butted in, "is that you two are planning to escape this awful place and leave me behind without even so much as a goodbye."

Caleb could see the anger on her face turn to pain. She was genuinely hurt.

"Rava... I'm sorry, I didn't—"

"You didn't what? Didn't think to tell me I'd never see you again after this suicidal plan of yours? Didn't think to ask for advice from the one person you know who has actually *been* to Aridor?"

Caleb glared at Dusty, who shrugged.

"Yeah, he told me everything. I swear, Caleb, for a literal genius, you can be so stupid sometimes."

Silence fell over the room. Caleb fiddled with the zipper on his backpack. He could feel the heat from Rava's stare.

Dusty spoke up first. "I apologize, Caleb. I was merely attempting to help. I didn't want you to leave without saying goodbye to her. She started asking me all sorts of questions and —well—she's very persuasive."

"*You* don't have to apologize for anything," Rava snapped, pointing her finger at Dusty. "You at least had enough sense to come to me. Caleb, on the other hand, has some explaining to do."

"I—I didn't want to hurt you, Rava," Caleb said as he forced himself to look into her eyes. He could feel tears beginning to well up. "After everything that happened, I guess I figured that it would be easier for you if I just disappeared from your life."

She relaxed her scowl and took a seat at the table as Caleb continued.

"I knew you would be angry with me, and I thought it would help you heal. But with you here in front of me, I now realize the real reason I didn't tell you I was leaving."

Rava leaned forward in her seat, placing her arms on the table in front of her. Caleb locked onto her piercing eyes.

"I was afraid you would be able to talk me out of going."

He blinked and a tear rolled down his face.

Rava shifted her gaze and spoke softly. "Caleb…"

"But I have to go. I know that now," he said, wiping the tear away with his sleeve. "There's no changing my mind. But I'm sorry I didn't tell you. I should have."

"I know," she said. "And you *should* go. Your mother needs you. But if you think I'm going to let you leave here without me, you've lost your mind."

Caleb looked at Rava in disbelief. "Really?"

"Is it that surprising? I want out of this wretched place as much as you do. Besides, how do you think I'd feel sitting here knowing the two of you were wandering around my homeland without me?"

She cracked a smile, and Caleb couldn't help but smile back. He couldn't believe he was lucky enough to have two friends who were willing to risk everything to help him.

Dusty took a seat at the table. "Shall we begin?"

Caleb nodded, pulling schematics and maps from his backpack as he began recalling the escape plan for them. Once they were all comfortable with the details, they moved on to the topic of Aridor.

When Caleb explained to Rava their rationale for believing the facility was in Jorence, she disagreed.

"You got us going to the wrong place," she said. "The facility isn't in Jorence. Most of the tech companies were located on the east coast, and unless you think they hauled all of that equipment there, I'd say we're looking for a building that was previously a tech research facility. I wasn't alive then, but my father told me all about what Aridor used to be like. Apparently, the beautiful beaches and vibrant nightlife of the coastal cities brought the best talent there. According to your research"—she leaned over and pointed at one of the three circled cities on the map—"it's probably in Portan."

"That's *improbable*," Dusty said in a know-it-all manner. "The map Caleb drew of his mother's facility doesn't match the layout of the building in Portan as much as either of our other two prospective choices. And how do you explain the damage to the building? We know for a fact the capital city was bombed."

Rava gritted her teeth. "You know for a fact, huh?" She stood up from the table, towering over Dusty. "You know only what the history books *told* you. Did you know they bombed more than just the capital city? I saw the damage with my own eyes. Every major city was bombed when Aridor was attacked, not just the capital. And those that weren't bombed were ransacked and destroyed by gangs. *That's* how I explain the building damage."

Taking notice of the rising tension between them, Caleb tried to be the voice of reason. "Dusty, the map I created was based on incomplete information. It's entirely possible my calculations were somewhat off. Don't you think we should factor in the information Rava is giving us?"

Rava sat back down and Dusty nodded begrudgingly, keeping his head down. He couldn't deny the logic, but Caleb could tell the uncertainty of the location bothered him. He needed to *know* they were going to the right place, and being unsure only made him more uncomfortable.

Caleb went on. "Okay, well if we assume the facility is in Portan rather than Jorence, we would need to find a way to get an extra two hundred miles south. I don't think a boat would get us there in time."

"I know someone who can help us," Rava said. "Let's just say not everyone who came here from Aridor came here *legally*. I know a guy who flies a small seaplane back and forth, transporting immigrants. He's not cheap, though. We might have to pool our credits together. How many do you guys have?"

Caleb answered first. "I think I have around forty thousand."

Dusty and Rava both snapped their heads to Caleb, their mouths gaped.

"Forty *thousand*?" Dusty replied.

"It's settled," Rava said. "Caleb pays for everything."

That was okay with him. After all, it was all in an effort to save *his* mother. His friends were risking their future. He felt like the least he could do was pay for the trip.

"That's fine, but how do I withdraw my credits from here?"

"They can be transferred to your brain drive storage using one of the terminals," Dusty said.

"Yup." Rava nodded in agreement. "You can even pay for things using the credits stored on your brain drive."

"Really?" Caleb said, his eyebrows raised. "Why haven't I

seen people do that before?"

"Because it's not *entirely* secure. Credits can be stolen from your brain drive by malware on any terminal you plug into. It was an intended feature that never took off."

Dusty must have noticed Caleb's unease and chimed in. "But for the purposes of transporting your credits out of here, it should suffice. Once outside the walls, we can convert your digital credits into physical notes at a bank."

Caleb nodded. He would prefer not to use his brain drive for this at all, but he took comfort in knowing he could convert his credits after he escaped. He began thinking about all of the bills he could help John pay.

Then a stark realization came crashing down on him. If everything went according to plan, he wouldn't be able to return home. If he was lucky enough to save his mother and make it back alive, he would have to go into hiding. Meeting up with John would only put him in danger.

Caleb pushed those thoughts aside. He needed to take things one step at a time. Right now, the most important thing was saving his mother.

After further discussion about the facility's most likely location, Caleb ultimately sided with Rava. They were headed to Portan. He was taking a leap of faith, but he trusted her intuition.

Next, they took a trip up to the fourth floor, where Rava and Dusty helped Caleb transfer his credits using the terminal. He had 40,950 credits stored in his brain drive.

They shared their last meal together in the cafeteria before heading back to their dorms. It was only a matter of time. Tonight, they would escape OASIS.

~*~

As midnight approached, Caleb and Dusty made their way down to the bus stop in front of their dorm.

When the shuttle arrived, they boarded it, passing by Rava, who was near the middle of the bus, and taking a seat in the back as planned. Sitting together would only serve to raise suspicion this late at night. Caleb's leg tapped furiously as the vehicle pulled away.

As they were leaving the GI residential area, the bus came to an unexpected halt. Caleb stood up and leaned over to look outside and see what the problem was. He caught a glimpse of a security officer leaning into the bus doorway.

He looked at Rava to see if she could see what was going on, but she turned around and shrugged at them. Caleb's heart began to race as he sat back down. He wondered how they had been found out already.

Their bus driver spoke casually with the security officer. Much to Caleb's relief, after a brief exchange they were back on their way. He looked out of the back window to see a silhouette of the security officer walking in the opposite direction. He let out a sigh as he turned back around. It was a close call.

Once they arrived at the Hub, they headed right for the north elevator. Caleb swiped his badge, and they began their descent to floor C1.

The elevator opened up to a pitch-black hallway. They stepped out, provoking the motion-activated lights to light the path ahead of them. Caleb led the way, swiping his badge again when they reached the doors that separated the bunker from the peripheral tunnels.

The moment they crossed the threshold into the tunnels, alarms on the ceiling began to scream, filling the air with blaring sounds. Red streaks of light flared out from above, lighting the darkness in front of them in a scarlet hue.

"Follow me!" Caleb yelled before he took off in the direction of the exit.

It was unclear to him how they'd set off an alarm. Maybe they were time-sensitive, he reasoned. Or someone who was monitoring the cameras could've taken it upon themselves to manually trigger an alarm. Either way, it didn't matter. Their only chance at that point was to make a run for the exit and hope they were fast enough.

They sprinted forward, following the tunnels north. Rava had no trouble keeping up, but Dusty appeared to be struggling to breathe. Even with an alarm sounding above them, Caleb could hear Dusty wheezing as he took in large gulps of air.

As they approached the locked door that separated the peripheral tunnels of floor C1 from the emergency exit tunnels, Caleb reached for his badge. His heart sank. It was gone. He frantically checked his pockets, but came up empty. It must have fallen off along the way.

Caleb looked at Dusty and Rava, his mistake written on his face. Dusty was too busy catching his breath to notice what was going on, but Rava quickly realized what had happened.

"Seriously, Caleb?" She tried her badge and nothing happened. Without a word of explanation, she pulled out a multitool from her backpack and began taking apart the card reader.

"What are you doing?" Dusty asked before reality sank in. His face turned pale in an instant.

"If I can access the internal wiring, I might be able to make something happen. It's better than standing around waiting to get caught."

"Hold this." She pulled a flashlight from her bag and thrust it toward Dusty. He took it and followed her directions.

"I'm going to go back and see if I can find it!" Caleb yelled over the blaring alarm.

As he turned to head back down the hallway, a security officer rounded the corner, running in their direction.

Caleb stopped in his tracks. It was all over, he thought. They had been caught.

Officer Thorington continued toward them. The scar over his left eye looked even more menacing under the flashing red lights. Behind him, Ricky Gunther came around the bend.

Officer Thorington looked back at Ricky before tossing Caleb's badge to him.

"Run, CJ!" he shouted as he turned around and held Ricky back.

Caleb spun around and sprinted for the door, hurrying to scan his badge over the card reader as Rava was still trying to remove the cover. The door slid open.

Then Caleb froze in place. *CJ?*

He turned back around, scanning the hallway for Officer Thorington only to find an empty tunnel. Red lights danced across the walls as the alarms continued to sound-off overhead.

"Come on!" yelled Rava. "What are you doing?" She grabbed the back of his shirt and yanked him through the door just before it closed.

His initial thought was to try to go back and find Officer Thorington. He wanted answers. He needed to know if that was his father.

Rava pulled on his shirt again and he looked back at his friends, their eyes begging him to run before they were all caught.

For a moment, Caleb felt like time had slowed. Dusty was waving him forward but his arm was moving far too slow. Rava was saying something, but he couldn't hear it. His mind was processing his predicament, and although it occurred over a fraction of a second, it seemed like much longer.

Ultimately, he knew what he had to do. His friends and his mother needed him. The rest could be sorted out later, he decided. Caleb tuned out his thoughts and broke out into a dead sprint alongside his friends.

Eventually, they came to another door. Caleb was sure not to make the same mistake again. He loosened his tight grip on his badge and swiped it.

They poured out of the tunnel into another pitch-black one. Dusty, still wielding the flashlight, cut through the darkness with his beam. The passage they were standing in was cylindrical in shape and made of metal, continuing to their right and left for about fifteen feet in either direction. A small stream of water sat idle in the bottom of it, running from one end to the other. Although the tunnel opened on both ends, the light from their small flashlight didn't allow them to see beyond it.

Caleb turned and jogged toward the opening, Dusty and Rava close behind, their footsteps clanking against the metal floor as they ran. After stepping out into the brisk night air, Caleb realized the metal tube they'd just emerged from was actually a culvert. The emergency exit tunnel was cleverly hidden, but there was no roadside nearby. Instead, the culvert was surrounded by nothing but trees.

Guided only by moonlight and their low-powered flashlight, they continued north.

CHAPTER FOURTEEN

Derek lifted the hatch door, climbing through and into the security office above. The access point was well hidden, located behind a heating unit in a utility closet.

He was hoping Caleb and his friends had made it out all right. Ricky had almost ruined everything when he spotted them in the emergency exit tunnels on the security feed. Luckily, Derek was able to get there first to ensure they weren't stopped. It was even more fortunate that he happened to spot Caleb's badge on the ground along the way.

Although Ricky was furious, threatening to tell his father George everything that had happened, Derek kept reminding him of their current objective: find the intruder that was spotted near the dormitory buildings.

Before the alarm was triggered, Derek was driving to the staff residential area following back-to-back shifts when he saw someone walking in the opposite direction. At a glance, he thought he'd seen his old friend John dressed in a black uniform. He brushed the thought aside and drove on, convinced his exhausted mind was playing tricks on him after pulling a double. But as soon as he heard an intruder was spotted in the same general area, disguised as a security officer, he knew it had to be John. It was just like him to do something like this—and he had to find him before anyone else did.

Derek slipped out of the back of the security office, leaving Ricky and the others to scour security feeds for the intruder. He had seen John walking from the north end of the compound earlier, so he would begin his search there. Since the intruder was spotted wearing a security officer uniform, he could have gotten it from the laundry facility. Derek would check there first.

As he was approaching in his work-issued truck, Derek took notice of a swarm of security officers searching a delivery vehicle parked at the loading bay. He pulled over to the side of the road and parked. He needed to think.

With no discernible way for him to escape easily, it was becoming even more important for Derek to find John first.

~*~

From the shadows, John peeked around the corner again, watching the security officers tear through the laundry bins that had been pulled from the delivery truck.

Still frustrated by his failure, John was having a hard time thinking at the moment. After weeks of preparation, he hadn't once considered a scenario in which Caleb wasn't in his dorm room. There was no need to—he was always there, or so he thought. One of the major benefits of a night mission was better control over where Caleb would be.

Racking his brain for a solution to his predicament, John ducked his head back into the alley.

Without a solid escape plan, he'd have to find somewhere to hide before dawn. He would be caught in no time if he stayed out in the open like this. Once he found a safe place, he could think up a new way out.

Deciding it would be best to distance himself from the laundry facility, John crept in the opposite direction, making his way across the street into another alley. He continued sneaking between buildings as he passed two more streets, sticking to tight corridors to avoid detection.

Although he was moving farther from the laundry facility, he didn't feel like he was making any real progress toward finding a hiding place, only finding himself more lost among the countless buildings that all looked the same. John started scouring his surroundings for potential places to hide.

He briefly considered hopping into a dumpster. He couldn't imagine they would check in every one. Better yet, if he could find a way to the top of a building, he was sure to be safe from search parties up there. That would also give him a good vantage point over the north end of the compound.

He began scanning the alley for anything he could climb. Busy looking up, he nearly missed the beams from two flashlights bouncing off of the sidewalk right next to him. The light caught his attention out of the corner of his eye, and before he could process what it was coming from, he took cover behind a dumpster. The officers carried on past the alley without even looking his way.

John stood up, continuing his search for scalable fixtures on the side of the building when something else caught his attention. This time, it was a shadow. He looked to his left to see a man standing at the end of the alley, his dark silhouette painted against the canvas of light provided by the streetlamps.

The man clicked a flashlight on, shining it in John's direction.

"John. Is that you?"

Blinded, John had an even harder time seeing the man, but he recognized his voice immediately. "Derek?" John asked, sounding both confused and relieved, as he attempted to shield his eyes.

Derek clicked the light back off. "John! I'm so glad I found you. We have to get you out of here. Follow me. I have an idea." Derek turned and John followed. As they neared the street, two more security officers stepped into the alleyway.

One of them was short and slim, while the other was average height and dressed in a suit, street lights glaring off of his bald head.

"Thorington, you want to introduce us to the fugitive you're attempting to harbor?" asked a stern voice coming from the bald man.

"Head Officer Gunther. Good, I was just looking for you," replied Derek. "I found this guy lurking in the shadows here—"

"Cut the crap, Thorington. My son told me all about what happened in the tunnel. I'm not exactly sure how you're mixed up in all this, but I'm going to find out. You two are coming with me."

John considered making a run for it. He was sure he could outrun them all, but where would he go? Then he noticed the bald security officer had drawn his pistol and he decided to comply.

After placing a pair of restraints on John's wrists, the bald man turned to Derek. "You too, Thorington. Turn around."

Walking under the streetlights, John was able to get a better look at the others. Derek looked nearly unrecognizable to him. Time had certainly aged him, but beyond that, a large scar covered the left side of his face. He wondered how he'd gotten that. He'd also never seen Derek with short hair or a beard. There was no way he could have picked him out of a lineup if he hadn't heard his voice.

Officer Gunther appeared younger than he'd imagined, although his handlebar mustache did its best to make him look older.

His small, skinny accomplice was a woman. He had initially mistaken her for a man because her brown hair was pulled back tight into a ponytail, giving it the appearance of a crew cut in the dark alley.

Even in the unfortunate situation John found himself in, he was still able to find humor in the fact he'd imagined all three of them differently than they actually were.

John and Derek were stuffed into the back seat of George's truck and driven to the large four-story building in the center of the compound, where Caleb worked.

They were escorted inside and down to what appeared to be some sort of fallout shelter. He couldn't help but admire the craftsmanship that went into designing the bunker as George ushered them through and into an unmarked room.

As they entered, John's eyes were immediately glued to the man in the navy suit. Without a doubt, he was looking at the president of the nation, Avery Blake. At first, he was stunned. After the initial shock wore off, he felt a mix of anger and fear: anger for the years he'd spent watching his fellow people starve because of the president, and fear for what might happen to him and Caleb now that their fates might be decided by the same heartless man.

President Blake scanned them with his dark-brown eyes before turning his attention to George, a relaxed expression on his face.

"I see you managed to apprehend the intruder," President Blake said in an even tone, seemingly unimpressed. "May I ask why you have restrained one of your subordinates?"

"Of course, Mr. President," George replied, his voice an octave higher than before. "I found Officer Thorington with him, and I have reason to believe he had intentions of helping him escape."

"I see. And what reason would that be?"

"Well"—George reached up and rubbed the back of his neck —"it looked like they were walking together when I found them. They seemed awfully friendly toward each other."

President Blake paced back and forth, listening as George continued explaining.

"And my son saw him let a few GIs make an escape earlier in the tunnels. I don't trust him one bit. Call it a gut feeling, but I know he's involved somehow."

John perked up at the news of GIs escaping, hoping the

conversation would continue in that direction. He'd feel much better if he knew Caleb was among them.

President Blake turned his attention to Derek. "Would you care to explain yourself, officer?"

"Yes, sir, Mr. President," Derek answered in a commanding voice. "In the early hours of the morning, I had received direct orders from Officer Gunther to join the on-duty officers in a compound-wide manhunt. Finding the intruder was to be our number one priority. When I encountered the GIs in the tunnel, it was clear to me they were not the subject of our search. While that, of course, was a security concern, it was not my top priority at the time. So I made a split-second decision to ignore the GIs and continue looking for the intruder. Shortly after that, I encountered him in a dark alley. After sizing him up, I decided against using force to apprehend him. Instead, I chose to act as an ally, promising to help him get to safety. To my surprise, he agreed and began following me. That's when we ran into Officers Gunther and Renick, and luckily, I might add. I'm not sure if he would have ambushed me from behind, given the chance."

John couldn't blame Derek for trying to protect himself. It was his own fault that he was in this situation, not Derek's. And if Derek could clear his name, he would have a friend on the inside.

President Blake looked back at George. "You see? There's a perfectly good explanation for his actions."

"Sir, you can't possibly believe—"

"I'm not finished," President Blake interrupted sharply. "*Your* actions, on the other hand, are not… *representative* of your given title as head security officer. Your number one responsibility is to maintain the security of this compound. Today, you failed miserably in this regard."

"But sir, I—"

President Blake slapped George across his face with the back of his hand. The sound reverberated through the room like the crack of a whip. John and Derek winced in unison. George instinctively cowered and put his fingers to his cheek before hurrying to stand back at attention with his arms at his sides. A trickle of blood ran down from his lip, coloring the edge of his handlebar mustache crimson.

"*Still. Not. Finished,*" President Blake said coldly. "Then, when the intruder was located, you not only took credit for finding him, but you also chose to punish the security officer who followed your direct orders and made his apprehension possible?"

George nodded reluctantly. "Yes, sir."

"Well, Officer Gunther, you've demonstrated a... *remarkable* inability to perform even the most basic duties of your job. You've failed. And failure has *consequences.*"

Suspense hung in the air as George's eyes followed President Blake back and forth over what felt like several minutes of silent contemplation. George's fear was palpable. Sweat ran down his face, forming small streams that traveled parallel to the red river streaking down his chin.

President Blake appeared to enjoy every second of George's mental anguish, stopping and glancing at him occasionally as if he was going to continue speaking, only to resume his pacing, rubbing his chin as though in deep thought.

Eventually, President Blake came to a stop and turned to face George, gesturing with his hands as he spoke.

"When I was a child, my father used to beat me senseless every day when he got home from work. *Every* day. I tried to make sense of these beatings. Certainly, I had done *something* wrong to deserve such a punishment.

"In my childish mind, the world had order. Good choices were rewarded, and poor choices were punished. As they should be. So in my efforts to identify the source of my father's... *displeasure,* I tried my best to make sure the house was spotless every day. Some days, I would clean from the time I got up until he got home. I even resorted to having dinner on the table when he returned from work. Do you want to know what I got for my efforts?"

George stared ahead silently, seemingly afraid to even blink.

"I got beaten. Every. Day. Harder and harder and *harder*." President Blake continued, his voice raising in a crescendo as he smacked the back of his hand into the palm of his other one with matching intensity.

"Eventually," he continued at his normal volume, "I stopped trying to appease a man whose only joy came from my suffering. My inner child died that day, along with my naive idea of a fair and just world." President Blake paused briefly before going on. "Until one day, I was busy cutting my father's steak up for him when walked up behind me and smacked me clear across the kitchen. Then he lunged at me, and I... *instinctively* extended my hand forward, plunging the steak knife into his neck. I still remember the blood gushing from him, soaking my clothes as I watched the life slowly leave his eyes. That *exact* moment was when I realized my true purpose in life."

He began walking around again as he spoke, his voice becoming more animated. "You see, I wasn't wrong in believing in a fair and just world. No, such a world *was* possible. The piece that was missing, the thing that took me so long to figure out, was that it was *my* destiny to ensure the world is fair and just. The knife in my hand that day was fate. I was chosen to give my father the justice he deserved; to restore... *balance* to the world."

Again, he turned to face George, looking him in his eyes. "The point I'm trying to make, George, is that I was born to lead. And what kind of leader would I be if I didn't punish you for your failures?"

President Blake nodded at the security officers standing behind George. They approached him from behind, forcing him to his knees and restraining him by his arms. President Blake reached into the inner pocket of his navy suit's jacket and pulled out a small knife with a brown wooden handle and a serrated edge.

"This might hurt a little," President Blake said, staring down at the knife in his hand while he caressed the flat of the blade with his fingertips. He pointed the knife at the kneeling man's left side. "Left hand."

The officer restraining George's left arm wrestled it forward.

George struggled against the weight of the three men holding him in place. "No, no, no, you don't have to do this. I got the message loud and clear!"

"Oh, but I do," President Blake said, reaching down and grabbing George's pinky finger. A loud crack was followed by a blood-curdling howl from George.

"It's easier if it's broken first," he said plainly before lowering the knife down to George's hand.

George began hyperventilating, eyes wide with shock at what he was witnessing. His quickened breathing turned to a deafening shriek. John had to look away.

Then, suddenly the screaming stopped as George lost consciousness and his head flopped forward; his body was dead weight to the men holding him in place.

"There we go," President Blake said as he tossed George's pinky finger to the ground like a mechanic tossing out an old part before replacing it with a new one. "Get him out of here." President Blake waved his hands dismissively, blood dripping from his fingers to the puddle on the floor. They hauled George away, leaving a trail of crimson along the floor behind them.

Two additional security officers approached President Blake, offering handkerchiefs. After wiping his knife and hands clean, he returned the knife to his pocket and straightened his jacket.

He spun around to face John and Derek. "My apologies. I haven't exactly been the best host," he said with a smile, running his fingers through his brown hair. "Due to the nature of my work, I'm often forced to tie up loose ends during what should be a more... social affair."

"So," President Blake continued, shifting his eyes back and forth between John and Derek, his eyes eventually settling on the former. "Johnathan Shaw, what brings you here?"

CHAPTER FIFTEEN

Light flickered through the crack in the freight car door as the sun rose over the horizon, shining between the trees as the train rushed full-speed ahead. Caleb battled his eyelids, raising his eyebrows to help force his eyes open. He glanced down at his watch. A few more minutes and his shift would be over, and he could finally get some rest.

When they snuck aboard the southbound cargo train, they all agreed it would be best to have one person always awake in case it stopped. They didn't know where it was headed—they just needed to get far away from OASIS as quickly as possible. When it reached its destination, they could reassess their situation and find better transportation. Caleb volunteered to take the first shift, a choice he had been regretting for the last hour or so.

If there was one positive thing about being required to stay awake it was that he had a chance to process the events of the last night.

The interaction with Officer Thorington played through his mind on a loop. He could still hear "CJ" as clear as day. But the more he thought about it, the more he convinced himself Officer Thorington wasn't his father. If he was, Caleb imagined, he would have just told him, or at least come with them. It didn't add up.

Caleb also considered the road ahead. Imagining meeting his mother for the first time sent a jolt of excitement through him, but it was quickly dampened when he remembered she was in danger. They still didn't have a solid plan to reach her. He could only hope Rava's contact was good.

All of his current problems aside, his plan had *worked*. They'd escaped OASIS. The feeling of freedom was surreal.

With fatigue threatening to shut his mind off after a long night of navigating through a thick forest, Caleb positioned his head so the pulsating sunlight hit him directly in his eyes. He thought it would help keep him awake, but instead the strobing rays felt quite soothing, like a massage for his eyeballs.

Just as he was about to lose the ongoing battle for consciousness, his wrist began to vibrate. His shift was over.

Caleb made his way over to Rava, who was nestled up against a pallet of steel poles, using a sandbag as a pillow.

He nudged her awake gingerly. "Hey, Rava, time for your shift."

She inhaled heavily, squinting up at him and then took in her surroundings as though she had forgotten where they were. She silently nodded before crawling over to her post in the middle of the train car.

His face hit the sandbag and he was out in an instant.

Caleb was awoken to Dusty hollering and shaking him frantically. "Wake up! Let's go! The train stopped. We need to disembark before we're found."

It felt as if he had just fallen asleep. Although he wanted to roll over and ignore his friend in favor of more sleep, he pushed himself up off the floor and lifted his bag onto his back as Rava did the same.

They jumped to the ground. Caleb wasn't sure where they were, but it was clear to him they were farther south than he had ever been before. The air was at least twenty degrees hotter and rich with the scent of fresh pine.

It was common knowledge that the southern half of Materra was warmer, rarely seeing snowfall during the winter months. In fact, outside of northern Materra, the only other places where it regularly snowed were the northern tip of Crayna and atop various mountains.

Looking down the tracks, Caleb could see the locomotive bend around a corner and disappear behind trees. They had to be close to a city, he reasoned.

Following a brief discussion, they all agreed on the best course of action. They set off through the woods in the direction of the front of the train, reaching the other side within minutes.

The forest opened up into a wide clearing of overgrown green grass that was sloped slightly down, providing them with a great view overlooking the city from the tree line.

Red brick buildings littered the compact cityscape with houses of various colors peppering the outskirts. It was a relatively small town. John used to refer to these sorts of places as "railroad cities," implying they only existed because a train needed a place to stop. Taking in the sights, Caleb guessed he was right.

As they scoured the landscape for a building that appeared to be a bank, Caleb instinctively started forming a map of the city's layout in his mind. Then he stopped. While he technically could have done so without the use of his cartography module, he wasn't sure he was doing it completely on his own. He was finished with the brain drive. They would be able to find their way around the city just fine without it.

After withdrawing their credits at the bank, they visited a local department store for a change of clothes. Traveling together in OASIS clothes would draw too much attention. Even if people didn't immediately recognize them, three kids traveling together in uniforms would look strange on its own.

Dusty chose to buy plain white T-shirts and a few pairs of tan cargo shorts. "White reflects sunlight better than any other color," he assured the others. "Well, it's technically not a color itself, but—"

"We get it," Rava said, loading the cart with solid black tank-tops and jean shorts.

Caleb had chosen whatever he could find in the clearance aisle, ending up with an assortment of out-of-style T-shirts and jean shorts of various colors. While he had plenty of credits, an uncertain future loomed over him. He thought it wise to save all the money he could.

Now that they had new outfits, their next goal was to find transportation to Rava's contact, who was located near Yule, a large coastal city on the southwest border of Materra.

They located the nearest brain drive terminal, where Dusty and Rava each uploaded a general reference map of Materra. As a free module, it contained only gross information such as knowledge of major highways and the locations of cities. Caleb's refusal to use his brain drive to upload the module came as a shock to his friends.

"That's idiotic," Rava said. "You have an amazing piece of technology at your disposal, and you're refusing to use it because *other* people abuse it for nefarious purposes?"

"You guys should understand better than anyone what I'm saying. You were both at OASIS much longer than I was. What they justify doing to kids there in the name of advancing technology is criminal. Besides, I got along just fine without it before."

"While I don't agree with the conclusion you've drawn," Dusty said, "I can respect your choice. I would like to point out, however, the irony at play here. The one member of our group who is trained in cartography is refusing to upload a map module." He chuckled, but neither Caleb or Rava joined in.

"I still think it's dumb," Rava added. "Regardless, we don't have time to sit around and chat about this. We have fifty-six miles to go before we get to Yule."

Caleb couldn't argue with that. They had yet to find proper

transportation.

"If we were to proceed on foot at an average walking pace, it would take us eleven hours—that is, assuming we're walking in a straight line and the terrain is fairly even," Dusty announced, as though he was going to start listing all of their options.

"We're *not* walking," Rava said before looking at Caleb. "Do you know how to drive?"

"Yeah, but where are we going to get a car?"

"Follow me," she said before taking off toward the department store.

Rava began walking through the parking lot, trying to open vehicle doors.

"Rava, what are you doing?" Dusty asked. "We could get in a lot of trouble for this."

"Calm down for once, Dusty. We're already fugitives who broke out of a classified government facility. Car theft would be the least of our worries if we're caught."

Dusty turned to Caleb as though asking for backup. He shrugged.

Just then, a door opened for Rava. She pulled her multitool out of her pack and bent down under the steering wheel. Caleb stopped her before she could even get started.

"Rava," he said, pointing at the back window. "Car seat."

She glanced into the rear and then lowered her head in defeat. Stealing a car was one thing. Stealing a car from a mother with an infant was out of the question. They'd have to find another.

The search didn't take long. The very next car she tried—a light brown sedan—was also unlocked. In less than a minute, she had it running.

"Full tank!" she called out from inside. "C'mon, boys, time to hit the road." Rava jogged around to the passenger seat and got in after throwing her bag in.

Caleb rushed over to the driver's side, doing the same. Dusty reluctantly plopped down in the back seat, next to all the backpacks, still clearly uncomfortable with lifting a car. Caleb shifted into gear and pulled away.

~*~

George Gunther woke from a cold sweat in a panic. He wiped his forehead with his hand to find it wrapped in blood-soaked gauze. A gasp accompanied the realization that his nightmare wasn't that at all. President Blake really *had* severed his pinky off.

He curled his remaining fingers into a fist. He could still feel all five digits moving, causing a strange disconnect between his physical sensation and his eyesight. He'd get used to it, he supposed. In reality, he'd have to. If there was one thing he knew about President Blake, it was that he had no use for unproductive individuals. The man was insane.

George sat up and swung his feet over the edge of his bed, sliding them into a pair of slippers. Once again, he found himself questioning whether or not he had played a part in creating the monster that tormented him to that day.

When Avery Blake was sentenced to his first stint in solitary confinement at the age of twelve, George had been the officer who was assigned to release him. He hadn't been thrilled about the task. Avery had a reputation for being an odd kid, and he gave George the creeps.

George had opened the cell to find the boy grinning up at him. A shiver ran down his spine. He'd ushered Avery to a brain drive terminal and pulled the interface cable toward his head. Avery snatched the man's wrist, startling him. He'd looked down and met the boy's dark eyes. "Leave them," Avery said with a smile. "I like them." George had hesitated, but in the end, he let him keep the modules.

Over the years, George had reflected on that decision multiple times. Every time he came to the same conclusion; he'd made a terrible mistake. In his mind, he'd helped cultivate Avery's brazen attitude and fearlessness. If he could go back in time and change one choice in his past, that would be it. He would return to that moment and refuse to let Avery walk out of there with those memories.

But he couldn't go back. He could only move forward. And he had a son to look after. George stood up and made his way into his closet, fetching a work suit. He didn't want to be late for his shift.

~*~

John was startled awake by the sound of the door opening. He lifted his strained neck to see President Blake enter the room, activating the overhead lights. Sleeping while cuffed to a chair was easier than he expected, but his neck hated him for it. It reminded him of when he used to fall asleep while watching boxing films of his opponents.

President Blake mimicked an announcer as he spoke. "In the red corner, fighting at a whopping two hundred and twenty-five pounds, Johnathan Shaw!" He began clapping boisterously, a smirk on his face. The sound echoed off the concrete walls.

"What happened to you, John? I remember watching you dismantle every heavyweight fighter Materra could produce. You held that title for what, five straight years?"

John didn't respond, his face expressionless. He didn't owe the man any explanation.

"Then one day I turned on the television to see you'd abruptly entered into an early retirement, sending the boxing world into a frenzy overnight. It didn't make sense to me. You were on top of the world, and you just threw it all away."

President Blake sat down in a metal folding chair opposite John, the only other piece of furniture in the room. But unlike John's, his seat wasn't bolted to the ground. He leaned back, crossing one leg over the other and running his hand through his slick hair.

"But now, I've figured it all out. You see, there was one

other… *significant* piece of information I remembered about the day you announced your retirement. On the same day you left boxing for good, a certain… *treasonous* couple mysteriously disappeared." His voice was filled with disgust.

"At first, I didn't make the connection. I understood why *you* were here. A determined father trying to free his son from the clutches of the big, bad government. Really, a truly heartwarming story. And you were *so* close."

President Blake leaned forward and began to speak almost in a whisper. "But once I realized the link between your retirement and the disappearance of Derek and Emily Foster, I've got to say, my mind was… *tickled*. I mean, what an ingenious plan. They fake their deaths and go into hiding while you raise their son for them, keeping him a secret. I honestly wish I had advisors as cunning as those two."

He stood up and began walking around the room. "Of course, I knew from the beginning they had faked their deaths. What are the odds that they would die in a freak accident right after I ordered their execution? At the time, it was to our advantage to let them think they'd gotten away with it. I knew one day they would resurface, and I'd have my chance to deliver justice. And guess what?" he said with a hint of excitement in his voice while he looked at his reflection in the large mirror on the wall. "I was right! In more ways than one, actually. But can you blame me for being thrown off? Because *that*"—suddenly, the mirror faded away, turning into translucent glass—"does *not* look like Derek Foster."

John could see his best friend handcuffed to a similar chair in the room next door. His head was hanging forward with his chin to his chest, his face bloodied and badly bruised. Red streaks ran down his face and neck, dripping into his lap.

"And not because of what I did to him," President Blake said. "Even before all that… *work,* he looked like a completely different person."

Anger flared through every fiber of John's being. He lunged

forward, his strength testing the durability of the handcuffs that bound him, ultimately coming up short. He sat there, seething, his breaths coming quicker as if preparing for a fight, and his eyes staring daggers at President Blake. Gone was the typical boyish look to his face, replaced with a feral expression like that of an aggravated lion.

"There he is," President Blake exclaimed. "*That's* the Johnathan Shaw I remember from twenty years ago."

"Take these cuffs off, and I'll introduce you," he growled.

President Blake waved his hand in a dismissive fashion. "Oh, don't be so dramatic, Johnathan. Unfortunately, I can't *kill* either of you. How else would I lure Caleb back here?"

John's anger faded as quickly as it arrived, replaced by equal parts concern and confusion.

"No need to worry; Caleb is safe. He's currently on his way to Aridor to find his mother."

"What?" John replied, his narrow eyes conveying his skepticism. "Aridor? There's nothing over there."

"That's what they want you to think," President Blake said, beginning to pace again. "As it turns out, that *traitor*, Emily, is heading up a research facility out there. She's been working on some interesting technology. Technology that I'd very much like to get my hands on. However, my inside contact never made it to the last rendezvous, leaving me with no way to locate her. Now, I could go kicking down doors out there and eventually find her, but I don't want to draw attention from the rest of the world and I would also... *appreciate* her cooperation in the matter. She may prove to be useful."

He stopped to face John directly. "And that's precisely why I convinced Caleb to find her for me."

John tensed up again, his icy glare fixated on President Blake. It was one thing to toy with him. It was another thing altogether to put Caleb's life in danger. If given the chance, he swore to himself he'd make sure Avery Blake understood that very clearly.

"Like I said, he's in good hands. I have my best special operations team tailing him and his friends as we speak. They have direct orders to... *diffuse* any situations that may arise."

John looked President Blake directly in his dark eyes. "If anything happens to my son, I promise you I will make you swallow that cute little knife of yours."

President Blake chuckled and shook his head as he reached his hand into his inner jacket pocket. He pulled out a brown-handled blade and began gently stroking it. "I wish you wouldn't have said that. Choices have consequences, Mr. Shaw."

~*~

"There it is," Rava said, pointing at a sign that read *Seaside Motel*. Caleb pulled the car up to the front of the building and parked.

"Are you sure this is the place?" Caleb asked, studying the building's exterior with a skeptic eye. The motel was two stories high and covered in white aluminum siding that was riddled with dents. The bottom two feet was stained a faint yellow color as though the lower part of the building had once been submerged in liquid for some time. A crooked wooden staircase led to a rickety balcony that allowed access to the rooms on the second floor. When looking beyond the motel at the ocean, it felt entirely out of place. It looked as though someone had plucked two metal mobile homes from a run-down trailer park and stacked them on top of one another on a bluff overlooking the ocean.

"This is it," she responded with certainty, an endearing smile on her face.

As they exited the vehicle, a warm sea breeze brushed over Caleb, blowing his shaggy black hair out of his eyes. The salt was so heavy in the air that he felt like he could taste it.

Walking toward the main entrance, they were caught off-guard by a portly old woman in a blue bathrobe that was staring at them out of room four. Her squinted eyes followed them all the way to the entrance.

Dusty pulled at the neck of his new T-shirt as they entered the motel, as if the hole was too tight.

The interior of the motel was even more run-down than the exterior. Striped green wallpaper bubbled and peeled away from the walls like it was melting off. The white and green vinyl flooring was marred with cracks and stains. Sparsely-placed light fixtures provided a bare minimum amount of light, adding another element to the ramshackle feel of the motel.

Rava approached the front desk and rang the bell. A door behind the desk opened and the old lady in the blue bathrobe waddled out.

"How can I help you?" she said, grunting.

"I'm looking for Marcus," Rava answered.

The old woman scratched her mole-covered neck. "No Marcus here. Sorry, you must have the wrong place." She turned around and began walking back toward the room she came from.

"Wait," called Rava, "Tell him…"

The woman stopped but didn't turn around.

Rava looked from Caleb to Dusty and then back at the woman. "Tell him his *daughter*, Rava, is here."

The woman, without turning around, opened the door and went back through it. Rava backed up from the desk to find both Dusty and Caleb staring at her blankly, mouths hanging wide open.

"Your dad?" Caleb asked. "Your contact is your *dad*? Why didn't you tell us?" It wasn't a total surprise to him. Rava was extremely tight-lipped about her family. But it was shocking to Caleb that she hadn't given them a heads-up.

"Technically, no. Remember when I told you we came over to Materra on a refugee ship when I was ten?"

Caleb nodded. Dusty stared and listened intently.

"Well," Rava looked down at her hands as if they held the words she was searching for, "I didn't tell you the whole story."

She swallowed hard and continued. "My family needed out of Aridor badly. We boarded the first ship available, and it happened to be run by sharks."

"Sharks?" Caleb asked.

"Yeah, sharks. They're smugglers that prey on naive and desperate people, not unlike my parents. They find ways to extort them, like promising to take them to Materra for a reasonable fee and then hiking the prices up after the ship arrives."

Dusty looked appalled. "What if they can't pay?"

"Refugees who can't pay the additional amount are either taken back to Aridor or forced to work off their debt to the sharks here in Materra. If they don't make payments on time, the sharks pay the family a visit and *remind* them, often through violent means."

Rava paused before carrying on, her voice shaky. "You should have seen the look on my father's face when the shores of Materra came into view. He was so… proud."

A tear ran down her face. She wiped it away before going on.

"The sharks had us right where they wanted us. When we tried to get off the ship, they demanded we pay them triple the agreed-upon rate. They even threatened to send me and my mother back to Aridor until my father could earn enough credits to pay the fee. My father was known to have a fiery nature—my mother used to tell me I got her eyes and his temper—and he was having none of it. He started screaming at them and rallying the rest of the passengers around him. Everybody was waving their fists in the air and shouting. So the sharks decided to make an example out of my father."

Rava sniffed and wiped at her eyelids, fighting back tears. "One downside to having an eidetic memory is I can still see it all happen as if it was yesterday. The leader of the sharks pulled out a gun and aimed it at my father's head. He never even saw it. He turned around to look back at me and my mother, and he must have seen the look of horror on my face because his expression changed immediately. He looked worried and confused. It was like he thought something was wrong with *me* and his fatherly instincts kicked in. And then the shark pulled the trigger, and he was just... gone."

This time, she lost the battle with her emotions, and tears flooded down her face.

Unsure of the proper reaction in this situation, Caleb trusted his gut and pulled Rava in, wrapping his arms around her. She covered her face with her hands and nestled into his chest.

"I'm so sorry," Caleb said. "I had no idea."

Dusty reached up and patted her on the shoulder.

Seeing Rava so vulnerable was new to Caleb. He viewed her as a strong person with unshakable resolve, someone he respected for always knowing what she wanted and expressing it unequivocally. But as he held her, he felt like he was getting a peek behind the veil of her tough persona, seeing the real Rava— a scared girl whose past still haunted her.

After a few minutes, she gathered herself and stepped backward. "Marcus was at the dock that day, hoping to hire a few refugees. He saw everything. After my father was killed, he generously paid them for our freedom and gave us a place to stay."

She looked down the hall. "We stayed in room six. He also gave my mother a job at the motel. She vowed to pay every credit back, but he would have none of it. He never accepted a single credit in return. A year later, my mother was diagnosed with late-stage kidney cancer and she passed away shortly after that. Marcus let me stay here after my mother died, and he treated me as one of his own. I haven't seen him since I was taken away to OASIS. Sorry, I should have told you guys this sooner."

"You don't need to apologize for that," Caleb said.

"Yeah," Dusty agreed. "You had every right to your privacy."

Out of the corner of his eye, Caleb saw a man walking down the hall toward them. He looked past Rava to get a better view of him.

He was a short man who appeared to be in his fifties or sixties, wearing a tight neon yellow and green full-body wetsuit, though he appeared to be dry at the moment. His tan skin was a few shades darker than Rava's, and he wore his salt-and-pepper hair in a tight buzz cut. Beneath a pair of bushy gray eyebrows were droopy eyelids that draped over the outer corners of his deep-set eyes.

Rava noticed that Caleb was looking past her, and she whipped around.

"Marcus," she exclaimed, sprinting down the hall and bending down to hug him tightly.

"Rava, it's so good to see you! My, you've grown. Last time I saw you, you were shorter than me. Now look at you." Marcus stood back, looking Rava up and down as though admiring the person she'd become. A broad smile illuminated his clean-shaven face, revealing numerous missing teeth.

He grabbed both of her hands, holding them in his. "Are you well? You look like you've been crying. Are these your friends? Are you in danger?"

Rava chuckled. "I'm fine, Marcus, really. I was just telling my friends here how we met. This is Caleb, and this is Dusty. They're my friends from OASIS."

Caleb smiled and waved at Marcus while Dusty nodded in his direction.

"Listen, can we go somewhere to talk?" Rava asked. "I have a favor to ask of you."

Marcus smiled at her. "I'll put on some tea."

CHAPTER SIXTEEN

"No, absolutely not!" Marcus slammed his mug down on the kitchen table, which appeared to be carved from a large piece of driftwood. He wiped his mouth with the sleeve of his wetsuit.

Marcus's apartment, occupying nearly a quarter of the motel's first floor, was filled with repurposed items masquerading as furniture and fixtures. Two benches made of old surfboards and stumps surrounded the driftwood table. Various chairs, shelves, and tables were fashioned out of retired dock wood. Multicolored wind chimes made of fishing line, polished seashells, and broken glass hung from the ceiling. To say he was crafty would be an understatement.

That struck Rava as odd. She had no recollection of Marcus building furnishings before. He must have picked up the hobby over the years. It had been five years since she had last been there, and Marcus's apartment looked completely different.

"C'mon, Marcus, his mother is in real danger!" Rava pleaded. While that was true, she couldn't help but feel a little guilty about her ulterior motive. Of course, helping Caleb locate his mother was her top priority, but she'd be lying if she said she wasn't excited about revisiting Aridor again for the first time in seven years.

"You have no idea what it's like over there now. Gangs have taken over the entire continent." His voice was firm with conviction. "I haven't flown there in over a year now. It's too dangerous. I won't risk all of our lives for this."

He paused, letting his words sink in before continuing in a softer tone. "I'm sorry, but his mother chose the wrong place to go into hiding." He looked at Caleb with sympathy, his bushy eyebrows furrowed. "No disrespect to you or your mother, but I can't help you."

Rava leaned back against the surfboard that made up the back of the bench, crossing her arms. Caleb shot her a look that told her he was surprised to see her abandon the argument so quickly. But he didn't know Marcus like she did. Once he'd made his mind up, there was no changing it.

Caleb leaned in, resting his forearms on the smooth tabletop. "Is there *anyone* you know who could help us get to Aridor? My mother needs me, and with or without your help, I'm going."

"No. Unfortunately, I don't know a single soul who's making trips there these days. Back when I first started bringing refugees over, there were still camps and makeshift cities. It wasn't much of a society, but it was at least something. Over the last ten years or so, the populations dwindled down to nothing due to pressure from gangs looking to seize more territory. Some refugees immigrated to other countries, while those who stayed were forced to either become nomads or join a gang. These cities were the final heartbeats of a dying nation; when they fell, Aridor died. Of course, people still live there and call it home, but the way I see it, they are maggots living in the rotting carcass of a once great nation. I'm surprised gangs haven't taken over your mother's facility at this point." Marcus took another swig of his tea, finishing it before putting the cup back down.

It was shocking to hear Marcus talk about Aridor like that. Of all of the immigrants Rava knew, Marcus took more pride in his heritage than any of them. It must have been much worse over there than she remembered.

"You wouldn't happen to own an aviation module that I could upload to operate a plane, would you?" Dusty asked.

"I don't have any flight modules. But even if I did, it would never substitute for experience. Just like describing a sunset to a blind person wouldn't mean they could draw one."

Caleb looked up at the ceiling as though he was pondering the analogy before looking back at Marcus. "How did you learn to fly?" he asked.

"My father taught me at a young age. I first learned in a little two-seater he bought and fixed-up himself. Eventually, I graduated to a small passenger plane. My father was a fighter pilot for Aridor. He died defending our country in the Great War."

Marcus paused for a second, staring down into his empty mug before producing a light chuckle through a smile. "That man made sure I knew how to fly before I knew how to drive a car. He always talked about how planes were safer and being in the cockpit was the best way—"

"He was right," Dusty blurted out to no one in particular. "Statistically speaking, air travel is over a hundred times safer than automobile travel." He suddenly pulled a notebook from his backpack and began scribbling furiously as if struck with an inescapable urge to put his thoughts onto paper.

Rava rolled her eyes. She wondered if she was going to be able to put up with Dusty for the duration of the trip. It wasn't so much his behavior that annoyed her—it was his arrogance that rubbed her the wrong way. Though she guessed he might feel the same about her.

"Anyway," Marcus said.

"Yes, moving on," Caleb said before reaching into his bag and pulling out his hand-drawn maps of Aridor. He spread them out over the table and pointed to a marked city on the east coast. "Can you at least tell us everything you know about the current state of Portan?"

"Never been there. What I do know is that this entire area"—

Marcus circled a large part of the eastern coast with his finger—
"is all under the control of a gang known as the Scorpions."

"Scorpions?" Caleb asked. "Anything we should know about
them?"

"Not much I can tell you, I'm afraid. As you might imagine,
ammunition is hard to come by out there, so most gangs stick to
using handheld weapons. I don't know anything about the
Scorpions, though. I never had to travel that far south."

Caleb met her eyes and she knew he was thinking the same
thing. "Everyone at your mother's facility was armed with a
gun, right?"

He nodded. "As far as I could tell. They must be pretty well-
hidden to still have ammunition at this point."

She returned a nod.

Caleb sat up straight, gathering his maps up off the table.
"Well, I appreciate all of the information you—"

"Heart disease, cancer…" Dusty's eyes were glued to his
notebook as he spoke, but he was facing Marcus, who was
seated next to him. "Stroke, pulmonary disease, degenerative
brain disease, automobile accident, hurricane. Statistically,
taking into account your location, age, and lifestyle, you are
most likely to die from one of the causes I just listed. And if
you're curious as to which is most probable, I listed them in
order of highest to lowest probability. Heart disease was most
probable by a wide margin."

Marcus stared blankly at Dusty.

"Dusty!" Rava snapped, glaring in his direction before turning
to Marcus. "I'm so sorry, Marcus. He can be rude sometimes."

Dusty scowled in Rava's direction. "I was simply stating
statistical facts in order to help Marcus reevaluate his decision.
Marcus, I ask you this one question for your consideration: if a
life isn't worth risking, is it even a life worth living?"

Rava's embarrassment bubbled over into anger. He had no
right to speak to Marcus like that, she thought. She leaned over
the table to give Dusty an earful. "What is wrong with you? If

you knew how many times this man has risked his life for others, you wouldn't—"

Marcus raised a hand and gently pushed Rava back down into her seat. "Calm down."

She sat back down, but kept her cold stare fixed on Dusty. She'd definitely overestimated her ability to put up with him.

"He's... actually got a point," Marcus said.

Rava's gaze darted from Dusty to Marcus, a dumbfounded expression on her face. "What?"

"I guess it's true that my life *has* lost some of its purpose lately. In my younger years, I was fearless, probably to a fault at times. I had so much drive and passion. I wanted to save the people my father died defending. It was all I wanted for such a long time. It was my calling. Ever since I ran out of refugees to rescue, I guess I've been trying to find myself again." While his eyelids were normally droopy, they seemed to be sagging a bit more now. "I've been keeping myself busy here with the motel, but the truth is I go to bed every night and wake up every morning feeling the same: unfulfilled. I even tried my hand at crafts and woodworking." Marcus gestured around the apartment as though his handiwork didn't speak for itself. "Now it just feels like I've been wasting what little time I have left decorating my coffin. What *life* am I even worried about protecting?"

Rava looked sympathetically across the wooden table at the man she'd grown to admire. He looked deflated. She'd never seen him like this before. He was known for his positive attitude and near-permanent smile. In her opinion, he shouldn't have to feel like that. He'd already dedicated so much of his life to helping others. Rava believed if anyone deserved to relax and enjoy their elderly years, it was Marcus.

Her anger raised back to the surface. She felt like this was all Dusty's fault. Not only did he insult Marcus, but he had managed to make him feel bad about himself in the process.

She reached over the table and took Marcus's hand, holding it firmly. "Without you, I wouldn't be here." An encouraging smile formed at the corner of her lips.

As a formality, Marcus smiled back.

She knew he appreciated her kind words, but that wouldn't be enough. He needed a change; something to bring him *purpose*. It wasn't something that would come from words in a greeting card. And Rava understood it wasn't something she could give him.

He met Rava's gaze. "I'm in. We leave at first light tomorrow."

Rava's eyes went wide, and Caleb let out a celebratory cheer. She looked over at Dusty to see his reaction. He was smiling to himself as he closed his notebook and packed it away. Maybe she hadn't given him enough credit.

~*~

The six-seater seaplane came to an idle crawl, the power of its propeller pulling it slowly across the choppy waves.

Having no former experience flying, Caleb felt a rush of joyous relief to be alive. He wasn't sure if landing was always that rough, or if it was because they were landing on water, but he was too polite to ask. Besides, no one else seemed phased at all.

If there was one thought Caleb clung to as the plane descended, it was that crashing in the water would probably be safer than crashing on land. He didn't dare to ask Dusty if that was true. Instead, he just clung tightly to his life jacket.

Portan's marina had seen better days. Lack of upkeep had left most of the docks crumbling and falling into the water. Not a single boat floated in the harbor. Only fully or partially sunken watercraft remained, making the waters difficult to navigate. Although Marcus seemed to have no trouble docking the plane on a half-submerged aluminum dock.

"All clear," he called out from the dock. "Watch your footing down here. If you can't swim, keep your lifejacket on."

Rava was the first one out. She climbed down the metal rungs on the seaplane's legs. Caleb removed his lifejacket and followed. Dusty kept his firmly strapped on until they reached land.

They navigated the flimsy pier carefully. After they made it to shore, a palpable feeling of shared relief washed over the group. It had held up under their weight.

Rava looked down the beach with a fond smile on her face, taking a deep breath as though she loved the way the air smelled. To Caleb, it was the same as where they came from.

"All right, you have four hours to get her and get back here," Marcus reminded them. "I can't risk sticking around too long."

They all exchanged nervous glances.

Caleb gave a firm nod. "Let's go."

From the beach, the city of Portan made a better impression than from the sky. Buildings that were taller than any Caleb had ever seen before towered over the city, gleaming in the sunlight. These enormous skyscrapers carried on as far as Caleb could see down the shore in either direction, forming a luminous silver skyline, a stark contrast to the sparkling beaches of white sand that stretched along the coast.

A row of untrimmed palm trees separated the city from the beach, their sagging dead leaves hanging from the green canopies like gray beards, obscuring any view of the streets.

They made their way from the shore to the pavement. "I bet there are tons of bird nests in here," Dusty said as they passed through the wall of palm trees to the other side.

Up close, the city was much less impressive. Winding cracks crawled through the uneven streets, weeds and grass sprouting up to fill every inch of them. Once-busy thoroughfares were now clogged with broken-down cars, rubble, and trash. Old storefronts were marred with torn canopies and shattered windows, the glass shards adding to the debris below.

It was a bizarre sight. Parts of the city looked frozen in time, like the sign that was still flipped to *Open For Business* on an old pastry shop, while other parts of the city looked aged, such as a van with vines growing into and through its smashed-out windows.

Fortunately, they had yet to see any locals. Caleb figured the Scorpions would have no need to patrol near the sea, since it was a natural barrier to attacks from rival gangs.

Aside from the chatter of birds and other animals, the streets were filled with a haunting silence.

The lack of other people in such a large city made Caleb uncomfortable as he led the way through the empty streets. Dusty must have been feeling the same because he kept his head on a swivel, constantly checking behind them as he followed. Rava appeared at ease, strolling along while casually swinging her arms and looking at the storefronts as though browsing for a place to shop.

When they were about half way to their destination, all of the animals suddenly fell silent. Dusty noticed immediately, stopping in his tracks. "I'm not so certain we picked the right city," he said, unease straining his vocal cords.

"We *picked* the right city," Rava said.

Just then, a loud choppy sound echoed from above, growing louder by the second. A black helicopter appeared over the rooftops and continued on in the direction they were heading. Caleb shared a confused glance with Rava. "They have a helicopter?" he asked. He knew the answer, but he was hoping he was wrong.

"It's highly unlikely," Dusty answered.

"It's Blake," Rava said with certainty. "He must have sent his team to your mother's compound already." She was right, and he knew it. But something didn't add up. They were way too early for the operation.

"Let's pick up the pace," Caleb said before taking off after the helicopter. He didn't have time to try to make sense of the situation. He needed to play the cards he was dealt. Whether it was President Blake's team or not, someone was heading toward his mother's facility, and he had to find it before they did.

A few blocks later, Caleb stopped in his tracks. Rava and Dusty caught up a few seconds later, bending over to catch their breath. "What's going on?" she asked. "We can keep up."

That wasn't the reason he stopped, but Caleb looked over at Dusty, who was wheezing heavily once again, and wondered if that was actually true. He saved his breath and instead pointed.

The two-story brick building at the end of their block had boarded up windows. A large symbol roughly resembling a scorpion enclosed in a circle was spray-painted on the side of the building in red spray paint.

"Scorpions..." she muttered.

"We could go a couple blocks that way and circle back," Dusty suggested, pointing to their left.

"We don't have time for that," Caleb said. "This could be an abandoned hideout. We could take our chances, try to sneak by."

"Could be," Rava said, sounding much less hopeful than Caleb.

"*Could* be?" Dusty screeched. "It could be their main base of operation for all we know. Let's go around."

Caleb stared at the structure, looking for any clues that suggested it had been deserted. He knew Dusty was right—the safest choice was to go around. But every minute they wasted was another minute his mother was in danger. If it was only him, he'd sprint past the building and hope for the best, but he had his friends to worry about.

"How about this? I'll scout the area ahead. You two wait in that bus stop." He pointed to a shelter down the street that had a clear view of the building.

"If I make it safely, I'll signal you guys. If I get into any trouble, I'll make a run for it and you guys sneak around the other way and we can meet up there."

Rava hesitated, but agreed. Dusty accepted the compromise with a half-nod.

Caleb approached the intersection with caution. The building in question had every window covered, though as he got closer, he noticed small holes in the wood. Peepholes, he imagined. He could see why they would pick such a place for a hideout. Compared to its neighbors, this one was basically brand new. There were no cracks in the walls and no chunks of brick missing. It appeared to be a bank, so there was probably a vault of some sort for storing valuable resources.

Sneaking along the edge, Caleb decided to peek through one of the boards to look inside. It was no use. All he saw was darkness. That could be a good sign, he thought.

"Whatcha doin'?" asked an unfamiliar voice from behind him.

Caleb spun around to find himself staring down three people approaching him slowly from across the street.

The woman who spoke was tan-skinned with long, wild black hair. She wore a red bikini top and jean shorts that looked like they had been cut from pants. In her left hand she carried a metal claw hammer while her right hand was balled into a fist. A crude black pincer was tattooed on the back of both of her hands.

To her left was a man about the size of Caleb who had the same shade of skin as the woman. He was shirtless and wearing stained khaki shorts. A good majority of his bare, muscular chest was covered in scars. Short, jagged black hair covered his head like a mop. He carried a baseball bat in his hands, bringing it up and down to slap it against his palm in a menacing fashion. Like the woman next to him, both of his hands also bore pincer tattoos.

Another tan-skinned man was to the woman's right, but he was much shorter and skinnier than his counterpart. His slick black hair was pulled back into a short ponytail. He wore an oversized, dirty white T-shirt with the sleeves ripped off. Caleb assumed he was wearing shorts, but the T-shirt draped around him like a dress so there was no way to tell. He tossed a small switchblade knife back and forth from one tattooed hand to the other as he approached.

"Hey," Caleb said as he put his hands into the air. "I mean you guys no harm. I'm just passing through. I'm looking for my mother, and I believe she's here in Portan."

The woman burst out into boisterous laughter, looking back and forth at the two men flanking her. "I don't know about you guys, but I haven't seen any people around here who look like *him*." Her laughter cut off abruptly, her face settling into a stone-cold expression. "You'll have to try better than that."

"I'm telling the truth. I understand this is Scorpion territory, and I appreciate you giving me a chance to explain. I don't have any way to prove I'm being honest, but you have my word. I will be out of your hair before you know it."

"Your word, huh?" The woman stared at Caleb for a moment. "Get him."

The two men lunged toward Caleb at once.

The larger man made it to him first, swinging the baseball bat at his head. Caleb ducked under the bat, and the man lost his footing under the momentum of his swing. This gave Caleb a brief moment to turn his attention to the smaller one.

He stood up and faced the man with a ponytail, who was pulling his knife back, readying it to stab him. Caleb hit him with a quick left jab. The man stumbled and fell backward, catching himself and landing on his rear, blood gushing from his nose.

Caleb turned back toward the shirtless man to find a baseball bat swinging at his midsection. He leapt backward in the nick of time, barely avoiding a hit to his gut.

He took his opening and sprang forward again, launching an uppercut that caught the shirtless man on his chin and sent him flying onto his back. The bat flew from his hands, clanking on the pavement as the man reached up and covered his face.

Caleb spun around to see the skinny man lunging at him again, holding the knife. With one arm, Caleb grabbed the wrist of the man's knife-wielding hand and twisted it behind his back.

At the same time, he wrapped his other arm around the man's neck, putting him in a headlock. He twisted the arm he had pinned until the man dropped the knife and then hurled him to the ground.

"Please, stop," Caleb pleaded. "I'm not here to fight."

As he glanced over his shoulder to check on the larger guy, Caleb caught a glimpse of a wooden baseball bat inches from his face before his vision went black.

~*~

Caleb woke up to Rava shaking him. "Caleb! Wake up! We have to get out of here. Dusty, grab his legs!"

His vision was slowly coming into focus as he struggled to uncross his eyes. A throbbing pain radiated from the side of his head, clouding his thoughts. He raised his hand to his head, running his fingers over the large lump on the side. He winced and retracted it immediately. Still battling for control of his eye muscles, Caleb looked down to see two blurry right hands with blood running from the fingertips.

"Where are we? What happened?"

"You got cracked in the head pretty good with a bat," Rava answered, helping Caleb to his feet. He clung to her while he tried to regain balance, his vision finally snapping into place.

Caleb surveyed the scene. A small knife and a baseball bat lay on the ground next to a bleeding, shirtless man. It was coming back to him now. He had gotten into a fight with a few Scorpions.

Dusty bent down to gather the weapons on the ground. "After you lost consciousness, someone shot the guy who knocked you out, and the other two ran off."

He looked at the man on the ground again. At first glance, Caleb had assumed he was bleeding from his nose, but now he saw it. He had a bullet wound on his chest.

"We need to go before we get shot," Rava said. "Are you okay to run?"

"Yeah," he answered, peeling his gaze away from the man.

He'd never seen a dead person before. He'd seen his fair share of dead animals over the years, and that'd never gotten to him. But something about the look of a deceased person felt unnatural, like they weren't real.

The rest of their trek through the city was surprisingly uneventful, and a few minutes later, they stood in front of the building they were searching for.

It was massive, occupying almost half of the entire block. The exterior was made of glossy steel, and large windows covered the front, though all of them were broken.

Caleb's heart sank as he concluded it couldn't be the right place. The lack of boarded windows wasn't the main reason he'd lost hope. It was because it was obvious that the property had suffered a devastating fire.

The upper half of the eight-story structure was covered in black soot, while the top two floors were nothing but a melted metal frame.

As Caleb walked closer, he got a better look at the charred interior, a colorless tapestry of black and gray with debris scattered about. Most of the interior walls on the first floor were burned down to the steel frame, though a few chunks of drywall remained standing among the wreckage. The ceiling of the first floor sagged in some areas, while it was completely gone in others, revealing a second floor that looked much the same.

"Well, this certainly is unfortunate," Dusty said, a hint of superiority in his voice.

"Not helping," Rava said, shooting an annoyed glance in his direction. "Caleb, I know maps are your thing and all, but is it possible we're off by a block or something?"

"No, this is it."

Caleb tipped his head forward into his hands, rubbing his eyes as if it would magically change the building into something else. It was supposed to be here. And yet he stood staring at a pile of incinerated junk instead of a research facility.

"I know she probably isn't here, but I *have* to make sure," he said. "We came all this way. Let's at least walk through and see what we find."

Dusty didn't object, but he stuck mainly to the perimeter, claiming the interior was too "structurally unsound" and he needed to be able to jump out quickly if the second floor collapsed onto the first for any reason.

Rava and Caleb searched the inside, looking for any clues that might indicate the facility was there. The more they searched, the clearer it became: they were in the wrong place.

Right when they were about to give up and head back empty-handed, Dusty found something interesting.

"Caleb, check this out! This part of the floor appears to have been swept." He pointed to an area that looked like a path had been cleared from a door to a large piece of charred drywall on the ground.

Caleb lifted the slab to reveal a concrete staircase leading down into pitch black.

Dusty pulled a flashlight from his backpack and tossed it to Caleb. He pointed it down into the darkness and saw a concrete hallway that continued left at the bottom of the stairwell. He couldn't see beyond the bend from where they were standing.

A nervous excitement blossomed inside Caleb as he descended down the stairs, Dusty and Rava close behind. It was difficult to imagine a research facility being down there, but *something* was.

Just like above, the dark hallway appeared to have been swept clean. The walls were littered with cracks. Metal light fixtures resembling small cages lined both sides of the corridor, though he had yet to see any switches or pull-chains to turn them on.

The path forked in both directions at the end. When Caleb came to the intersection, he looked to the right only to see another concrete passage that continued for a while before turning left. As he was in the process of turning to check in the other direction, he heard a noise that made him freeze in place. It was the sound of a gun cocking.

A deep voice came from his left. "Don't move, or I shoot."

Caleb couldn't help but smile.

CHAPTER SEVENTEEN

Out of the darkness barked a voice. "Give me the light." Caleb handed it over while keeping his hands raised. Complying would be his best chance at getting real answers—not that he had much of a choice with a gun to his back.

The stranger scanned all three of them with the flashlight. "On the ground, all of you. Now! Hands flat out in front of you. Is it just the three of you?"

"Yeah," replied Caleb.

"Tallie, get their bags. Han, pat them down. Do you have any weapons on you?"

"There's uh… a knife and a b-b-baseball bat in my backpack," Dusty stammered out.

Then he stood up.

"Hey! I said on the ground!" The man aimed the pistol at Dusty.

Dusty began pacing back and forth along the width of the hallway, shaking his head back and forth. "I'm sorry, I can't. I can't. I can't."

"Get down! Now, or I'll shoot!"

Caleb couldn't believe it. Dusty was going to get himself killed.

Rava hopped to her feet and put herself between Dusty and the man with the gun.

"Please, don't shoot! He's autistic. Trust me, he's harmless. Can you just let him stand?" Now Caleb really couldn't believe what he was witnessing. Rava was risking her life for Dusty.

Dusty was still pacing back and forth, crying and whispering to himself. "I can't. I can't. I can't…"

To Caleb's relief, the man lowered his weapon. "Han, pat him down first. You." He turned to Rava. "Back on the ground."

After they were searched, the stranger with the deep voice pointed the light at Caleb's face. "What are you doing here?"

He squinted through the brightness, unable to make out any faces. "I have a message for Dr. Olivia Birch."

There was a brief silence.

"We don't know anyone by that name. Take your things, and get out of here. Forget you were ever here. If we see you again, we *will* shoot you."

"Wait!" Caleb pleaded. "Please, just tell her that Emily Foster's son is here to see her. She'll know what it means."

Another pause was followed by faint whispering. Then the lights came on.

"Get up. Follow me," the man said. "You try anything—"

"You'll shoot us. Got it," Rava said.

They scrambled to their feet. Rava put her arm around Dusty and held him close as they walked. That seemed to help calm him back down.

One of the people stayed back to tail them from behind. He was a short tan-skinned man with spiky black hair.

In front of them, two people led the way. One of them was a black man with a clean-shaven head and face who was slightly taller than Caleb. The other was a fair-skinned woman of average height with curly red hair that flowed down her back in waves.

All of them were armed with pistols.

While they followed their leaders, Caleb took notice of the

security cameras strategically positioned overhead to see down every hallway. He imagined that was how they knew the three were there. He wondered if they also had security cameras above ground that he'd missed.

After leading them down a few corridors and around a couple of bends, they turned down a hallway that looked a bit different. The walls were still concrete, but there were boarded-up windows along the right side.

They rounded another corner and came to a set of double doors. Like the windows, the glass on the doors had also been replaced by boards. After pushing past them, they were escorted to the first room on their right.

"You three," said the tall muscular man with a deep voice. "Stay in here."

The door was shut behind them, leaving them alone.

"This the place?" asked Rava, a hint of excitement in her voice.

"I'm not sure," Caleb said, his brow furrowed as he studied his surroundings. "Nothing I've seen so far was in the video footage. But it's got to be, right? I mean, what are the chances there would be another underground base right where we expected to find my mother's facility?"

"I'd have no way of calculating that probability without further information on the demographics of the city in its current state," Dusty said as he began shuffling through boxes in the room.

"I wasn't really—never mind." There was no sense in explaining himself. Dusty could be a bit too literal at times.

The room they were put in appeared to be a storage closet of some sort. It was a cramped space full of junk—mostly old computer parts—in boxes that were stacked high.

"This *could* be it," Rava said, sifting through the clutter.

The door swung open. It was the same man that had shown them to the room. "Dr. Birch will see you now."

Caleb's eyes lit up and his heart leapt with excitement. It was actually happening. He was going to meet his mother. He looked at Rava and she flashed a smile at him. Dusty stood up and brushed the dust off his tan cargo shorts.

As they were leaving the room, the man blocked Dusty and Rava's path with his arm. "*Just* you," he said, looking at Caleb. "You two sit tight."

Tallie and Han were standing guard next to the door. Caleb gave them a nervous nod as he passed by.

"My name is Gregory," said the man Caleb was following. "I'm the head of security here. I apologize for sending you away initially. I didn't know you were a friend of Dr. Birch. I'm sure you can understand why we have to be cautious around here— especially with all the Scorpions running around."

"Yeah, we had a run-in with a few of them on the way here." Caleb pointed to the lump on his head.

"I was wondering what happened to you. Did they stick you?"

"What?" Caleb asked.

"They carry around hypodermic needles full of poisonous substances—anything from cleaning products to antifreeze—and if they get close enough in a fight to inject you, they will. Hence the name Scorpions."

Caleb shuddered at the thought. He didn't recall seeing any needles on the people he had fought earlier, but that didn't mean they didn't have any. He felt lucky to be alive.

While they were walking, Caleb noticed for the first time that Gregory was wearing diamond stud earrings. They sparkled under the soft lighting, giving off a lustrous emerald glint. He had never seen anything like them before.

After following through another set of double doors, Caleb began to recognize his surroundings from the video recordings.

Gregory gestured to an open door nearby. "Here we are."

Caleb's nerves peaked. He took a deep breath before stepping through.

~*~

The large room contained five computer desks, one in each corner and one along the back wall, opposite the door. Every workstation was full, its occupant intensely focused on a screen filled with seemingly endless text of various colors against a black background. A large wooden table covered with toppling stacks of paper dominated the center of the room and was surrounded by six empty chairs.

Working at the middle computer was a dainty woman in a lab coat with long dark-brown hair. When Caleb entered the room, she spun around in her seat, locking eyes with him.

Caleb just stared, unsure of what to say. He felt like he was looking into his own ocean-blue eyes. Her facial features were petite and soft. The corners of her mouth perked up to form an endearing smile. "Caleb. I…"

"Mom?" Caleb forced out through a lump in his throat. He needed to hear her confirm it. He had to know.

Everyone in the room stopped what they were doing and turned around to watch her response.

"Let's, uh, go talk somewhere a little more private." She turned back to the others. "Back to work! That bug isn't going to find itself!"

She led Caleb to a room down the hall that he assumed was her living quarters. It had barely enough space for a full-size mattress, desk, and a wardrobe. It reminded Caleb of the room he grew up in.

"Please, sit." She motioned to a chair and Caleb sat. "I know you must have gone through a lot to get here, so I figure I owe you an explanation." She cleared her throat. "Yes, I am your mother."

It was as if every muscle in Caleb's body had loosened up at once. He had actually found his mother. He almost couldn't believe it. Questions began flooding his mind. There was so much he wanted to know.

"But," Emily continued, "when you were just an infant, your father and I were working as physicists in a top-secret nuclear research facility in Amahl. It was located underneath a manufacturing plant. The government only built it there to serve as a front for the research facility."

"You lived in Amahl?" Caleb wondered aloud.

"Yes. Your father and I wanted to return to his old hometown after our time at OASIS. We were contracted to essentially run the facility. The pay was great, and we were able to strike a good balance between work and life. We figured if we had to work for the government, we could at least do it on our own terms. When we found out I was pregnant, it was like the stars were aligning. Our life was coming together perfectly."

Caleb smiled. It was nice to know he wasn't an afterthought. His parents had actually wanted him.

Emily smiled back, but looked down at her hands immediately.

"Then, we started getting visited by strange people from Aridor who were trying to recruit us to provide them with information about our government. At first, I repeatedly declined to even meet with them. But one day, they left an envelope with classified information."

She shook her head back and forth slowly. "That day changed the trajectory of my life entirely. The envelope contained evidence that suggested the Great War was all a lie. It was intel I couldn't ignore."

Caleb leaned forward with a furrowed brow, confused yet intrigued.

"According to the documents, Materra, Crayna, and Feraxia conspired to steal technology from Aridor. They used propaganda to convince their citizens that Aridor was developing nuclear weapons with the intent of overthrowing the rest of the world. Thus, the Great War was born, which allowed them to bomb Aridor, steal the technology they were developing, then blame it all on them. The thing they sought would eventually be known to the world as the brain drive."

"Wait, you're saying that they *weren't* developing nuclear weapons?" Caleb asked. He had read at least twenty books on the Great War. He didn't understand how so many authors could've gotten their facts wrong.

"I can't be sure, but I would guess not any more than the rest of the world at the time. Aridor viewed technology as the future, and they were developing so quickly it scared the rest of the world. They feared they would eventually be overtaken if they didn't intervene."

"So it was all true then? The Great War was a big cover-up?"

She nodded. "I believe so. I was never able to fully verify all of it, of course, but you've seen it over here. They didn't just bomb the capital city like the history books claim. They *destroyed* this country. And after that, the brain drive technology became utilized all over the world practically overnight. People were so amazed by it that they quickly forgot about the millions of people who had lost their lives in the tragic war."

"Then you started working with those men?" Caleb asked, still unsure how this all connected.

"No, actually, I didn't. I knew in my gut what the truth was. However, I had a baby on the way, and I wasn't going to risk my life. But those people were relentless. They *kept* coming. They'd show up at the places we would frequent, or just be sitting outside of our house when we got home. They weren't threatening us in any way, but we were forced to repeatedly turn them down. They even showed up to the hospital the day you were born."

Emily paused, looking Caleb in the eyes. He could feel the hurt behind them.

"Then one day, President Blake must have caught wind of it all. I was alerted by someone I trusted in his inner circle that he considered us a liability and was planning to have us executed. So we were forced to flee Materra, and I couldn't think of anywhere that would be safer than Aridor. So Derek and I faked our deaths by staging a car crash, and we changed our identities. Then we joined the team from Aridor that had been trying to recruit us all along. It wasn't ideal to become part of the group that put our lives in jeopardy in the first place, but they offered us protection, and we believed in their cause. As you know, we left you with your father's best friend, John. John is a great man, and we knew he would take care of you."

"Is my father here too?"

"No, he's not. He had been keeping tabs on you. Once he got word that you were being sent to OASIS, he left here to try to get you out of that place under his alias, Chris Thorington."

So Officer Thorington was his father after all. Again Caleb wondered why he'd stayed behind. If his father's goal was to free Caleb, why hadn't he come with them when he had the chance?

"We didn't want that life for you, but we figured it was only a matter of time with your genetics. I haven't heard from him since he left. I figured he made it, but—wait, if he didn't send you here, then how did you find me?"

"While I was at OASIS, I was given a classified assignment in which I was tasked with creating map modules of top-secret facilities around the world. The maps were then to be used to perform covert operations, with the intention of taking out specific targets."

Caleb noticed his mother shift uncomfortably. She had already connected the dots.

"This place—*you* showed up on my list." He paused, then continued. "They had a spy on the inside. Her name was Judy, and she wore a silver bracelet with a heart-shaped ruby pendant."

Emily nodded quickly. "Yes, Judy. I haven't seen her in about two weeks. She went out on a supply run and never came back."

"We saw a helicopter fly over Portan on the way here. I think Blake's team is close. We have to get you out of here and to safety. I'd recommend everyone—"

"No," she interrupted him, avoiding eye contact. "I'm not leaving. We are *so* close to finishing development on the AR mod. It could literally put Aridor back on the map. Wait until you see what it can do."

Caleb stared at the woman blankly for a moment before speaking. "Mother. Or Emily..." he said. "I understand you'd like to complete your project, but you'll have to bring what you can with you. You won't survive here. This facility is well-hidden, but it's only a matter of time before they find this place, kill you, and steal your work."

"Caleb, you *don't* understand," she replied, her voice growing firmer. "I've been developing this technology for seventeen years! I can't abandon my team. The AR mod has the potential to revolutionize the brain drive. I believe I could convince the people here to unite behind it. If I could bring them together again, civilization could return. Can you imagine it? We have the opportunity to restore a lost nation. And if they were attacked, they could fight back and—this time—be able to defend themselves. It's the only way they can rise up again. The odds may be against us, but these people deserve a chance."

Frustration continued to build inside Caleb, his words sounding more combative. "I'm not sure when the last time you've been above ground was, but you should take a trip up there and look around. What are you trying to save, exactly?"

As soon as the words left his mouth, he wished he could have them back. That wasn't the argument he wanted to make, but he was finding it hard to reason with his mother.

Emily looked at Caleb, a scowl on her face. "You've been here all of five minutes and you think you've got Aridor figured out, huh? Well, let me remind you that everyone up there is a human being. They didn't *choose* this. They have a right to a life just like you and me. And that's been stolen from them."

Caleb slumped over, resting his face in his hands, searching for the words to convince his mother to leave.

"I don't have time for this," she said, turning for the door.

"Look, I'm sorry you came all this way to warn me. And that I couldn't be there for you while you were growing up. But these people *need* me. This is my calling, and I'm done running and hiding." She paused with her hand on the door handle and looked back. "Oh, and could you please refer to me as Dr. Birch while you're here? I can't afford to lose their trust now."

Caleb didn't look up from his hands until he heard the door close behind her. For a while he sat there, in his mother's room, crying.

~*~

After Caleb was able to gather himself, he made his way back to the main work area, where he found his friends.

Dusty was standing next to a man seated at one of the corner desks, talking his ear off about the western starling, an apparently invasive species of birds originally native to Aridor which had since migrated around the world. The man nodded along politely but kept his eyes glued to his computer monitor. Dusty didn't seem to take offense to the fact that the guy was only offering a fraction of his attention.

Rava was hunched over the table in the center of the room, flipping through the pages of research sprawled out in front of her. She looked up as he entered, an excited smile plastered on her face. "Did you see this? It's amazing!"

Caleb, still sorting through his emotions after the conversation with his mother, shook his head. "No, what is it?" he said as if he was truly interested. He didn't want to rain on her parade.

"The technology they're developing is incredible. It's an augmented reality modification to the brain drive. If I'm understanding this correctly, it utilizes hardware that already exists in the brain drive to interface with the vision centers of the brain and provide visual cues of some sort to the user."

"That's correct," Emily said.

Rava's eyes snapped up to see Emily standing in the doorway, smiling. The whites of her eyes were pink and her eyelids were slightly puffy. Caleb sat down, crossing his arms and looking at the wall as if he'd suddenly lost interest in the research.

Emily joined Rava, looking down at her years of hard work spread across the table. "Project Ariel was launched by our team seventeen years ago in an effort to continue development of the brain drive—specifically its visual capabilities. The human brain subconsciously processes millions of visual stimuli every second. Project Ariel's main focus was to tap into those and use them to give the user meaningful feedback when desired. Some is provided to the user as direct knowledge, while other information is provided as visual cues in the form of augmented reality."

"You mean it flashes information directly into your vision?" Rava asked.

"Not exactly. You could say it *enhances* aspects of your vision to draw your attention to areas of interest. Sometimes, that's in the form of visual feedback, such as highlighting part of your vision. Other times, it's in the form of subconscious awareness, to look in a general direction or at a specific object. But the AR mod relies on your brain to ask for the information; it doesn't interject any unsolicited."

Rava was now staring at Emily in awe. "Wow, so what does that look like to the user?"

"That's a tough one to answer. Generally speaking, it will be a mix of what is necessary to convey the desired information and the user's preference. I have no doubt two people may experience the same scenario in completely different ways. It truly is up to the user's brain to provide the data the way it sees fit. And that's only scratching the surface of Project Ariel."

Emily shuffled around papers on the desk, searching for something specific. "Ah, here it is. These are the original reference materials for phase two of Project Ariel. It was implemented to create a way for the user's brain drive to interface with peripheral technologies via the wireless chip embedded in it. This relationship between the brain drive and other devices, such as cameras or microphones, could be revolutionary!"

"I had no idea the brain drive was equipped with a wireless chip!" Rava exclaimed. "That's huge!"

"Yes, it is," she agreed. "The brain drive was designed with the future in mind, but those who are in control of the technology now don't fully understand it's capabilities. Unfortunately, it seems we might run out of time before we're able to find the bug that's preventing the software from operating properly."

Rava's head snapped up from the papers on the table. "Can I see your code?"

Emily looked over to her computer. "I guess a fresh set of eyes wouldn't hurt. You know Lex?"

Rava nearly sprinted over to the computer. "I am proficient in over twenty different coding languages."

Caleb looked at Rava in disbelief. "Rava, we don't have time —"

"Shhhh," she rode over his words, waving her hand at him in a dismissive fashion. "I see the error code being thrown by the debugger. Your notes are impeccable. Hmm, let's see..."

Overtaken with frustration, Caleb got up and left the room in search of a place to clear his head.

He found a break room down the hall and stepped inside. The small space contained three benches made of metal chairs that had been bolted together, a short wooden table in the center of the room, a half-empty wooden bookshelf, and a television mounted on the wall. He sat down on one of the bench's worn, red plush seats.

Dusty entered the room and sat down opposite him. "I couldn't help but notice some tension back there. Are you doing all right?"

Caleb tipped his head back, studying the imperfections in the concrete ceiling above. "She confirmed that she's my mother, and"—he looked at Dusty—"she's refusing to leave. She'd rather risk her life staying here to finish this project than leave with us and be able to get to know her son." He shook his head back and forth. "I guess I imagined this being so... *different.* I thought that once I met my mother, once I finally knew the truth about my past, I would somehow come to know myself better. Now I feel even more lost."

Dusty stroked his chin for a moment before speaking. "There are species of birds that lay their eggs in the nests of other birds."

Caleb rolled his eyes and tilted his head back again. He wondered if Dusty was seriously going to compare his relationship with his mother to that of *birds*?

"They are referred to as 'brood parasites.' By leaving their young to be raised by another bird, it relieves them of the responsibility of child-rearing and nest-building, giving them more time to forage and lay even more eggs, effectively increasing the chances of survival for their species as a whole." Dusty pushed his glasses up his nose, going on. "I am not, in any way, trying to take sides here, but it sounds like your mother is sacrificing her own happiness, her own life even, for the chance to make a positive change in the world."

"*Is* it a positive change though?" Caleb asked rhetorically as he stood up and began walking around the room. "Am I the only one who thinks the brain drive was a mistake? Sure, the technology is amazing; you can upload information with the click of a button, no learning required. But at what cost? You know OASIS better than I do. Is *that* place good? Is forcing a bunch of kids to work full time for the benefit of everyone else a *good* thing? All of the jobs lost, the increased wage gap, the world-wide technological arms race—are those good things? I know you've practically spent your whole life in a government facility, so you may not know this, but we have a continent full of people who are hurting."

Dusty stared into his lap like a child receiving a lecture as

Caleb continued ranting.

"And how do you think this new AR mod will turn out? I can't wait to see how our children are exploited to make the most of that technology. Our world is so reliant on the brain drive already that I'm afraid of what would happen if everyone's stopped working overnight. All I know is that the moment I got this thing put in my skull, my life became way more complicated." He sat back down, the bench creaking as he leaned back abruptly.

After a tense moment of silence, Dusty spoke softly. "Complicated isn't always a bad thing. Simplicity often leaves little room for growth. I know change is difficult—as you know it's actually something I struggle with quite often. Me coming here with you complicated my life tremendously, but it was worth it to help a friend in need. And like it or not, the brain drive is here to stay. If your mother doesn't develop the AR mod, someone else will. All we can do is find our place amid the chaos."

Caleb wished everyone would stop trying to convince him that the brain drive was a good thing. That device was the reason he grew up without his real parents. Not only did he believe it was the reason his life was messed up, he thought it was responsible for the whole world being out of whack.

The door flew open, and Emily burst in, followed closely by Rava. "Caleb, you have to see this! The AR mod works. Rava found the bug in the code!"

Rava was nodding furiously with a giant grin on her face.

"This is incredible. I can see—"

Her face went pale, and she started looking around as if she could see through the walls.

"They're here."

CHAPTER EIGHTEEN

"I knew it!" Caleb yelled, slamming his fist down on the wooden table in front of him before looking at his mother. "I told you we should have left already!"

Dusty jumped in his seat, startled by the loud bang.

"We can still get out safely. Follow me!" Emily sprinted out of the room, leading the way back down the hall to the computer room.

"Caleb, sit," she demanded.

He followed his mother's command, and she thrust a cable into his brain drive.

"Rava, run the update on Caleb, and get him synced to the network like you did for me."

"But—" he contested.

"Caleb"—she looked at him, her dark-blue eyes meeting his—"I need you to trust me right now. This is our only chance of getting out of here."

She turned back to Rava. "After the update finishes, transfer all of the files onto this." She handed Rava a lime-green memory stick. "I need to go warn everyone. You"—she pointed at Dusty—"come with me."

The two of them left the room, and Rava began clicking and

typing at lightning speed. With every second that passed, Caleb found it more and more difficult to fight the urge to rip the cord out of the back of his head. It all felt so unnecessary. If President Blake's team had really found the facility, they didn't have much time before the enemy was busting down the doors. Besides, he didn't plan on using his brain drive anyway.

"All right, it's done," Rava said, and Caleb reached for the cable.

"Wait! I need to test the—" She was too late. He had already unplugged himself from the machine.

"It's fine. We need to get out of here," he said, standing up and starting for the door.

"Hold on, I need to finish up here. First, I need to connect you to the—there we go. Did anything happen?"

Caleb looked around. Everything with his vision seemed the same. "Nothing yet."

"Try asking it for information. Maybe wonder to yourself where your mother is or something."

"We don't have time for—"

"Just do it, Caleb. Trust her."

He let out a sigh and tried it. At first, he noticed nothing different visually, but he suddenly knew with certainty that his mother was behind him, exactly two rooms down.

Caleb spun around to see a rough silhouette of her body in his vision as though the walls between them weren't there. As she began to move around, he noticed she looked less like a flat shadow of herself and more like a three-dimensional rendering made of blue mist.

"Whoa," Caleb muttered. His imagination began to run wild with the possibilities. Then he stopped himself. No, he wasn't going to get sucked into this again. He was done with the brain drive.

As he turned to face Rava, she slipped something into her pocket. While he didn't get a good look at it, for some reason he knew it was a blue memory stick. A few seconds later, she pulled a lime-green memory stick out of the computer and held it up to show him.

"Done," she said with a smile. "Let's go."

He wondered what she was hiding. He'd clearly seen her pull two memory sticks out of the computer.

"Rava, what was—"

Caleb was interrupted by Emily poking her head through the door. "They're closing in. You done?"

"Yes," answered Rava, shooting Caleb a sideways glance before following Emily.

Caleb filed out behind Rava. He decided he could ask her about the second memory stick later. It wasn't the time.

Emily and Dusty were poking their heads into rooms as they continued down the hall, ensuring no one was left behind. Emily was directing Dusty to skip certain doors. She must have been scanning them with her brain drive beforehand, Caleb thought.

Caleb looked ahead at the group of people being herded forward and wondered how many were among the crowd. Fourteen, he answered himself instantaneously, as though he'd just done a mental headcount in a fraction of a second. And it wasn't a guess.

Suddenly, a thunderous crack rang out from behind them, like that of a tree being struck by lightning. Caleb turned to look for the source of the noise and noticed a small, pyramid-shaped black object bouncing across the floor, coming to a stop in the middle of the hallway.

His first thought was that it was some sort of smoke bomb, but it looked nothing like a grenade—at least none he'd ever seen before. Its surface was covered in tiny holes, giving it a sponge-like appearance. Rather than gas, a white light radiated from the peak of the pyramid, forming a small hologram of President Blake.

The evacuation was paused as everyone turned to look at the image, mesmerized.

"Emily. Caleb. I hope this message finds you well," the

miniature President Blake began. Even as a hologram, he was able to convey a charming demeanor.

"Please know that I do not wish to hurt either of you. I am merely interested in the technology you possess. I've asked my team to avoid causing harm in every way possible. All I ask of you in return is complete cooperation in your... *surrender*. If you walk toward my team with your hands raised, they will politely take you into custody, unharmed. You have my word. And, of course, for your troubles I will spare both of your lives. Now, in the event that you choose not to cooperate, my team has been authorized to use lethal force."

A second hologram joined the first, depicting a man slumped over, handcuffed to a chair. "Oh, and one more thing, Caleb. John came by to see you, but you *just* missed him. Don't worry, I'll look after him until you return."

Thanks to the level of detail provided by the device, Caleb could tell with certainty that the second image was, indeed, John. Angst built up in his chest at the sight of his adoptive father next to that man.

The hologram of President Blake walked over and placed his hand firmly on John's shoulder. "Cheers!"

The message cut off, leaving a moment of silent suspense lingering in the air.

"Run!" Emily called ahead to the others as she pulled a pistol from under her white coat. She fired two shots, seemingly at random, into a board covering a window near her.

"What are you doing?" Caleb yelled at his mother.

Before he could get a response, a flurry of return fire came through another boarded-up window down the hall. If before sounded like a lightning strike, this sounded like they had their heads in a cloud during a thunderstorm.

Almost reflexively, Caleb tackled his mother to the ground as bullets and wood chips soared through the air around them.

Caleb looked up after the gunfire ceased to see a few people clutching at their wounds, screaming in pain. Others had taken cover or were lucky enough not to be hit. Dusty was on the ground, hyperventilating as he ran his hands over his body checking for injuries. Caleb couldn't see any. He was also relieved to see Rava unharmed, but she appeared to be mortified as she looked in his direction. But her eyes weren't fixed on him. She was staring at Emily.

Caleb looked down to see his mother's limp body sprawled out, blood pouring out of a bullet wound in her neck and from the corner of her open mouth.

"No!" he shouted, searching for any sign of life in her wide-open eyes. He found none—she was gone. He began sobbing and shaking as he laid his head on her chest.

Rava crawled over to them and put her hand on his shoulder. She was saying something, but he couldn't hear her. He was too focused on the injustice of his mother being ripped from him already. Fate was cruel. Everything they'd done in the name of saving her was all a waste. He'd failed.

He was naive to think he could ignore technology in a world that revolved around it. Like Dusty said, he needed to find his place amid the chaos.

Rage began to fill every inch of Caleb's being. The crying stopped, and his eyes blazed open. *Where are they?* he screamed internally as he grabbed his mother's gun from her lifeless hand and steadied his own.

His vision was filled with five silhouettes of red mist lining both sides of the hall—three on the right and two on the left. The closest one on the right disappeared immediately. He was already dead.

Caleb stood up, shaking Rava off his arm and darting forward.

He ran up to a boarded window on his right and fired a single bullet at the head of the red silhouette. The shadow slumped over, and by the time it hit the ground, he had rolled into position for his second shot. He pulled the trigger.

Two down, two to go.

Caleb dove across the hall in an attempt to stay low to the ground. To his surprise, no return fire came. He could hear the confused voice of a man trying to get the status of his fellow comrades. Caleb took aim at the unsuspecting soldier and let a bullet loose.

As the silhouette of the man crumpled, the last began running away down the hall. He must have picked up on what was happening.

Caleb sprinted down the hall in the same direction as the red figure. He ran past them and waited at the next boarded window, his gun raised to the level of their head. As the red misty form crossed his line of fire, he shot his pistol and watched the stranger fall to the ground.

Four members of President Blake's elite special operations team had been eliminated by Caleb in all of eight seconds.

Falling to his knees, Caleb's hands began to tremble again. He looked up to see a cramped hallway of faces staring at him as if he was some sort of monster. Even those who were nursing injuries looked on with a mixture of horror and shock, appearing more worried about him than their potentially life-threatening wounds.

Caleb walked over to his mother's body and knelt beside it, squeezing her hand as he wept. As much as he wished it did, avenging her death by killing President Blake's soldiers didn't make him feel any better. There was nothing he could do to get her back.

His friends gave him space to grieve, tending to those in need.

After a few moments, Caleb stood up and turned to Dusty and Rava. "Let's go. We better get back before Marcus leaves."

At the end of the hall, Caleb stopped and put his hand on Gregory's shoulder. "Please see to it she gets a proper burial."

Gregory nodded solemnly.

It felt wrong leaving his mother's body to be buried by people he thought of as strangers, but they weren't strangers to her. For the last seventeen years, they had been her family. They would be sure to take great care of her body, ensuring her life was dignified with a ceremony.

Without looking back, Caleb carried on forward. Dusty and Rava followed, neither saying a word.

~*~

After emerging from the facility back into the blistering heat of the midday sunshine, Caleb continued to lead the way back to the plane. He'd decided to take a different route in an effort to avoid the Scorpions, and his efforts nearly paid off.

With the marina in sight over the top of the palm trees, Caleb was alerted to sudden movement in his peripheral vision. He turned his attention to an alley as Scorpions began spilling out.

"Uh, I don't imagine we can take them all on," Dusty said. "Let's make a run for it."

Caleb looked at Rava. The look in her eyes told him all he needed to know: she would back his decision, whatever it may be.

"You two stay here," he said firmly. Then he began walking directly at the Scorpions without any hesitation.

As he approached, he tested the power of the AR mod. *Are they armed?* he wondered. Suddenly, red mist highlighted suspected threats in his vision. In all, there were eight Scorpions, all armed with various melee weapons.

As Caleb marched steadily toward them, armed with nothing but the look of determination on his face, the two men closest to him found it increasingly difficult to hold their arrogant grins.

Noticing their hesitance, he took his opening and headbutted the first Scorpion so hard he heard his nose break. Then a warning flashed in the side of his vision in the shape of a red arc. He ducked his head in response and a golf club brushed through his hair, barely missing his skull.

Caleb straightened back up and grabbed the second Scorpion

by the throat with both hands, slamming him into the ground without breaking his stride. The golf club was sent rattling away on the asphalt as the man gasped for air.

He turned his attention to the next two gang members approaching, both tall men, one holding a rusty wood-handled hatchet and the other wielding a syringe filled with blue liquid like a dagger. They both charged at him at once. The man with the hatchet swung down at him as the man with the syringe attempted to plunge it into Caleb's side.

He grabbed the outstretched arm holding the syringe and pulled it above his head as he ducked down slightly, using the man's arm as a shield. The hatchet buried itself into the man's arm, and he let out a loud cry.

Red flared out of the right side of his vision, and Caleb diverted his attention to see the syringe falling from the screaming man's hand. He snatched the falling needle out of midair and stuck it in the hatchet-wielding man's neck in one fluid motion. Then he depressed the plunger. The man collapsed almost immediately, grasping at the syringe in his neck as he began shaking and foaming at the mouth.

When Caleb looked up in anticipation of the other four Scorpions advancing, he instead saw them scurrying back into the alley like a pack of wolves who had just witnessed their alpha get torn apart by a predator.

A wise choice, Caleb thought.

~*~

Rava's heart was racing, and her eyes were peeled open, watching on with apprehension as the large man fell to the ground and began convulsing.

Caleb's reflexes were sharp, but there more to his methodical movements than that. She figured it was the power of the AR mod in action. He certainly wasn't holding back from using his brain drive anymore.

Seconds later, she was happy to see the rest of the Scorpions retreating. It was smart of them to run. They had nothing to gain by killing Caleb even if they could—and she wasn't so sure they could.

Caleb looked back in their direction, wearing the same expression he had after killing the entire special operations team by himself: pure determination.

Honestly, the look frightened her. While Caleb was never short on confidence, he was typically level-headed in his approach to solving problems. Measured. Calculated. But this was entirely different. This was the look of someone who couldn't be stopped.

Rava glanced over at Dusty, and his face suggested he was at least as uneasy as she, if not more. Probably more, she imagined.

Caleb nodded his head toward the marina and began trudging in that direction. They caught up with him and walked next to him in silence until Rava's curiosity won out.

"Where did you learn to fight like that?" she asked.

He didn't bother to look in her direction, simply answering, "John," as if that was all the response the question deserved.

They walked the rest of the way to the dock in complete silence.

As they approached Marcus, he bowed his head slightly and closed his eyes, as though he could feel Caleb's pain. Without them uttering a word, he already knew his mother hadn't made it. He'd always had a gift for reading people. Although Rava was never one to be subtle with her emotions, he had a knack for knowing when something was off even when she tried her best to hide it.

Marcus put his hands on Caleb's arms as though he was steadying him, his squinted eyes meeting Caleb's. "I'm sorry, son. I've seen a lot of kids lose their parents over the years. Do you want to know the difference between those who recover from it and those who don't?"

"No," he said, moving past Marcus and onto the plane.

Marcus's smile broadened like a proud father.

While Marcus was untying the plane from the dock, readying it for takeoff, Rava looked back at Caleb, who was sitting alone next to the empty seat that was supposed to be carrying his mother back to safety. "So how are we going to get John out of that place?"

"I already have an idea, actually." He looked at Dusty. "What are the chances your parents would be willing to help us?"

~*~

The Harding estate was nothing short of extravagant. The three-story white-brick house sat atop a hill overlooking a sprawling, meticulously landscaped yard. Its black roof and shutters provided a striking contrast to the bright exterior. Perfectly trimmed hedges surrounded the house like a green skirt. The driveway, also made of white brick, stretched across the front of the house in a wide U-shape and was capped at both ends by a black elegantly crafted wrought-iron gate. A wall made of white brick surrounded the entire property, save for the black gates.

"Wow," Rava exclaimed under her breath as they walked up the driveway. "You used to live here?"

"Nope," Dusty said. "But it looks as though they've made good use of their monthly stipend from OASIS." He hadn't grown up poor, but the house he left when he was six years old looked nothing like this.

Caleb and Rava shared a look of astonishment. Since they were both technically orphans, their "families" had probably received nothing.

Dusty reached for the doorbell and then stopped, turning to his friends, eyes glued firmly to his shoes. "Maybe I should do this alone."

"Whatever you think," Caleb reassured him.

"We'll wait in the car," Rava agreed, tugging at Caleb's arm before they both turned to walk back down the stone driveway.

Dusty took a deep breath and rang the doorbell.

A woman with shoulder-length curly blonde hair answered the door wearing a plush pink bathrobe. She called back over her shoulder. "Rob! You left the gate open again!" She turned back to Dusty. "I'm sorry, dear, we're not interested."

She went to close the door, and Dusty stuck his hand out to stop it. She shot him a glare and opened the door again.

"Excuse me?" she snarled. "I said we're not—"

"Mom," he interjected, unable to look at her face. "It's me. Dusty."

The look of disgust slipped away and was replaced by confusion. "Oh, I'm sorry, honey. Are you in trouble? You didn't get kicked out of that government place, did you?"

"Not exactly. I'm here to ask you for a favor. Can I come in?"

She paused and looked back over her shoulder again. "Your father and I were getting ready to go out to dinner. I'm not sure…" She slipped out of the front door and closed it quietly behind her, joining Dusty outside.

He already knew where she was going with this. His father had always been ashamed of him. When he'd left for OASIS as a child, his father had refused to even see him off. Surely, he wouldn't be happy to see him now.

"I get it, Mom. Listen, I've never asked anything of you. My friends and I need your help with something. Please, just hear me out before you give me an answer."

~*~

As Caleb and Rava waited in the car, they watched Dusty and his mother talk.

"They seem so… *formal*," Rava observed aloud.

"Yeah. There's definitely tension between them." Caleb wished he knew more about body language. He was sure his new AR mod would be able to help him pinpoint exactly what seemed off about their interaction. He made a mental note to look into getting a body language module, if it existed.

"So, what's John like? I remember what you told me about the memory stick and him lying to you about the brain drive and all. But you never really told me about him beyond that."

That's a fair question, Caleb thought. If she was going to be risking her life to save his, she deserved to know what kind of a man he was.

"He's..." Caleb thought for a moment. "He's like if you took the soul of a dog and put it into a grizzly bear."

Rava let out an explosive cackle. "I'm sorry," she said, trying to hold back her laughter.

"Don't be." Caleb couldn't help but chuckle himself. "He's fairly mild-mannered and humorous. Prepared for anything. And loyal to a fault."

"And the grizzly bear part?"

"Oh, he's a *big* guy."

They shared another laugh.

"Seriously though, before me, he was the heavyweight boxing champion of the world. He told me he gave up all of that when I was born. With everything I know now though..."

She gave him a reassuring smile. "Marcus always used to tell me the test of a man's character isn't what he's able to accomplish himself. It's what he's willing to sacrifice to allow those around him to succeed."

"I like that," Caleb said, a faint smile forming at the corners of his mouth.

Dusty opened the back door of the car, startling them both. "She's in," he said in a business-like manner as he took a seat.

"Awesome," Caleb exclaimed, attempting to make up for Dusty's lack of enthusiasm, though it wasn't difficult for him. He actually was excited, to an extent. All of the pieces were now in place for his plan. Whether or not it would work was another matter altogether.

"Yeah, that's great!" Rava added.

Dusty didn't respond. Instead, he stared out the window at his parents' house as they pulled away.

CHAPTER NINETEEN

President Blake buttoned up his navy-blue suit jacket and proceeded to run a hand through his dark-brown hair in a combing fashion. He'd always loved mirrors. More accurately, he loved the way he looked in them.

"It's done, sir."

President Blake spun around to face his advisor, a heavyset man well into his sixties. "Thank you, Simon."

Simon Vertif had been his senior advisor on technology and innovative sciences ever since he'd taken office twenty-two years prior. He was one of three of his original advisors who still remained from that time. Back then, his hair wasn't gray, and he had more of it. Now, the man was balding on the top, and his face was little more than a pile of wrinkles.

"I know I already told you this, Mr. President, but results aren't guaranteed with such a rushed timeframe. More effort spent on pattern-recognition could have yielded far better results with greater accuracy."

This was the part about being president that Avery Blake loathed. Subordinates were always so afraid of him that they felt the need to constantly justify their failures. Why couldn't they simply get results like he did?

"There's no need to repeat yourself, Simon. I understood you the first time. Now quit making excuses and wake him up. I need to test this out."

Simon unplugged the cord from the back of Derek's head, allowing it to retract back into the spool it came from. Then he injected him with a syringe. "It may take him a few hours to become fully coherent."

President Blake bent down in front of Derek as he sat, slumped over and handcuffed to the metal chair. He steadied himself at Derek's eye level and watched as Derek lifted his head and opened his eyes.

At first, he looked around through half-opened glazed eyes. Dry blood caked the lower half of his face, which was cracked and flaking as if he was shedding a layer of crimson skin.

The scar stretching down the left side of his face granted him a frightening expression that made President Blake envious. If only he looked like *that*, he mused, he wouldn't need to work as hard to constantly strike fear in the eyes of his subordinates. He pondered that thought for a moment before deciding he preferred being handsome instead.

Derek slowly pried his eyes the rest of the way open and looked directly at President Blake. "C-Caleb?"

A wide grin spread across President Blake's face. He straightened up, nodding to Simon in approval before sweeping out of the room.

As he opened the door, he saw a hand covered in gauze and medical tape reaching for the handle on the other side.

"Officer Gunther," President Blake said as he slid into the hallway, still wearing his cheery smile. "Tell me you've come bearing good news."

"Yes, sir. Minutes ago, I received word that Caleb Shaw was captured at the front gate. I instructed them to bring him down to you. They're on their way now."

Interesting. He wasn't captured by the special operations team, so he must have slipped away, President Blake imagined. But he hadn't attempted to sneak in. He had walked right up to the front gate. He wondered if the boy was really *that* naive.

"Very good. Be sure to tell your men to allow him to keep any of his possessions, aside from weapons. I need him to trust me." George nodded firmly. "Consider it done, sir." Then he was off down the hall in the opposite direction.

Although he was working harder than ever, President Blake still sensed anxious tension in George. In his experience, that usually took a while to subside after having a finger cut off. If he failed to get over it, then the man would be no use to him—which was a shame, because he did like George.

Overall, he was satisfied with the outcome. George had learned a valuable lesson, and he was getting the results he desired in the form of a more dedicated employee. In the president's mind, it was a win-win.

~*~

Pamela Harding drove her black sedan up to the visitor entrance of the OASIS compound. It was visitor's day, and she had every right to visit her son. At least, that's what she kept telling herself in an attempt to get into character.

She was no stranger to confrontation, but for some reason, she had to continuously psych herself up for her role on the ride over. She needed to be convincing.

As she pulled up to the security checkpoint, an officer approached the vehicle. She'd never been there before, but Dusty had briefed her on how the interaction would go.

"Hello, ma'am. I need your ID and the name of the GI you're here to see today."

She thrust an identification card in the man's direction. "Dusty Harding."

The man glanced up from the tablet he was holding at the sound of Dusty's name. He handed her the card back and pointed forward. "Thank you. Please pull through the gate. Park to your right in one of the open spots, and stay seated in your car. My supervisor will need to speak with you."

Pamela mustered up a friendly smile. "Thank you."

She drove into the compound, taking care to park with another vehicle to her right, as planned.

Shortly after, a heavy-set security officer approached her, bent down next to her window, and glanced around the empty back seat before speaking. "I'm sorry Mrs. Harding. We haven't had a chance to contact you yet, but your son Dusty has escaped from the premises with—"

"Escaped?" she roared, ripping off her sunglasses for effect. "You can't be serious."

"As I said, I apologize. We are—"

"What kind of shoddy operation are you running here where a sixteen-year-old child can break out so easily? And where do you suppose someone his age would venture off *to*?"

"Actually, we were hoping you had heard from him."

"Ah, I see." The sarcastic tone grew in her voice with every sentence. "You lost *my* son and now you are wanting *me* to find him for you. I need to speak with your supervisor."

"That's not at all what—"

Pamela opened the car door and got out.

"Mrs. Harding, please, I need you to get back into your vehicle," he pleaded, keeping his voice even.

"Your supervisor," she snapped. *"Now."*

The man put himself between Pamela and the security office, holding his hands up in a calming gesture. "My supervisor is tied up at the moment, but if you take a seat in your car, I can bring him over as soon as possible."

Pamela weaved around him and marched steadily in the direction of the security office. "Where is he? In there?" She pointed to the building. "Let's go get him, shall we?"

She had to admit, she was having fun playing the role of an angry mother. Hopefully, she was making enough of a scene.

~*~

From the trunk of Pamela's sedan, they could hear her storming off toward the security office. That was their cue.

Rava pushed the seat forward and crawled from the trunk into the back of the car. She didn't want to spend any longer than she had to in that confined space. She peeked out of the window to see another security officer rushing from the office as Dusty's mother continued storming forward, ignoring the large man who was still pleading with her to return to her car.

"What's the hold up? Let me out of here," Dusty whispered from the trunk.

Rava quietly opened the back door and poured out onto the ground. Dusty followed close behind. He closed the door gently and mimicked her movements as she darted out from behind the car and crouched behind a row of shrubs that ran along the edge of the parking lot.

She looked over at Pamela, who was now struggling to break free from two security officers. A third was watching intently from the window of the office. That was good—he would be too preoccupied to bother watching the monitors.

"Fine, I'll leave," she heard her call out. "But you'll be hearing from me. I expect your supervisor to call me personally and explain to me how my son managed to escape and what he plans to do about it!"

By the time Pamela was done ranting and walking back to her car, Dusty and Rava had already snuck past the security office and were in the main compound.

Now on the inside, their gray GI uniforms and badges would allow them to blend in. Dusty's OASIS-issued backpack was also a nice touch, and though he argued he needed it, she was certain he only wanted it for comfort. She couldn't come up with any other logical reason why he would risk bringing a bulky backpack along on a stealth mission.

Dusty looked down at his watch. "Approximately twenty

minutes. You got everything you need?"

Rava side-eyed Dusty. "Last I checked it's all up here." She tapped on the side of her head with her finger. While not strictly true—she had the wireless transmitter and multitool in her pocket—it made her point clear. They had gone over the plan numerous times together. He should know she was prepared.

"Okay. Good luck. And don't worry about me. I'll be fine," Dusty said just before they parted ways.

"Okay…" Rava had no intention of worrying about him. They were past the worrying stage. From here on out, they needed to stay focused on their objectives.

For Rava's role, she first had to find a way into Ricky Gunther's personal shack—or any security office for that matter, but they figured his would be the easiest target. She couldn't let herself be caught trying to break in, though. That was a mistake she couldn't afford. Stealth was crucial.

When she got there, she peeked into the window to see an empty office. Rava made her way over to the card reader next to the door, pulling out her multitool. She'd have to work quickly to avoid detection.

The housing popped off easy enough, revealing six colored wires that connected the card reader to its power supply. As Rava studied the device to determine the purpose of each wire, the door to the security office opened.

Ricky Gunther loomed over her, looking down on her with red eyes and a puzzled look on his face. "What are you doing, Garza?"

He swiped at his eyelids and Rava noticed they looked heavier than normal. She latched onto that detail. "Are you okay, Ricky? It looks like you've been—have you been crying?" She did her best to sound sincere. Anything that would make Ricky cry was probably a good thing for anyone else, she surmised.

His expression changed to disdain but it immediately softened as though he didn't have the energy to maintain a facade. He opened the door further, slumping his shoulders as he retreated back inside.

Rava stood up, pausing briefly to glance around before following the sulking boy inside. She glanced down at her watch. Twelve minutes left.

"So, are you going to tell me what's going on?" she asked.

Ricky sat down and leaned back in his chair as he ran his hand across his buzzed hair. "I'm honestly not sure. My father had a finger cut off by President Blake a few days ago. But that's not entirely unexpected. And he seems to be handling it well." His eyes were darting around the room while he spoke as though he couldn't bear looking at her.

Rava winced. "That's gruesome. Are you *sure* that's not what's bothering you?" Her time was limited, but if she could gain some trust with Ricky, maybe she wouldn't have as much trouble convincing him to help her.

"Maybe it is. I don't know. The thing is, I don't feel that broken up about it. And maybe a part of me feels guilty about that." He stopped, looking up at Rava like he'd just realized who he was talking to. "What did you say you were doing here again? I thought you had escaped."

She tried to keep the focus of the conversation on him. "Is it possible that this little glimpse into your future showed you you're not meant to walk in your father's footsteps?"

His brow furrowed. "Cut the crap, Rava. What are you doing here?" He raised up to his full height and looked down at her.

"All right." The natural firmness of her voice had returned. "I need your help to free Caleb Shaw's father from President Blake. We have about ten minutes."

He rubbed the back of his neck for a couple of seconds, mulling over her words.

Rava glanced around the room for objects she could use to knock him unconscious if needed. There was a lamp on a desk that she imagined would do the trick.

"Okay, I'm in," he said at last. "What do you need, Garza?"

~*~

Caleb glanced down at his watch as he was being escorted through the concrete halls of C1 by four security officers. About ten minutes left. That should be enough time, he thought. He hoped his friends were finding success with their tasks. His life, and the lives of others, depended on it.

It was always fairly chilly down here in the bunker, but that didn't stop Caleb's hands from clamming up, forcing him to continuously wipe them off on his GI uniform.

In theory, his plan would work. In reality, there were more ways it could go wrong than he could count on his sweaty fingers. He did his best to push his doubts aside. President Blake was cunning, but he wasn't all-knowing—and he certainly wouldn't be expecting what Caleb had prepared.

As they entered the room, the officers took their posts. Two guarded the door and another two perched along the back wall next to George Gunther, who stood firm like a statue behind Blake.

Caleb immediately locked eyes with John, who was seated next to the president, bound by handcuffs, the metal chair bolted to the ground. He'd have to find a way to get him out of the handcuffs if his plan was going to work.

"Caleb! Don't trust—"

President Blake slapped a hand over John's mouth. "Uh-oh, John. We talked about this. No spoiling surprises. Do I need to pull my knife out again? I'd hate to do that in front of your son."

Is he hurt? A yellow mist drew Caleb's attention to John's hands. Dried blood covered his knuckles. When Caleb looked closer, he saw that the webbing between all of his fingers had been cut. The incisions were rough as if they were done with a dull, jagged blade.

Caleb fought to suppress his primal urge to charge forward at President Blake. He couldn't let the man see him shaken—his plan relied on his confidence. Besides, he was untouchable while surrounded by his bodyguards. It wasn't like threatening him would do any good.

President Blake slowly released John's face, his words lingering in the air. A wide grin grew across his face. "There we go. That's better."

He turned his attention to the boy, eyebrows raised and arms fanned out to his sides. "Welcome back, Caleb," he said in a jovial tone.

He brought a hand up to his chin, tilting his head back and tapping with one finger. "Although, I couldn't help but notice that Emily isn't here. I would have... *loved* to have had her here for this."

"She's dead." Caleb shifted his gaze from President Blake to John. John's eyes closed, and he shook his head as he processed the news.

"You see," President Blake continued, "I was told that once before. Forgive me if I choose to wait until I get confirmation from my special operations team before I take you at your word."

Caleb's eyes flicked back to Blake, staring into his nearly pitch-black eyes as he kept his face deliberately emotionless. "They're dead too."

For the first time, Caleb saw the President thrown off. It wasn't disbelief on his face, it was a brief look of pure surprise. Then he began to grin again. "Okay, you've got my full attention, Caleb Shaw. Now, tell me why you've come here."

Caleb felt a sudden change in his awareness, almost like he could see *everything* in the room. Rava had come through in getting his brain drive hooked into the security feed.

Hopefully Dusty was in place and ready. When he tried to wonder where Dusty was, nothing happened. He must have been out of range of cameras, Caleb assumed.

Is my father still here? He knew as quickly as the thought crossed his mind: he was in the room next door. A blue silhouette of a man handcuffed to a chair was visible through the mirror on the wall. The space was identical to the one they were standing in, but aside from his father, it was empty.

Caleb nodded toward John. "I came here for him." Then he tilted his head to the side, motioning toward the room with his father in it. "And him."

"Impressive," President Blake said as he glanced toward the mirror, attempting to sound genuine, but Caleb detected a sting in his voice. "So did you expect me to simply *let* you take them?"

Caleb reached into his pocket and pulled out a lime-green memory stick. "I believe you offered a trade. The technology from Project Ariel for both of them. It's completed, as you've probably guessed by now."

President Blake let out a condescending chuckle. "As you may recall, I offered the technology in exchange for John. I made no mention of Derek. I'd like to keep him. He and I have a longstanding... *score* to settle. I am, however, willing to allow you and John to walk away scot-free for the data, as promised."

"I'm afraid that won't work for me," Caleb said, tucking the memory stick back into his pocket, discreetly checking the time left: less than four minutes. "I'll need both of them."

In an instant, President Blake's demeanor switched from annoyed to agitated. He began slapping his own forehead with the palm of his hand as though he was trying to shake an idea loose. "Enlighten me, Caleb, because from where I'm standing, you have no leverage. You're lucky I haven't put a bullet through your head and just taken what I want. Do you understand *who* I am? *What* I am capable of?"

President Blake was in Caleb's face, more and more anger pouring out with every word, but Caleb just stared at the man with a stone-like expression. Though his appearance never let on to his nerves, Caleb desperately hoped President Blake couldn't hear his heart pounding against his chest.

Despite his steadily increasing rage, Caleb needed to push him further, and he was running out of time. "It must be frustrating to be so powerful and yet feel so powerless at the same time. I get it. I'd feel the same if I was outsmarted by a child more than half my age, surrounded by witnesses, in my own top-secret facility, no less."

"Outsmarted?" he snarled as he backed up and held his hand out in George's direction, never breaking eye contact with Caleb.

"Gun," he demanded. George unholstered his sidearm and handed it over to the president. Blake cocked the pistol and pointed it at John's head. "Cards on the table. I'm done talking."

"I wouldn't do that. You see, as we speak, copies of this memory stick"—Caleb pulled it back out of his pocket and checked the time: two minutes and twelve seconds—"are on their way to both President Sun and President Jackson. It's also encrypted, and only I know the password. So, I would think very carefully about whether you want your adversaries to have access to this technology before you get your hands on it, because the only way I tell them not to deliver those copies is if I walk out of here with both of them."

President Blake's face transformed into a twisted smile as he lowered the gun. "As you wish." He held up his other hand and waved a security officer over and then pointed to John. "Release him." Then he motioned for another guard to go next door.

The officer scanned his badge on John's ankle cuffs, and they fell off his legs. John rose to his feet, dwarfing President Blake like he was a child, hands still bound behind his back. Caleb watched through the wall as a red silhouette unshackled his father.

A moment later, a security officer entered with Derek, who was still handcuffed behind his back as well. Caleb watched as his father, who appeared utterly confused, took his place next to John.

"Well, a deal is a deal. Now hand it over, and you'll all be free to go. You have my word."

Caleb looked down at his watch: four seconds. Perfect. He approached President Blake, extending his left hand forward, the lime-green memory stick in his palm.

President Blake stepped forward and reached out for the memory stick. Just as he was about to grab it, Caleb closed his hand around it and hit President Blake with a right hook, sending him toppling backward to the floor. Every security officer in the room reached for their weapons at once.

Then the room went pitch black.

CHAPTER TWENTY

Caleb's plan was working. Both of his friends had come through for him, and for that, he was grateful. Otherwise, he was sure he'd be dead already.

Relieved Dusty was able to shut the lights off, Caleb burst forward into action. He was in an even tighter time-crunch now. But he had one advantage that no one else in the room had: the AR mod. Dusty had only cut power to the lights, leaving the cameras functioning. Caleb could literally see in the dark.

His first task was to remove the handcuffs from John and Derek. Locating a security officer was easy enough, as every one of them had rushed forward in a blind panic to check on President Blake.

Caleb snatched a badge from one of the security officers as the man bent down. He hurried to swipe it over John and Derek's wrists, and the cuffs dropped to the floor with an audible clank. "Don't move," he whispered to them.

Caleb sprinted for the door and pulled it open. Then he slammed it shut.

"Don't worry about me, you *idiots*. Go get *them*," President Blake barked at his subordinates.

Caleb watched as the security officers rushed out of the room in a frenzy, tripping over one another as they spilled out into the hall and dispersed in both directions.

After the commotion settled, the only people left in the room were Caleb, John, Derek, President Blake, and a lone security officer, George Gunther.

Caleb had expected all of the officers to clear out. Although George hadn't left, Caleb figured he could improvise and still make an escape. But he had to get the gun. He wondered if President Blake still had it. A green flare flashed in his vision near George's feet, and Caleb moved toward the gun-shaped mist. As he ran toward it, the lights came back on, and George Gunther abruptly bent over and picked up the weapon.

Caleb put his hands in the air and began backing away slowly as he stared down the barrel of the pistol.

President Blake, who had now worked his way onto his knees, began laughing wildly as blood poured from his nose, staining his maniacal grin. "How *stupid* are you? You're all dead. Officer Gunther, kill them all."

George hesitated as he toggled his aim between all three of them, gripping his gun tighter.

"You don't have to do this, George," Caleb said in a calm voice. "This is *your* choice."

"No, it's not," said President Blake. "Do as I say, or I will see to it that your son is pulled apart in front of your eyes."

George aimed the pistol at President Blake.

President Blake smiled. "Oh, you're going to shoot me, huh? Go ahead, do it." His words were sharp as he stared at the bald man in disgust. "Do it!" he yelled.

George's hand began to tremble, and he lowered the weapon.

"Coward," President Blake said.

As President Blake began to rise to his feet, he was forced back down to his knees by a hand on his shoulder.

John stood next to George and pried the gun from his hand. George didn't fight him over it, he just let it go. He fell to the floor and broke down into tears. Caleb found it strange to see the typically stoic man in such a fragile state. He supposed not everyone was built for enduring the pressure of such high-stakes situations.

President Blake didn't bother pleading or trying to weasel his way out of his fate. Instead, he used his final breath to look Caleb in the eyes. "You have no idea what you're doing. You think this ends with me?"

John pulled the trigger and Caleb watched the life leave the president's dark eyes. The look on John's face was all too familiar to Caleb. He'd watched John put down rabid animals on their property before, and he wore the same painful expression on his face each time.

Derek was completely unfazed by the scene, staring straight ahead at a blank wall, head tilted to the side as though admiring a complex work of art. The dried blood on his face in addition to the curious look gave Caleb the impression that Derek wasn't all there.

"Let's go!" Caleb shouted. "It's only a matter of time before they find us." He looked over to George. "You should get out of here, too, so they don't pin anything on you."

John nodded and started pulling his best friend toward the door by the arm. George crumpled up into a ball next to the wall, frozen in place.

Caleb led the way through the maze of concrete corridors with John dragging Derek close behind.

They were heading for the peripheral tunnels. Using his brain drive, which was still connected to the security cameras, Caleb saw nothing but empty hallways ahead of them. But something wasn't right. Dusty wasn't waiting where he was supposed to be.

Where is Dusty? He didn't know. Dusty must have still been out of view of a camera. Caleb had a sinking feeling in his gut. It wasn't like Dusty to veer from a plan.

Where is Rava? Caleb immediately knew where she was— waiting in the peripheral tunnels where she was to meet up with them.

As they neared the room where Dusty should have been waiting, Caleb swiped the badge he stole from the security officer and pulled the door open. Even though his brain drive *should* have told him whether Dusty was in there or not, he still had to check for himself. No sign of Dusty.

Where is he? he wondered again. Right then, he knew. He turned his head to look at him and saw a small blue figure walking alone in the opposite direction almost a quarter mile away.

"What's going on?" John asked.

"My friend was supposed to be here." Caleb knew his only logical choice was to leave Dusty behind. But it wasn't a decision he was thrilled to make.

John could see the pain on Caleb's face. "It's your call, bud. We can wait if you think—"

"It's no use. We don't have enough time." It hurt Caleb to say those words out loud, however true they may have been. They had to carry on without Dusty.

Caleb led the way through C1 and into the peripheral tunnels. He did a mental scan again before proceeding, and he spotted security officers in the north and south tunnels. The east and west ones were clear, with the exception of Rava waiting under an access point in one of the west tunnels.

"This way," Caleb said, looking back at John, who was hoisting Derek over his shoulder.

"We won't make it out of here at this rate," John said. "I'll carry him."

Caleb checked the tunnels again as he began to run and noticed the officers were converging on their location. "Security is headed this way. We need to go faster!"

Caleb picked up the pace, and John matched it, the weight of another man hanging over his shoulder only slowing him slightly. Having never raced his father before, Caleb was impressed by how fast he was.

In no time at all, they made it to Rava. "You must be the grizzly bear," she said to John as they caught their breath.

He twisted his face in confusion and then looked at Caleb.

Caleb spoke through deep breaths. "Rava, this is John. John, Rava. She's one of my best friends, and she helped me orchestrate all of this. And I'd love for you guys to get to know each other better, but I think it's best if we cut the introductions short for now."

The security officers were gaining on them. They were now in the west tunnels and headed their way.

As they turned to continue running, Rava stopped. "Wait, where's Dusty?"

Caleb briefly wondered about his exact location and got an answer immediately. "He never showed up, and we couldn't wait for him. I'm not sure why, but he seems to be heading back to our dorm."

Rava looked just as confused as Caleb felt. Although both of them understood that they had to keep moving, it still didn't feel right leaving him behind.

~*~

Dusty swiped his ID badge across the card reader outside his apartment. To his pleasant surprise, it still worked.

He pushed his way inside, the door feeling heavier than ever before. The stale air hit him like a strong stench as he entered.

The apartment had been his home for over a year, but now it felt so *cramped*. For the first time ever, he had the urge to open a window, and he wasn't even sure if they opened. He'd never checked before.

Dusty sat down on his couch and started digging through his backpack. After shuffling a few things around, he finally found what he was looking for. He pulled out a test tube full of white sand, tipping it back and forth so the grains tumbled over one another and glistened.

While trapped in that storage closet back in Portan, he had been digging through boxes of old computer parts when he happened upon a glass test tube with a rubber stopper that had gotten mixed in by mistake. He took it and filled it with sand at the beach before they left. He had never been much of a collector, but a souvenir to remember the trip by seemed appropriate after all they had gone through together.

Clutching his memento, he made his way over to his bookshelf in his bedroom. He knew the perfect spot for it.

When Dusty had been dropped off at OASIS at six years old, he didn't fully comprehend what was going on. His parents had explained it to him like he was going on a vacation, but they failed to emphasize the permanence of it all. So, in his childish brain, he thought it would be a good idea to bring items from home that reminded him of his parents while he was gone on his trip.

To remember his father, Dusty had brought one of his pipe stands. Dusty's father would smoke his pipe twice per day: every morning while reading the paper and every afternoon while watching television. His father had never paid him much attention, but when he would call through the house asking for someone to bring him a pipe stand, Dusty would rush to the rescue, wooden cradle in hand and with a beaming smile on his face. When Dusty was packing for his vacation, he had taken one of his father's pipe stands in case his father ever came to visit him and needed a place to set his pipe.

With great care, Dusty placed his vial of sand onto the pipe stand. The bottom of the test tube fit perfectly in the divot on the base, and the test tube rested at an angle against the brace that normally housed the stem.

He stood back and admired it with a smile on his face. Finally, he had a use for that thing.

He wished he could have gone with his friends and escaped this place for good, but he'd made a deal with his mother: she would help him with Caleb's plan to free John, and in exchange, he would return to OASIS and resume his work so they could keep their stipend.

Sure, he could have broken his promise and left anyway, but for some reason he couldn't quite explain, he still longed to please his parents. He wanted them to be proud of the person he'd become. He wanted to feel loved by them. And if keeping his word to his mother brought him any closer to that, then he wanted that too.

Caleb and Rava would understand. Not right away. But someday, they would.

~*~

The western exit of the underground tunnels was tucked behind a natural rock formation on the side of a hill.

"Is he okay?" Rava asked as John lowered Derek down from the cove nestled in the stony slope and into Caleb's arms.

"Not sure," Caleb said, grunting as he steadied himself against the weight of his father in his arms. "He's been in a weird daze the entire time."

John landed with a thud next to them. "We have to keep moving. We can worry about all that later." He lifted Derek from Caleb with the ease of a father lifting a toddler, hoisting him over his shoulder again, on the other side this time. A knot was already forming on his right side, where he had carried Derek through the tunnels.

"Follow me," John called back as he started west. "My truck is probably still parked this way."

Even if it wasn't there, it was the direction of the closest city for miles. They ran the risk of being caught quickly by traveling straight there, but John was sure OASIS would have bigger issues than chasing them down when they discovered the president was dead. They may have wanted to find them even more after that, but it didn't seem likely. Either way, the choice was already made for him. They had to run.

It surprised John that the president even had anything to do with that facility at all. In the grand scheme of things, it seemed so trivial. But what did he know? He wasn't a president.

John thought back to the look on Caleb's face after he shot President Blake in front of him. He'd looked on with an understanding that John had never seen on his face before. He'd grown *so* much since he'd left home. It made him wonder if his overprotective nature had been holding Caleb back before, keeping him from becoming the man that walked beside him today.

"Hey bud, I just wanted to say that—back there—I didn't—I guess what I'm trying to say is—"

"You did what had to be done." Caleb finished the sentence for him. "I know, *Dad.*"

Hearing Caleb call him that immediately warmed his heart as though he was hearing him speak his first words again. An unavoidable grin took over his face.

"Where are we going to go?" Caleb asked.

"I'm sure Marcus wouldn't mind taking us in for a while," Rava suggested. "I know his motel isn't much, but I don't think you'll be tracked there."

It was nice of Caleb's new friend to offer up shelter for them, but John had a solution to their problem long before it existed.

"Don't worry about that," John reassured Caleb and Rava. "I've got a place we can go."

When John had retired from boxing, he was wealthy beyond his imagination. Being the best meant he was paid like the best. For his last fight—the fight that cost him his brain drive—John's agent had negotiated more credits than his previous three fights combined. At the time, he had more credits than he had time to spend.

Of course, Caleb didn't know any of that, which was a point of pride for John. It's not that John preferred Caleb to grow up poor, but he certainly didn't want him growing up spoiled.

After he hung up the phone with his manager, who was

understandably furious at the news of John's sudden decision to retire, the first call John had made was to his real estate agent.

He gave her three tasks.

The first was to list the condo he had just bought. She urged him to keep it for a while. He'd be taking a loss if he sold it so soon after buying it, but he refused and told her to get what she could out of it. That was easy enough for her.

The second job was to find a nice piece of property in Amahl —somewhere remote with a bit of land, nothing fancy that would draw too much attention to it. Going back to his hometown was risky, but he wanted Caleb to grow up where he did. Finding a place that met his needs hadn't taken her long. There was a hunting cabin that had been passed down through generations of a local family which was up for sale. The two-bedroom house was fairly small, but the price was reasonable for the amount of land they were selling along with it. He'd given her the okay to purchase the property.

The third task had taken a while longer. When he'd first told her what he needed, she had stopped him halfway through and asked him to repeat it all while she took notes. He needed a sizable plot of land that couldn't be traced to him which included each of the following: access to a freshwater source, such as a private lake or pond; soil that was able to be penetrated by digging equipment up to thirty feet; a climate that was conducive to growing crops year-round; and access to an adequate power supply.

John had never trusted the government to protect him or his family. He grew up learning about the Great War. He had seen what happened to an entire nation of people who were unprepared for life after civilization broke down. And he could only watch as his two best friends had been forced to flee the country and leave their newborn son behind in fear of the government.

With access to funds he'd only ever dreamed about as a child, he would do whatever he could to ensure he didn't make the same mistake as those before him. He would make sure he was prepared.

When Caleb was two years old, John had finally broken ground on building his underground shelter. His real estate agent had found him the perfect plot of land in an undeveloped area about sixty miles north of the southern coast of Materra. The closest neighboring city was over forty miles away. It would be six years before they finished construction on the project.

And John had never been happier that he decided to prepare for a day like this.

~*~

President Deryl Jackson stood like a drill sergeant, spine precisely straight and arms crossed behind his back, at the largest of his palace windows. Exercising good posture was one of the many habits he'd taken from his time in Crayna's military. It wasn't possible to achieve the rank of lieutenant—let alone general—without certain behaviors drilled deep into your being.

It was President Jackson's favorite place in the palace, which was why he'd had his office moved there when he assumed the presidency of Crayna four years prior. His predecessor would be rolling in his grave if he knew that President Jackson converted the room that once housed the gallery of former presidents' portraits into a personal office. But he wasn't one to be bogged down by tradition. *He* was in charge, and it was what he wanted.

The large window, occupying an entire wall, overlooked the capital city of Goldberg and provided not only a broad view of the gleaming buildings but also an abundance of direct sunlight.

Due to the naturally rough and rocky landscape of Crayna, forests were anything but abundant on the eastern continent. Very few species of plants and trees were able to thrive in the soil, and those that could were regarded as drab by the nation's inhabitants. Pine trees, shrubs, and cacti could only be so beautiful.

As a result, President Jackson had imported the most beautiful plants he could find from across the world and displayed them proudly in his office. Everything from Western Sundrops to Southern Bells lined the walls in ornate white and gold pots of various sizes. The sunlight that poured into the room was crucial for the health of his prized garden, as were the servants that watered it regularly.

Many others found his obsession with rare plants strange, but to President Jackson, they were a status symbol, a display of his impeccable fashion sense. Secretly, they also served as a daily reminder that his goals reached far beyond the confines of his home continent.

Despite the fact that mining was Crayna's chief industry, its citizens considered fashion their true contribution to society. Men, women, and children of all ages worked tirelessly in the mines every day, soiling their clothes until they were caked in dirt and dust. Outside of the quarries, however, they wouldn't be caught dead walking the streets looking like that. Appearance was as important as air to the people of Crayna.

Even their architecture reflected their fashion sense. Nearly every building in the capital city was trimmed with gold. Some even glittered when the sun hit them just right, demonstrating a sparkling air of superiority that let onlookers know the owners had spared no expense for beauty.

President Jackson stared down at his beloved city, admiring the array of white and gold structures glistening under the cloudless afternoon sky. An occasional twinkle from a dangling piece of jewelry caught his eye as the streets bustled with citizens going about their business. The view would make any leader proud, he imagined.

A knock at the door stole his attention. Before answering, he checked his appearance in a full-body mirror on his wall, and it was a good thing he did, because the gold-trimmed collar of his emerald blazer—the national colors of Crayna—was folded down on one side. After adjusting his clothes, he took a seat in the throne-like chair behind his desk, glancing at a mirror once more before allowing his visitor in.

"You may enter," he called out in a stern voice.

His senior advisor on foreign affairs, Garnet Waters, entered, gasping for air as though he had just sprinted from the opposite side of the palace where his office was located. His hair was a mess. An added benefit of the tight crew cut that President Jackson inherited from his time in the military was he never had to worry about his hair looking disheveled. But if his advisor hadn't even stopped to straighten himself up, he figured the message must be urgent.

"Sir," he choked out between breaths. "President Blake...." He took a deep breath and gathered himself. "We just got word that he was assassinated."

President Jackson leaned forward, his brow furrowed. Depending on the circumstances surrounding his death, it could be excellent news for him.

"By whom?"

"It's unclear, but international interference is not suspected. All current intel points to an inside job."

"Very well." He tried his best not to let his excitement show through in his voice. "Prepare the interference beacons for deployment." It was time to see how well Materra would fare without access to their precious brain drives.

"Yes, sir." Garnet departed with a firm salute.

President Jackson wasn't surprised in the slightest that Blake had been murdered. What *was* surprising was that the man had lasted over twenty years at the helm of Materra. His arrogance rubbed people the wrong way—including President Jackson— but moreover, there was something *off* about the man. Certainly, he would have had no trouble making enemies during his tenure.

Regardless of the way he felt about him, he couldn't deny the man's effectiveness. He managed to cultivate production of brain drive modules that surpassed the annual output from both Crayna and Feraxia combined. Under President Blake, Materra seemed to have been thriving.

And now it was left defenseless, without a leader. It was there for the taking. President Jackson was not going to stand idly by and watch as President Sun took advantage of the opportunity. No, he would be the one to make the first move.

When the dust settled, he would ensure Materra belonged to him.

~*~

Relief settled over Caleb as he relaxed against the leather seats of John's truck, reflecting on his successful rescue mission. It was like his body was ready to shut down and finally rest.

It all still felt so surreal. His plan had actually *worked*. He hadn't set out with the intention of killing President Blake, but he figured Materra was better off for it. So he didn't dwell on that too much. He regretted not being able to save his mother, but if there was one thing that he'd learned through all of this, it was that he was not merely a product of his past, known or unknown. His fate was his, and only his, to decide.

His comfort was short-lived, fleeing him as he looked over at his father sitting in the seat beside him. Derek was still in a trance, staring aimlessly into the distance as they drove. He hadn't said a single word yet, only the occasional half-formed sound or grunt. It looked almost as if he was sleeping with his eyes open. President Blake must have drugged him, he thought. Caleb was sure it would wear off eventually.

Caleb's mind drifted to the other nagging worry on his mind: his friend Dusty. He racked his brain for a reason why Dusty would have stayed at OASIS but kept coming up empty. Though he couldn't find a motive for his actions, he was certain he had one. Dusty tended to think, and often overthink, before doing anything. Caleb was sure this was no exception. But knowing that didn't put his mind at ease at all. The fact remained they'd left Dusty back there, and no matter how much he tried to justify it, it didn't sit well with him.

John pulled into a gravel driveway and followed the winding path through the heavily wooded area. The forest opened up into a vast clearing of overgrown grass. At the far end of the patch sat a two-story log cabin with an attached three-car garage. Beyond the house was a large pond.

The truck came to a stop nearby, and they got out.

"This is it," John said through a pleased smile.

"This is yours?" Caleb asked, unsure if he was supposed to feel proud on John's behalf. He was looking at Caleb as if he was expecting some sort of reaction from him.

"Yup. Well, it's *ours*." John made a large circle with his hands, indicating that everyone was welcome there.

Rava glanced to both sides, looking at the forest that formed a border around the property. "You *really* didn't want to be disturbed, did you? Building all the way back here in the middle of nowhere."

"You could say that," John said, still beaming.

It occurred to Caleb that they had left Derek sitting in the truck alone. He made his way over to the passenger side and opened the door.

Derek slowly turned his head and looked at Caleb, his brow furrowed as though he was studying his face.

"Are you all right?" Caleb asked cautiously.

Red flared at the edges of his vision, and before he could react, Derek was on top of him, pummeling him with his fists.

Caleb held his forearms above his head in a defensive manner, attempting to block as many of the blows as he could. Still, quite a few punches connected.

"What—are you—doing?" he managed to yell while absorbing strikes with his face.

Suddenly, John peeled Derek off of him, immediately putting

him in a sleeper hold until he passed out.

Caleb regained his footing. "What was that about?"

"Hey, guys," Rava said while staring off into the distant sky.

"I'm not sure," John said as he cradled Derek in his arms. "President Blake must have given him a heavy dose of drugs or something—"

"Guys," Rava yelled this time. "Look!"

She pointed at the sky.

Multiple fiery projectiles were raining down around them as far as they could see. It was as though missiles were falling from the clouds, their smoky trails scribbling across the bright blue sky.

John started for the front door, carrying Derek. "Come on. We need to get inside."

Rava didn't budge, petrified in place. Caleb grabbed her hand and pulled her along as he ran by.

They followed John into the cabin and down to the basement. John set Derek down on the concrete floor, and he began running his hand along the wall, searching for something along the foundation.

Derek began to regain consciousness, glaring at Caleb and Rava as he tried to sit up.

John must have found what he was looking for because a cement slab of a door was open where a wall had been only seconds prior, revealing the entrance to a bomb shelter of some sort. He was motioning everyone inside when the ground began to shake below them like an earthquake. They steadied their legs against the trembling earth, trying to walk slowly into the bunker. Derek was crawling away from it and toward Caleb.

The rumbling came to a crescendo as a crashing boom reverberated through the entire cabin like a lion's roar. Suddenly, Caleb fell to his knees, cupping his hands over his ears as a debilitating ringing harassed his eardrums.

As the sound in his ears was letting up, Caleb looked around to find Rava and Derek in similar poses, hands clapped over their ears tightly. John was looking down on all of them with a confused face before he began lifting them one by one into the bunker, closing the door behind them.

Caleb looked at Derek as the ringing died down to a hum, and he was able to form thoughts again.

Is he hostile?

No response came to him courtesy of his brain drive, but his instincts told him that his father looked frightened and confused.

Derek looked into his eyes.

"Caleb."

THE END

Caleb's story continues in

NEW ARIDOR

Tom Hall lives in Michigan with his beautiful wife and two amazing daughters. *Brain Drive* is his debut novel, and he's eternally grateful to anyone who's given the book a chance.

He graduated from Ferris State University in 2014 with a Doctor of Optometry degree. Although writing is a passion of his, he spends most of his time as a practicing optometrist. In his spare time he also enjoys camping, fishing, chess, and video games.